HUNGRY
HEARTS

HUNGRY
HEARTS

FRANCINE
PROSE

Pantheon Books · New York

All rights reserved under International and Pan-American Copyright Conventions. Published in the United States by Pantheon Books, a division of Random House, Inc., New York, and simultaneously in Canada by Random House of Canada Limited, Toronto.

Library of Congress Cataloging in Publication Data
Prose, Francine, 1947–
Hungry hearts.
I. Title.
PS3566.R68H8   1983   813'.54   82-12568
ISBN 0-394-52767-4

Manufactured in the United States of America

FIRST EDITION

For Jessie and Phil

I would like to thank the Creative Artists
Program Service (CAPS) of the New York State
Arts Council for its assistance.

HUNGRY
HEARTS

1

I HAVE ALWAYS FELT blessed to have had the chance to play Leah in the Leon Dalashinsky production of *The Dybbuk*.

We opened in the autumn of 1921, on Stuyvesant Place, and by intermission the verdict was that we were turning a new page in the book of Art Theater history. A ten-minute standing ovation was our first review. Did our audience demand fifteen curtain calls? Ever generous, we gave twenty, bobbing up and down as if those footlights were the Wailing Wall.

The whole company bowed together; at that time we were under the impression that "ensemble" was a Yiddish word. Supposedly, our "revolution" had abolished the star system and left us so indifferent to who got top billing that we let the alphabet decide. The program, which listed our names from Appleman to Zipkin, made no distinction between principals and extras—and neither, supposedly, did we. Only now, sixty years later, has Leon Dalashinsky's influence worn off enough for me to admit it: That night, I was the star.

As Leah, I was the heroine, betrothed to Chonon since forty days before birth. But Chonon has grown up to be a poor student, a mystic—and Leah's father is determined to marry her off to a rich old man. Chonon dies of heartbreak, and his spirit enters Leah as a dybbuk. Eventually, the possessed girl is exorcised by Rabbi Azrielke, the wonder worker of Miropol. But Chonon's love is too strong, and as the final curtain descends, Leah collapses—and joins her true bridegroom in death.

Playing opposite me as Rabbi Azrielke was Leon Dalashinsky, founder and director of the Yiddish Art Theater. And starring in the role of Chonon was the brilliant Benno Brownstein —to whom I had been secretly married since the third Friday of rehearsal.

Our reason for keeping it secret was this:

On the Monday morning after the wedding, when Benno and I went to tell Dalashinsky the good news, he'd pushed us into his office, drawn the curtains, and shut the door. He lit a candle— only Dalashinsky would pick one of the black tapers we were using in the exorcism scene—then fished our contracts out of his file and held them over the flame. Fanning them so the flickering light threw ghastly shadows on his face, he'd talked down to us.

"Children. Allow me to remind you what this drama of ours is about. Someday, if you ever learn your lines, you will be playing Leah and Chonon, two souls betrothed in heaven and cruelly kept apart on earth. A tragedy, no? Correct me if I'm wrong.

"Now you tell me what will happen to our sense of truth if the audience knows that in real life this couple is married. What will become of our unbroken line when the curtain rings down on this heart-wrenching situation and the crowd thinks, 'So what? Now the newlyweds can run home and hop into bed?'

"You call this a marriage? I call it sabotage. It must be kept secret, even from the cast."

"The cast?" said Benno.

"Especially the cast. Do you want to ruin everything? Keep it under your hats"—Dalashinsky turned our contracts so we could see the back pages streaked with soot—"or there's no point going on."

To Benno and me, this made perfect sense. But not to my mama and papa.

"If that young man really loved you," said Papa, "he'd punch that Svengali in the nose and shout it from the housetops."

In private, Mama said, "Just between us two: For five generations, the women in our family have married handsome no-bodies."

I'd never thought of Papa like that. And the fact that Mama could speak so disloyally made me realize how bitterly she opposed the marriage.

"If that's the family curse," I said, "it's skipping me."

Because Mama was wrong. Handsome as Benno was, he was anything but a nobody. *I* knew he loved me—why shout? And besides, our match was so made-in-heaven, it made Leah and Chonon's look like the work of a cut-rate marriage broker.

Benno had been brought into the company to play Chonon, kidnaped out from under Maurice Abramowitz's famous hawk nose. The story was that Dalashinsky had caught Benno in Abramowitz's *The Jewish Seagull* and had sent a note backstage, very cloak and dagger, arranging to meet at a little stevedores' restaurant on Front Street where no one from the neighborhood ever went. The owners, however, were Jewish, and the owner's wife ran back to her own kitchen for dish after dish of noodle pudding with raisins for the visiting celebrities. Otherwise, they were left in peace for three solid hours of Dalashinsky holding forth on art, beauty, illusion, and the sense of truth sustained through the unbroken line.

Later, Benno would claim that what had moved him was the effort being lavished on wooing him when all the great Leon Dalashinsky needed to say was, "Come to Stuyvesant Place and wash floors." Which is not to imply that Benno didn't know Dalashinsky's reputation: He would charm a snake if he needed it to bite Cleopatra.

When Dalashinsky announced that Benno Brownstein was joining the cast, I shivered as if someone were pouring ice water down my back, and maybe that was why I cried, "No!" For I too had seen the Jewish Seagull which had inspired Dalashinsky to gain five pounds in one sitting from the *kugel* in that waterfront lunchroom.

Our spare time, such as it was, was spent (where else?) at the theater. For homework, Dalashinsky sent us uptown and down. A Chinese acrobat couldn't blow into town without our being warned that we would never understand movement until we had seen the Shanghai Ninepins bowling with a pyramid of human clubs and a human ball. On the Bowery, we watched hoofers in blackface tooting three harmonicas at once; on Broadway, the "standback" dramas. ("Stand back! That girl you're tying to the railroad tracks is your long-lost daughter Lou!") Safe at home on Stuyvesant Place, we shook our heads at the wasteland out there; then, with hearts full of hope, we'd go out again to poke the dust for signs of life.

And yet with all this theatergoing, I had never seen anything like Benno Brownstein in the role of Trigorinstein.

For the most part, Yiddish matinee idols ranged from the Persian princes to the Greek gods. So Benno stood out just by being a man. Pacing the stage, he looked more like an imprisoned Samson than a neurotic literary type, but that was all right with me. What could be nicer than a soft-spoken tough guy whose low voice reached without strain to the second balcony, where I sat with Ida Appleman?

Ida, whom I knew from the *Tevye* chorus and whose part in *The Dybbuk* was that of Leah's companion Gittel, was in those days my closest friend—but not close enough for me to confess that sin against art which I was committing there in the dark. I knew that Chekhov, even this plagiarized Yiddish Chekhov, deserved better from me. But I couldn't keep my mind on the play. Instead I kept daydreaming about what it might be like to eat breakfast with a man like Benno Brownstein.

Sometime during the second act, I abandoned myself to sin by asking Ida a question about dramatic technique which was really a question about Benno.

"Have you noticed," I said, "that Trigorinstein plays to the top balcony?"

"What I've noticed," said Ida, "is how he has to restrain himself from running up here and sitting down in your lap."

For such a sweet ingenue, Ida was awfully sarcastic. But I was used to it and let it pass. So what if my love was one-sided? Since when was love ever rational?

When Benno-Trigorinstein showed his passion for Nina-Celia

Adler by gently placing both hands on her elbows, I felt such a rush of hate for poor Celia; forty years afterward, I was invited to a banquet in her honor, and I couldn't make myself go.

Later, when Benno and I would tease each other about who had the head start in love, he would always maintain that my attraction to the Jewish Seagull didn't count. I'd been no more infatuated than several hundred other girls in that audience. Also, it was an insult to his acting to say that it was Benno I loved, when all that I should have been seeing was his Trigorinstein. Benno's version was: We both knew at the same time, the first minute we saw each other at rehearsal.

"Dalashinsky was what brought me to Stuyvesant Place," he would say. "But you were the reason I stayed."

It was company policy to begin every rehearsal with act one, scene one. ("Starting in the middle," said Dalashinsky, "is like climbing in the window when the playwright himself is holding the front door open for you.") So that first rehearsal began with the three *batlonim*, the professional students, comparing notes about their wonder-working rabbis.

Then from the dimmest corner of the gloomy *shul*, Benno-Chonon stepped forward and ended the discussion with a hymn to the glories of Kabbala. Speaking of how the soul can leave the earth and fly up to unravel the curtain of heaven, Benno was so convincing that, as I watched from the wings, my heart sank.

On such high flights, I thought, this man will never have room for me. But I stopped thinking as soon as Chonon began to mumble about the holiness of sin, the greatest holiness in the greatest sin, which was lust for a woman. And when he quoted from the Song of Songs—"Behold thou art fair, my love, thy hair is as a flock of kids that scamper down Mount Gilead"— my knees went so weak that Gittel and Frayde actually had to hold me up for my entrance.

After the opening, the critics praised me for making the whole dybbuk business more psychologically credible by playing Leah a little unbalanced from the start. But at that first rehearsal, it went unappreciated.

"Stand up!" hissed Clara Frumkin, who was playing Frayde. "The play's only starting and already you're on the floor!"

You would think that a group of actors trained to investigate every social nuance like the mysteries of the universe might have picked up something funny. But even Dalashinsky was so oblivious to the situation that he stopped the rehearsal at that point and introduced us—two soul mates recognizing each other from forty days before birth!—like a pair of strangers.

"Leah, this is Chonon. Chonon, Leah. You know each other already from the prenatal matchmaking, but also from more recently; from when you, Chonon—the yeshiva student, the charity case—used to take meals in Leah's father's home. Since then, you've thought only of each other, but you cannot even admit it to yourselves. Now, meeting in this drafty *shul*, you know. Your only desire is to warm yourselves in each other's arms. You talk about how sad and lonely the *shul* is, Leah. Really, you mean Chonon. And Gittel doesn't have to tell you that the strange young man is staring at you."

Despite our newness, our nervousness, that scene required no acting. Benno and I looked, we looked away. Our hands were shaking so, you could hear our scripts rattling. And when it came time for me to greet Chonon, my mouth wouldn't work.

From the front row, Dalashinsky yelled at me. "'Good evening, Chonon.' Three little words, Miss Rappoport. It's too much for you to remember?"

"Maybe Leah would have trouble saying them," I suggested.

"This isn't Second Avenue," said Dalashinsky. "Don't ham it up."

Somehow Leah and Chonon exchanged their inhibited hellos and how-are-yous. Talk about living the part! The script called for me to kiss the Torah passionately, as if it were Chonon. But I kissed it with the confused tenderness of a girl who doesn't know how to kiss but wants her lover, who is watching, to think that she does. It was so natural, so "organic" as we used to say, that even Dalashinsky was moved to cry, "Hot! For such an innocent girl, you can play it hot!"

And yet it was precisely this heat which gave me such trouble later on as I worked to capture the chill of the grave in the harsh tones of Chonon's dybbuk. My problem was, I didn't want Benno Brownstein to hear me with such an ugly voice.

In the legendary Vilna Troupe production, the dybbuk's lines were recited from offstage by the actor who played Chonon. Leave it to Dalashinsky to decide that the only natural place for them to come from was Leah herself. Leah was enough work without her dybbuk. But I never complained though that voice cost me months of rehearsal, of torture, of twisting my throat inside out and sweating blood while Dalashinsky hounded me.

"Again! Again! You think this dybbuk is the boy next door? The dybbuk comes straight from the tomb, with a noseful of death and the chill of the grave on its lungs!" Then he would turn to the rest of the cast and say, "This, children, this is what you get for casting an actress for her hair!"

With such encouragement, it was a wonder I could talk at all. And no one needed reminding that my part was originally intended for Alba Springer. The problem was that Alba had bobbed hair, and that Dalashinsky's heart was set on the braids of a *shtetl* girl. Without the *tzepelach*, he insisted, there was no illusion.

A wig was produced, but every rehearsal degenerated into Dalashinsky clapping the wig onto Alba's head and Alba tearing it off. Beneath this slapstick, something was going on between them; the most reckless gossips wouldn't venture a guess, not even after it ended with Alba flinging the wig onstage, where it lay, looking sillier and deader with every second of silence which followed her stormy exit. What melodrama! Alba slammed the door, and the whole theater shook. When, without so much as a head scratch, Dalashinsky shrugged and started looking us over for a replacement, it was all I could do to keep from waving the tips of my braids at him.

Still, I wouldn't have taken the part if I hadn't had faith: I was more than a hank of hair. Wasn't it an article of our religion that there were no small roles, only small actors? And I was a true believer, an Artiste with a capital A.

Stanislavsky was our god, and Leon Dalashinsky his prophet; after less than a year in the Art Theater movement, I could quote *My Life in Art* like Torah. Ask me about the unbroken line, about motivation, the "magic if," restraint and preparation. Don't ask and I would tell you anyway, in droning unsolicited lectures which irked Mama into saying, "Preparation? A good pot roast with onions and carrots—that's what takes preparation."

But to us, preparation meant creating a role, storing up "emotional memories," real-life experiences which we could summon up onstage to produce the desired feeling and save us from resorting to that dreaded admission of failure, the acting cliché.

So in the name of preparation I submitted to those exercises which Dalashinsky designed to help me live the part of a restless soul. For my noseful of death, I haunted the vestibule of Bellevue Morgue, inhaling the stench which reminded me of spoiled chicken with an edge of kerosene. For the chill of the grave, I sat for hours in overgrown cemeteries, shivering in the rattling October wind.

Through it all, I consoled myself with the knowledge that Dalashinsky had prepared for *The Lower Depths* by living two months in the grimiest Bowery flophouse. For *Othello*, he had colored his hands and face with chocolate syrup and walked the Lower East Side as a Negro. And yet I was inconsolable when, despite every effort, my dybbuk sang out like Chaliapin.

"Feivel!" Dalashinsky yelled to the stage manager. "Get me a coffin!"

We heard some sawing, some hammering, and then, with faces longer than the coffin, four stagehands bore it in on their shoulders.

"Miss Rappoport," said Dalashinsky. "Get in."

The contortions alone were pure humiliation. They'd made

the coffin too small, and as I squeezed in, I thought: Corpses get better treatment. Dead bodies can lie flat.

"Now," said Dalashinsky. "Let's try it from the dybbuk's point of view. Leah, your predestined mate, is about to be married to the filthiest pig in Brinnits. He's approaching her with the wedding veil, he's drooling, his sweaty hands are shaking to touch her, and what do you say?"

"You are not my bridegroom!" I cried out from my wooden box. "I have come to my predestined bride and will not leave her!"

"Children," said Dalashinsky. "Miss Rappoport here has worked a theatrical miracle. In just two lines, she has transformed a coffin into a chicken coop."

The next morning, we had an early call. Except for the watchman who let me in, I was the first one there. The theater was dark but for a spotlight shining down on center stage. And what was it shining on? Three guesses.

An empty theater is spooky enough without a spotlit coffin. But hadn't Dalashinsky told us that an actor must feel as comfortable onstage as a cook in her own kitchen? Why else had he made us do all that set decoration if not to teach us that the stage was no more intimidating than any other wooden floor?

With this in mind, I was halfway to the orchestra pit when that bloody hand snaked out of the coffin. Someone grabbed me around the neck from behind, and I screamed. It was more of a bellow, that animal roar you hear when you yell in a dream and wake up shouting. Even in a packed house, you could have heard me in the cheapest seats.

The hands which released my neck were those of Feivel Frumkin, our stage manager. Dalashinsky himself climbed out of that plywood box.

"Miss Rappoport!" He was beaming as he wiped the ketchup off his hand. "I didn't think you had it in you! *Mazel tov!*"

Mazel tov was right. That voice made my career. Even now, young actors and graduate students with tape recorders come begging me for an echo of it and I tell them, "Sorry. I'm old enough to be the dybbuk's grandmother." Older people stop me on the street to tell me how, sixty years ago, my dybbuk gave them shivers. Imagine, they say, when the chills were something we wanted.

Those first few rehearsals were exhausting. Afterward, it took all our energy to slink off in different directions. So it wasn't until the third or fourth afternoon that I left the theater to find Benno waiting. It was almost dark, he was leaning against the wall—and I sailed right past him.

In his own confusion, Benno called, "Leah!" But I knew who he meant, and I turned to see him blowing into his fists, his breath making white corsages for me in the chilly air.

My first reaction was to look around for Frayde and Gittel to faint on, but now I was glad that they weren't there. Benno and I looked, we looked away. We knew. And what did we do with this knowledge? Naturally: We took a walk.

Nowadays, the world is one big lover's lane. Leah and Chonon can tell their parents some story and rent a room at the Plaza. But in those years, love was an obstacle course of suspicious mamas and papas, nosy neighbors, overcrowded flats. Now the biggest thrill is to smooch in phone booths and doorways as if no one could see, as if no one had ever kissed before, as if no one else existed. But in my day, the challenge was to kiss in those busy doorways so that really, no one saw.

Even after that first innocent walk, when all that Benno and I made together was small talk, we staggered our entrances at the Café Royale. From the opposite end of our regular Art Theater table, I noticed that Benno couldn't drink his tea or hold up his end of the conversation. And this, believe it or not, excited me more than a whole suite of rooms at the Plaza.

Except for the streets, the doorways, and that public café, Benno and I had nowhere to go. But if it's passion you want, forget the Plaza and look to the finish line of an obstacle course.

On the third Friday of rehearsal, we cashed our paychecks and eloped to City Hall. The marriage bureau smelled of goat cheese, wine, and the two enormous Armenian families celebrating the wedding taking place inside. When the young couple emerged (how scared and saucer-eyed and lovely they were!), the whole crowd applauded, and so did we. Then our names were called, and though we'd agreed that all this was just a formality, Benno seized my hand the way children grab each other on line for the roller coaster.

An old ward heeler in shirtsleeves, with a pomegranate nose and hands which shook harder than ours, raced through the civil service in two minutes flat, pausing only to stumble over our names, as if a Rappoport or a Brownstein had never darkened his doorstep before. It didn't bother us in the least. In our hearts Benno and I were already married, betrothed forty days before birth. And this ceremony, we kept telling ourselves, was only a piece of paper.

That piece of paper seemed so unimportant, I half expected Benno to fold it into an airplane and sail it over the roofs of Lower Manhattan. For all the good it ever did us, he could have. And he probably would have if we'd only known: Benno and I would go on to get married to each other—three times! Not counting what may or may not have happened before we were born.

I still think of those two minutes in the judge's chambers as the time we got married for the landlord. The landlord? That pillar of morality we dreaded like the angel guarding Eden turned out to be a half-blind old man with two greedy sons who asked to see nothing but the color of our money before handing over the keys to our first home sweet home.

Dalashinsky had given us a concentration drill: Study a room, then close your eyes and visualize it in detail. Maybe it was peculiar to be doing such exercises on your wedding night, but the habit stuck. Even now, I can shut my eyes and see every inch of that apartment.

An aged Irish lady had lived there alone with her doilies and saints, then stepped out for groceries and died on the way. Everything was so orderly, so company clean, we felt like guests invited for tea and told to make ourselves at home till our hostess returned.

But not for tea. The cupboard contained a pinch of it in a tin, an empty jar of honey. The icebox held the miserly portions old people buy for themselves: two eggs, a cup of milk, three slices of bread. I shuddered at the toothbrush in the bathroom, the thin towel, the perfumed soap still wrapped with green ribbon and a card: "Merry Christmas to Auntie Lenore." And silently I thanked her for being so considerate that she hadn't even died in bed, which she'd left neatly made with a white chenille spread and fresh sheets.

After three weeks of courting on our feet, any bed was a bed, and we got right in. Sometime during the night, I remember Benno saying that we'd already beaten Auntie Lenore to heaven. How young we must have been to joke that way! How immortal we must have felt!

In the morning I brewed two cups of tea from that pinch, scraped a spoonful of honey out of that empty jar. And it was sweeter than any breakfast I'd dreamed of sharing with the Jewish Seagull. We stayed home all day, and in the evening invited Mama and Papa over for wine, cookies, and the accomplished fact that I hadn't spent the night at Ida's after all. Faced by the evidence, they came around; and we, understandably, took their acquiescence for more than it was. Breaking the news was so easy, we couldn't wait to tell Dalashinsky Monday morning—and that was when he held our contracts over the flame till we agreed to his terms.

Benno and I were so deeply in love, we would have agreed to anything; and we were almost as deeply in thrall to our Svengali. The great director told us to jump—we jumped. He told us literally when to breathe. And once we had promised to keep our marriage secret, torture couldn't have pried it loose.

The truth was, we liked it. The sneaking around gave our passion the very edge which marriage was supposed to dull. *Our* passion, needless to say, was ever sharp, with a lifetime guarantee. Since neither of us had the brains or experience to worry about familiarity and time, it was lucky we had the instinct to enjoy that final obstacle to our public happiness. We threw ourselves into that game of secret love and played our married life like one long audition for *The Yiddish Romeo and Juliet*.

At rehearsals it was Miss Rappoport this, Mr. Brownstein that, long after normal strangers would have been Dinah and Benno. We took separate routes home from the theater, and when we met at the apartment—my God! What material to draw from onstage!

When the cue came for Leah to kiss the Torah, I pretended that the velvet Torah cover was a certain spot on Benno's neck, and the coolest critics went into a sweat. Nearly every write-up used the word "electric" to describe the undercurrents between Leah and Chonon and marveled at the extraordinary fact that Miss Dinah Rappoport's dybbuk voice contained unsettling echoes of Mr. Benno Brownstein's. It was typical (they all wrote the same review) of the Dalashinsky genius that the dybbuk's voice came from Leah, yet sounded as Chonon's might if he were dead.

But really, it had nothing to do with Dalashinsky's genius, his hounding me, his jumping out of that coffin—and everything to do with love. In playing those scenes, I imagined that Benno had been taken from me forever, before our love got the chance to wear down. And the voice which came out of my mouth was the voice I wanted to hear in my head.

If that voice had conviction, it was Benno who'd convinced me: Should something happen to him, he *would* come back. He *would* talk. Which was also my "motivation" for the chills which the ladies can still feel, original strength, after sixty years. For at that time (and those same sixty years make it easier to say it) my Benno was monkeying around with Kabbala. And he'd managed to persuade me: Once he had learned to slip between two worlds, a final return as a dybbuk would be automatic.

This was what haunted me, and I wasn't superstitious. I didn't believe in dybbuks. For such an Artiste, I lived very much in this world. There were actresses who couldn't shake your hand without having to read your palm, but I wasn't one of them. In other words, I'm no mystic.

From this perspective, I see that Benno's mysticism was a phase; like a little boy, for six months he's a parlor magician.

But at that age there are no phases. Everything is forever. I wasn't used to being a newlywed, half out of my mind with love. And besides, it flattered us both for me to worry that Benno, in tasting those mystical delights, might bite off more than he could chew.

It's obvious how the whole thing got started. Chonon was a Kabbalist, so Benno had to be one too. For us, a part was never just a part, but a twenty-four-hour-a-day job, a whole new skin. I couldn't buy herring without wondering what sort of herring Leah would buy. Benno couldn't wash without guilt for bathing more often than Chonon. If Chonon was unraveling the curtain of heaven, Benno was right there behind him, balling up the thread. And if all that dabbling in the "holiness of sin" got Chonon into hot water? My Benno was prepared to jump in.

Overnight, the books appeared in our apartment: the *Zohar*, *The Perfume of Joy*, *The River of Life*. How I made fun of those titles! But now I see that I would have resented even a scientific journal for distracting Benno from me. I needled him: A man was supposed to have a wife, a full belly and be forty years old before he was allowed to study Kabbala.

"The wife and the belly I've got," said Benno. "But at forty, I'll be too old to play Chonon."

Such conversations should have reassured me: Benno wasn't totally lost in mystical speculation. But still I felt that his interest wasn't purely theatrical. In the same way you want your husband to criticize the pretty girl who's flirted with him at a party, I longed to hear Benno say that these studies were just research for the play—and I prompted him with his own stories. Wasn't this like the time he learned the violin for *Yiddel's Little Fiddle* and smashed it to pieces at the final show?

No, said Benno. These holy books made him feel like a kid with a buried-treasure map, like a chef with a stack of new cookbooks—except that these recipes were for minting gold and seeing God's face. How could he not try them out? And I felt like the woman whose husband tells her that pretty girl at the party made him feel young.

I wouldn't have been so uneasy if he'd saved it for the audience. But like an onion in the icebox, it got into everything, the most intimate corners of life. I couldn't squeeze a glass of juice without Benno telling me that our souls were like the two halves of that orange, destined to be reunited in one fragrant and perfect sphere. He called me his Shekhina, his mystical bride; he spoke of holy matings, refining fires, unions that would hurry the Messiah's coming. One night in particular, I was half asleep, exhausted from rehearsals and love when Benno said,

"Listen, Dinele, a story: Once, a man came to Rabbi Shimon of Breslau with a problem so embarrassing that he couldn't discuss it till all the rabbi's followers had been sent out into the courtyard. Then he said, 'Rabbi, I know it is forbidden by law to make love to one's wife in anything but total darkness. But every Friday evening, when my Chaya and I approach each other for our marital obligations, a bright light fills our bedroom —from nowhere! You can count the stitches in the pillowcase. Moths fly in.'

"Without missing a beat, Rabbi Shimon said, '*Mazel tov*, brother. Now tell me exactly: What do you and your Chaya do? And where precisely are these moths flying to?'"

I crawled up on Benno's chest and said, "*This* is the kind of story you read in those books? No wonder! Well, tell me: What exactly *did* they do? Where *were* those moths flying?"

Benno didn't answer, but his skin heated up like a baked potato. It scared me, but, oh, how I wanted to be scared like that. It woke me right up.

In two weeks Benno's whole vocabulary changed. When I met him, he talked quietly, his Yiddish and English beautiful. He was that one in a million, a modest actor. But now that everything was an emanation or a symbol, his voice got a little louder as he suggested: Maybe art was an emanation, maybe acting was a symbol of the million masks concealing truth.

You were either a spark or a husk or a vessel; I got confused. But there was no mistaking it when Benno stopped and gave money to every stumblebum on Allen Street, so that it cost a fortune and took forever to walk one block. Why? They might be hidden *tzaddiks*. All thirty-six righteous men might be sleeping it off on the sidewalk between Hester and Grand.

Like those Jews who can spot an assimilated Cohen in every Connelly, Benno saw Kabbalists everywhere. Dalashinsky, to take just one example, was a secret master who spoke exclusively in code. Why else would he go on about artists being like rain barrels, open to whatever falls from the sky? Pure Kabbala, said Benno.

To convince me that these studies were getting him somewhere, he played tricks. One afternoon, we left the theater at the same time. I took the shortest route home, but Benno was there before me, with an armload of dark red irises we'd admired the evening before in a florist's window on Broadway and Tenth, half a city away.

"How did you do it?" I asked.

"I flew," said Benno. "On the power of the holy name."

And I thought, If being a mystic's wife means irises, I can live with it.

I particularly remember a dream Benno had at this time. In the dream, he told me, the Prophet Elijah was lecturing on the geometry of the copper frying pan. If only you understood the secret, you could cook a five-course meal—pot roast, fried potatoes, green beans, honey cake, and coffee—in the same skillet at the same time. At the end of this lesson, Elijah rolled up the rug, and Benno and I danced the tango.

"At least we're tangoing in your dreams," I said. "If *The Dybbuk*'s a hit, we'll be old before we can dance together in public."

The understanding was that Benno and I had no secrets, but already, after two weeks of marriage, there were things I couldn't say. For an unsuperstitious person, I kept fighting the superstitious urge to warn him against flying so high that he couldn't come down for his cues. I would never have said such a thing—and luckily, I didn't have to. Benno's performances were letter-perfect, passionate and controlled. And at that stage of love, when someone does something without your asking, you can only assume he's reading your mind.

Onstage with Benno, I realized that this was where those dusty books were getting him. Even the critics noticed that he spoke about wanting to reach the heights like someone who has spent his whole young life climbing. Compared to the agonies you could see any night on Second Avenue, Chonon's death was so subtle, so underplayed, it was almost possible to miss. And yet (in that houseful of sophisticates) Benno worked like a magnet for handkerchiefs, drawing them out of every pocket and purse. The joke was that Benno—for the length of *The Dybbuk*'s run—pushed the *Zohar* to the top of the Yiddish bestseller list.

If so, those books should have been sold with the warnings they put now on cigarettes: Caution. Dangerous to your health. Knock on wood, spit three times, don't open till you're fat and forty, with a wedding ring.

We didn't even have wedding rings. We were crazy to be flirting with dybbuks and restless souls, insane not to learn, from Chonon's sad example, that there were reasons why such studies were restricted to the well-fed, the married, the middle-aged. Only from this vantage do I understand that the years, the family, the physical weight were meant to keep your feet on the ground and prevent you from getting carried away. But like Chonon, we were young. At that age you don't read warnings, you don't believe in dangers. Anyway, what would we have done differently?

What would *I* have done differently? Of all the scenes which remain with me from that time, the one I most long to redo is the conversation I had with Mama and Papa on *The Dybbuk*'s opening night.

That night, with those twenty standing ovations still ringing in my ears, I ran backstage to find my dressing room like Grand Central Station; everywhere, famous poets, painters, critics, and philosophers were kissing and running as if they had trains to catch. These were my Tolstoys, my Valentinos, but when I walked in, they stopped in mid-kiss and pointed their champagne glasses at me. I looked behind me to see what they were saluting, and everyone laughed.

"To Dinah Rappoport!" someone cried. "The Queen of the Yiddish Art Theater!" And I thought, They've got the wrong girl. Whom were they toasting, that little nobody quaking in her boots as she read for a walk-on in Dalashinsky's *Tevye?* That skinny greenhorn, fresh off the boat from Novyzmir, lugging kindling to Mama and Papa's Attorney Street flat? Once again, I was holding out my arms, but now the stars were stacking them with long-stemmed roses.

In no time, my right hand was black from handshaking, my cheeks smeared with fifty shades of lipstick not my own. Just breathing, I smoked fifty cigars, but what was a little smoke when that whole night was getting me drunk without champagne?

Yet I wasn't so drunk that I didn't know the minute Papa poked his nose in my dressing room door. Through the crowd of well-wishers dividing me from Mama, I saw that her eyes were puffy and red.

This was long before my Hannele was born, but already I understood what hell it had been for Mama to sit in that audience and watch a dybbuk possess her child. Years later, when my daughter, learning to talk, struck up conversations with every bum on Broadway, I remembered Leah's wedding, that dance of death with the beggars of Brinnits spinning me like a top. And I sympathized: How Mama must have longed to break up that dance, to rescue me from those lepers harboring God knows what diseases!

If we'd been playing Second Avenue, where you could bring the children and the pastrami sandwiches, Mama could have cried out to me—and had plenty of company. But this was Stuyvesant Place, where everyone but Mama could distinguish between life and art. Mama was on her best Art Theater behavior, and that—plus Papa's hand on her shoulder—had restrained her. You might say that her tears were a compliment on my acting, but I felt like a sniper, congratulated on my deadly aim.

In that roomful of giants, Papa shrank to half normal size, and I felt that I had to run help him. But Mama breezed right through. The funny thing was that, like me, she wasn't superstitious. She didn't believe in dybbuks. Yet somehow I sensed with your own child, it's different. You can worry about things you don't believe in.

While the champagne corks popped around us, we huddled together like three little soldiers in a trench.

"Mama, don't worry," were the first words I said. "If I can handle Dalashinsky, I can handle a dybbuk."

"Dinele," said Mama. "That voice."

"It wasn't my voice," I said, not helping at all. "It was my dybbuk voice."

"Be reasonable," said Papa. "It was coming out of your mouth."

From this distance, that voice sounds like the best work I ever did. But on that opening night, my parents' distress made me doubt the value of my art. All that preparation so Mama and Papa could hear a voice from the grave. Didn't they hear enough of them every day?

"For an artist, the world is a series of dybbuks." (It embarrasses me now to think how I lectured my parents.) "Every time an actor walks onstage, every new role is a different dybbuk."

"For a hot-air artist," said Papa, "the world's a balloon. Every time he opens his mouth he could blow up a zeppelin."

Five minutes before, our Yiddish royalty had crowned me— and this was how Papa mimicked the Queen? Yet really, I couldn't blame him. I knew he hadn't forgotten the little girl who dissolved when somebody looked at her cross-eyed and died with every sore throat. I thought, How Papa must be kicking himself for all the times he called me his Saraleh Bernhardt, his little Camille.

My theater for this infantile acting was Rappoport's Trimmings, on Essex Street. For a ribbon shop, it was a chaste kind of place, with only the bright tips curling through holes in colorless cardboard boxes. Customers paid by the quarter inch, but Mama and Papa indulged their only child. On the floor, in back of that closet of a shop, I wallowed in an orgy of remnants.

Those shiny scraps were my costumes, my currency; the imported felts, embroidered with tulips and sold for the fortune of ten cents an inch, were my foreign travel. And my growing up was the cruel discovery that grown-ups didn't dress up in ribbons like Lady Astor's pet horse. Why had I pestered Mama to teach me how to use her yardstick when all that it meant was that I could mete out those stingy lengths of grosgrain for the grandmas' baby sweaters, the pale satin, no wider than a shoelace, for the occasional nightgown, the crocheted bag? The only time we did business by the yard was at Christmas, and that was for presents, not people, for color-blind Gentiles who could only see red and green.

Then one afternoon (and who was Papa supposed to kick for this?), the great Bessie Thomashefsky swept into our store. By then, I think, she and Boris were separated, with separate theaters: his and hers. To this day, it's a mystery why she came in just that once, on business which should have been the wardrobe department's job. But I remember clearly how that little woman commandeered our shop.

"A yard of this orange!" she ordered. "Two of the violet—no, that magenta over there. And three of that peacock blue!"

As I ran, measured, cut, and ran some more, Bessie watched my every move. I was flattered, thrilled; only years afterward did I recognize this great compliment as the way an actress is trained to study everything. Had I realized, I would never have had the nerve to finally ask, "What's all the ribbon for?"

Bessie seemed astonished that I didn't know. Then she graced me with a smile and said, "For the colors, darling. The colors."

Ah yes, the colors. That day, Bessie bought up the rainbow and took it with her in four huge paper bags.

By the time I was old enough to audition, Bessie Thomashefsky's star was fading; the new thing was Dalashinsky. And when I heard the Artistes claiming to have begun their lives in art at birth, I pretended that I'd wanted to be an actress ever since I'd played Queen Esther in a Novyzmir Purim play. I felt guilty for having joined up for the ribbons. But I'd paid for this sin, early on. My punishment was to debut in Dalashinsky's *Tevye*, that production mounted completely in *shtetl* browns, in a cardboard-gray costume with grease rubbed in and charcoal smudged on my face for my part in the beggars' chorus.

"Begging a kopeck with a filthy neck in front of a million people," said Papa. "Some life." From these signs, he predicted a brilliant future for me: Spinsterhood. Solitude. Barrenness. Four bare walls and an old age spent sifting through garbage cans.

Well, thank God, his predictions never came true. Today my walls are covered with treasures—framed posters, playbills, photos of Benno and me in the roles we created. Even by that opening night, it was a little late for me to worry about spinsterhood and poverty; between us, Benno and I were earning not exactly like doctors, but enough to keep us out of the garbage cans.

Once again, though, I couldn't blame Papa. Had I married a doctor, he could have made a public announcement, accepted his share of handshakes and hugs, worked years at the trimmings store to pay for the wedding. But his daughter the artist had found another one just like her. And Leon Dalashinsky, their Svengali, had decreed that the marriage be kept secret till after *The Dybbuk*'s run.

Still, there were things to fear, perils which had nothing to do with pennilessness or four bare walls:

I have always thought that what happened would never have happened if we'd stayed in New York, where the very pavement felt solid, as reassuring beneath my feet as a tightrope walker's net. In New York, the routines of daily life conspired to make me leave my dybbuk at the theater. No matter what part I was trying to live, it wasn't Leah buying herring at Lebowitz and Sons, but Dinah Rappoport, who'd shopped there since my family's first *shabes* in America. I could have been playing Julius Caesar, and Old Man Lebowitz would still have given me a pickled green tomato to taste.

In New York, there was no such thing as too much preparation—not with Mama around to remind me that preparation meant browning the onions and carrots. And maybe if we'd stayed there, Benno and I might have sidestepped the dangers; we might have been idiot-lucky, like those canaries in children's cartoons, skidding past the dozing tomcat's paws.

But New York wasn't big enough for the Yiddish Art Theater. Our dybbuk had to possess the entire world. And so what happened happened because Leon Dalashinsky took us on tour to South America, to the other side of the world—where everything was upside down and a different gravity unsettled the sensible girl who'd sat in her dressing room on Stuyvesant Place and joked so cavalierly with her parents.

"The trouble with most dybbuks"—was it really me who had said this?—"is that they want a free ride. This dybbuk, at least, pays room and board."

Years later, when I was playing Mirele Efros, I would draw my sense of parental heartbreak and bewilderment from the look on Papa's face as he said, "The trouble is a daughter who invites dybbuks to her wedding—and not her own Mama and Papa."

2

A DOZEN BOOKS HAVE BEEN WRITTEN about Dalashinsky, the Jewish Stanislavsky. Only the two he wrote himself refer to Stanislavsky as the Russian Dalashinsky. Yet all of them agree that the Yiddish Art Theater sprang out of Dalashinsky's head like Athena from Zeus' brow. Dalashinsky was the midwife who lifted Jewish actors off Mama's breast and introduced the relatives; Ibsen was our Uncle Hennie, Shakespeare our Cousin Will, Faustus the family doctor. He was not merely an innovator, but a revolutionary—the Moses who led us out of the Egypt that was Second Avenue, the Abraham Lincoln who freed us from the chains of melodrama and trash.

Before Dalashinsky, the theatergoing public (which in those days meant the entire Lower East Side) got a steady diet of garbage and knew no better than to gobble it up. On Second Avenue, Othello couldn't smother Desdemona without both of them chewing the pillowcase and spitting it out. King Lear didn't rage—he chomped the scenery like carrot sticks. Playwrights stole from everywhere and gave their plagiarisms names like *A Mother's Tears, A Greenhorn's Dreams, Hungry Hearts.* To this day, millions of people still believe that "Hearts and Flowers" is a Yiddish song.

Anyhow, the plays hardly mattered. Personalities were the principal draw, and the biggest dramas took place offstage. Whenever ticket sales fell off at the Grand, the great Jacob Adler would fall desperately, publicly ill—then return from death's door to a sell-out house.

Onstage, improvisation was the rule, actors made up as they went along, and the stars were always playing themselves. Once when the Thomashefskys were still together, doing *The Taming of the Shrew*, the script called for Bessie to slap Boris, which she did, crying, "There! That's for Rosie Temkin!"—who, as everyone knew, was Boris's latest flame. Even Sophocles (not that they ever did Sophocles!) was written to be improved on; "improvement" meant that Oedipus would stop in the midst of blinding himself and, with one eye hanging out, turn to flirt with his fans. And if all this romancing the audience made him lose his place in the script? No problem—a regular Greek chorus of prompters was crouching in the orchestra pit, hissing to him from the wings.

When the revolution came, these prompters were the first to go. In the name of respect for the playwright, we sat down on our behinds and studied. We were forbidden to improvise; a full week's pay was the penalty for changing one word of the text, the sacred text. The star system was overthrown, the ensemble brought in. The most minor production decisions were opened up for general discussion; an actor couldn't blow his nose onstage without a whole committee, strict parliamentary procedure, and a vote.

Like Talmudists, we debated every line, while Dalashinsky presided in his soaring, cultivated, and (if the truth be told) affected rabbi's voice, preaching silence and a sense of truth, restraint, more restraint, and finally that most precious and fragile of mysteries: illusion. The stage was not a circus ring, decreed Dalashinsky. We were artists, not tightrope walkers, but the consequences of falling were as serious and severe. Art must continually refine itself, and ours had become so pure—Sarah Bernhardt couldn't have gotten a walk-on with us.

So Dalashinsky changed the theater—and the audience changed to match. "Art" meant shut up and listen. Screaming babies were out; white gloves and neckties were in. On both sides of the footlights, the ad-libbing stopped. With the actors treating every word like pure gold, who in the crowd had the nerve to play alchemist? Our illusion was so easily shattered that

Stuyvesant Place began to feel like a china shop, and no one was volunteering to be the bull.

Suddenly their idols would no longer court them, and like disappointed lovers, the audience retreated into silence, attention, respect. Their brains took over from their hearts, and why not? An ensemble is much harder to love than one shining star.

Of course, America helped with these changes, and (as is always the case with immigrant life) the last holdout to change was the food. But finally, inevitably, the carpetbags and picnic hampers stayed home. The smells of oranges, onions, spiced meats, the sweetness of fresh apple *kuchen* and mother's milk disappeared from the theater. Now, at intermission, the whole crowd trooped out to the lobby for thimblefuls of overpriced lemonade. I wanted to yell at them, "Dummies! For the cost of that lemon and sugar water, you could have bought a case of seltzer, a hundred Thermoses of hot sweet tea!"

Because right in the midst of this victory for civilization, I missed those oranges, that pastrami. For all my faith in Dalashinsky, in art, I mourned those hungry hearts. Nostalgic for a milieu I'd never really known, I imagined Second Avenue as a theater of happy endings where sweethearts were always reunited, kingdoms restored, prodigal children returned—and where the voices you heard were not from the grave, but from life.

Meanwhile, this theater was alive and well on Second Avenue. Any night I could have enjoyed a sandwich, a full meal, while watching *A Greenhorn Mama's Tears* at the Astor. But I was too caught up in our revolutionary zeal to realize that.

Many years later, our Hannele went through a phase of constantly criticizing Benno and me for leaving the Lower East Side. In her imagination, the old neighborhood was an Oriental bazaar out of the Arabian nights, a year-round Chanukah party with aunts and cousins and downstairs neighbors too. Compared to that vitality, that richness, said Hannele, the Upper West Side was as sterile as an operating room.

"Sterile!" I said. "Would you want your tonsils out on the corner of Broadway and Seventy-second?"

Yet I understood that Hannele was only doing what I'd done in holding Dalashinsky responsible for "killing off" the old audience, those lovers who'd torn their clothes and sat *shiva* each time Jacob Adler "died." I too needed someone to blame for history, for the chilly Americanization of those warm Yiddish hearts. And in my case, Dalashinsky was a likelier target than my own father, who with his hard work, his trimmings shop, his unassuming life, hadn't changed anything, much less the theater, the world!

If I resented Dalashinsky for all the reasons children resent their parents, this too was his own fault. My children, he called us, my spiritual children, with all the baby words of endearment. We were his *tzatkelach*, his *oyfelach*, his playthings, his little chickadees. It must have been easier than keeping track of our names. Also it put us in our places and established his claim.

For a while, I resisted adoption; I had a papa, thank you. But by the close of *Tevye*, I'd succumbed to the seduction of a papa who calls you his plaything one minute and might not recognize you the next. It must have been pathetic to see us racing, so to speak, for Papa's pipe and slippers, scrambling to sit at his feet. Why didn't we understand that all the endearments cost Dalashinsky nothing? Or ask ourselves why he needed so many spiritual children when, according to his wife Hinda, he required a prompter to remember the names of his biological ones? Because the explanation seemed obvious:

Dalashinsky was above all that. He was one of those cockeyed geniuses—nothing mattered but art. Which is not to say that he didn't have legions of women; to every premiere, he came arm in arm with a different arm. Still it was clear to us (if not to them) that Dalashinsky hadn't sought them out. These women pursued him, proposed and paid for the wedding ring too, while Dalashinsky checked the engraving inside to find out who he was marrying.

Eventually this obliviousness cost him four wives and countless girlfriends. A few years before I joined the cast, he'd managed to forget he was married and become a bigamist. Hinda, the second wife, was a little nothing who'd attached herself to him like a piece of pulp in the lemonade she'd sold at Stuyvesant Place. Single, she hadn't gotten many second looks; marriage made her nearly invisible. As the children came, one each year, she faded into a ghost who haunted the wings and moaned to anyone who would listen that her husband was the kind of monster who called other women's names in his sleep.

Once I asked Hinda, "What names?" Oh, what a clear conscience I must have had!

Hinda actually looked both ways, as if crossing a street. I remember wondering if it bothered Dalashinsky to live with a woman whose natural behavior was an acting cliché.

"*Schvartze* names," she whispered. "Ophelia. Cordelia. Like that." Again Hinda checked for eavesdropping spies. "At least, thank God, it's female *schvartzes*. When Leon and I first got married . . ."

I was startled to hear him called Leon, and slightly embarrassed, as if Hinda were naming some intimate part of his body.

". . . he was preparing, as he would say, for Othello. What this meant was that I never knew what color husband would walk out of the bathroom in the morning. But Leon was his own pale self on that day he took me (all right, so he didn't take, I tagged along) to that waterfront dive on the corner of Fulton and Front.

"Even there, in that desert of a neighborhood, they knew Leon, and I'll tell you: It hurt that I wasn't introduced. Though the place was hopping, the owner's wife brought special dishes, enough noodle *kugel* for an army. But Leon just pushed a raisin around his plate till finally he jumped up and went over to a table full of stevedores." Hinda's eyebrows drew together and her face "got dark."

"Blacks. I'd never personally met a *schvartze*, only heard—I got ready to run when the razors came out. But as Leon spoke, they got quiet. After a while, Leon said, 'Come with me.'

"The giant who stood was six feet tall, not black exactly, but a reddish black-purple which shone in that badly lit lunchroom like a ripe Bing cherry.

"With Leon, you learn not to wait for invitations. After he'd said a few words to the owner, I followed him and the Negro into a back room, a kind of walk-in pie safe where a ceiling fan kept flies off the pastries and the cradle wrapped with layers of mosquito net. Leon and the *schvartze* paid me no more attention than they did the slumbering infant.

"'If you please,' said Leon, and the black man took off every stitch. Who, who but Leon would permit this in front of his wife? If Othello treated *his* wife like that, no wonder they had problems! I was so busy trying not to look you-know-where, I could hardly see. But Leon looked everywhere.

"'Front,' he said. 'Back. Stand up. Sit down. Thank you.' When the show was finished, the *schvartze* dressed and paid with what seemed like the Yiddish Art Theater's annual budget, Leon sighed and said, "Now at least I know how Othello buttons his pants.'"

To Hinda this was not a lesson in movement, musculature, researching and building a role, but a personal illumination:

"From that day on," she said, "I knew I was in for it."

To me, it was a different kind of lesson: When a wife claims that her husband is calling other women's names in his sleep, don't ask whose. Some questions are better not asked.

Somehow I would rather not have heard this story from Hinda's point of view. But really, it wasn't so incredible. Because everyone had a Dalashinsky story, each more unbelievable than the next.

Feivel Frumkin's was that he was walking down Chrystie Street with Dalashinsky when suddenly the director stopped in his tracks and began outlining his ideas for *Tevye*. At some point during this monologue, a stray dog emptied its bladder all over Dalashinsky's foot—and he never quit talking. That incident, said Feivel, convinced him that it was his job as stage manager to get Dalashinsky moving when the puppy lifted its leg.

All this, I hope, explains why we were so surprised when Dalashinsky announced that one of his reasons for scheduling *The Dybbuk*'s South American tour was his desire to escape another New York winter. Since when did our director know winter from spring except as a flurry of cotton snow, a pink backdrop of tissue cherry blossoms? And why was I less shocked than I might have been when, thirty years later, Dalashinsky published his *My Life in the Yiddish Art Theater* without once mentioning the story of how, on *The Dybbuk*'s South American tour, his leading lady was possessed by an actual dybbuk?

It's funny how the traits of a lifetime will follow you into old age and beyond. While my Benno grew more and more modest, so self-effacing that at the end he weighed only a hundred pounds, Dalashinsky got vainer and vainer and died with a full trumpet fanfare of blood in the brain. Those memoirs read like the huffings and puffings of an old windbag who thinks that the world still cares if the Yiddish Art Theater ate Napoleons and Jaffa oranges with the chief rabbi of Uruguay. I lived it, and *I* didn't care. The menu—and the rabbi's social position—were the least of it.

How disappointing to read a great artist dropping more names than Hedda Hopper, as if the whole point of our foreign travels was the honor of being wined and dined by the international Jewish aristocracy. Insisting, like a shady travel agent, that our accommodations were never anything less than first class, Dalashinsky seemed to have lost all sense of restraint, of inner truths and unbroken lines.

You could almost feel the wind blow through the holes in those memoirs; but, oh, what I wouldn't give to have that windy life story in front of me now. I was crazy not to save those *Forwards*, to assume that those daily serializations would be collected and printed like Dalashinsky's earlier books; that no publisher was interested shows how fast things were changing.

In a way, though, I hardly need them. Searching in vain for some reference to my dybbuk, I studied each installment so closely—thirty years later, whole sentences stick in my mind:

"When the Yiddish Art Theater set sail, Cleopatra's barge wasn't good enough."

Now this is why I remember so well. Soon after that chapter appeared, I ran into Clara Frumkin on Orchard Street. By then, poor Clara looked like a walking shipwreck herself, but politeness made me ask, "Clara, how are you?"

"Only so-so," she said. "My memory's going. Last week I lost my glasses and found them in the fridge. And as for the past . . . Dinah, tell me: Didn't touring used to mean taking your life in your hands? What about that time we loaded *The Dybbuk* onto that leaky Mexican shrimp boat? Am I making this up? Am I wrong? Because just a few days ago, I read in the *Forward* it wasn't a shrimp boat at all. It was Cleopatra's barge."

"Glasses in the icebox sound bad," I said. "But as for the rest, your memory's still terrific and so's your imagination. The truth, let's be honest, was somewhere in between. Anyhow, saying a barge isn't saying a luxury liner."

"Isn't saying a shrimp boat," said Clara.

So there we were after thirty years, still debating the seaworthiness of the *Veracruz*—and me still defending Dalashinsky. Though maybe I was just guarding my own memory of that boat, which lies docked forever, somewhere in between.

Mexican-owned, with a Mexican crew, the *Veracruz* was a far cry from Cleopatra's barge. But the chef was strictly Continental, and we did eat and drink like pharaohs. On those first chill mornings out, the deck stewards (slight, good-looking Indian boys with Jewish noses) wrapped blankets around our legs and served tea with cinnamon and lemon. Two to a room, we shared comfortable cabins with portholes which opened and shut. When the weather got warmer, we could switch on electric ceiling fans that cooled us better than a bargeful of palm-frond-waving Nubian slaves.

But in fairness to Clara's memory: The tea had an oily film on top and an aftertaste of meat consommé. When the stewards shook open those blankets, a cloud of fine yellow cornmeal sifted onto our laps. For though the *Veracruz* wasn't leaky—or, for that matter, a shrimp boat—it was a plain little freighter, bringing cattle corn to Argentina, where it would pick up beef for the voyage back.

After hefting those giant feed sacks, the stevedores tossed our crates of costumes and disassembled scenery up one-handed.

"Careful!" yelled Feivel. "Can't they tell theater from fodder?"

As we boarded, the dapper young captain took the men's hands, the ladies' elbows, and right in front of him, Clara yelled, "We're not on the boat yet—and already these pirates are making us walk the plank!" I remember Zalmen Hirsch (that slob of a character actor who was playing my "intended," Menasha) flicking the hull and groaning, "Swiss cheese!" The anchor wasn't up yet when the speculation began: The return cargo, the so-called beef, would actually be the tender flesh of innocent Yiddish actors.

To watch those innocents poking at their dinner rolls (biscuits so light, it was a wonder they didn't fly off our plates) and screaming at the waiters, "Muchacho! What do you call these? Tamales?", you'd never believe that they'd all crossed the Atlantic, not so very long before, on a steerage diet of boiled potatoes and salt. To hear them sneer about cattle, you wouldn't dream that they'd come to America on what amounted to three-week floating stampedes.

Or maybe if you dreamed about immigrants, you would. For an immigrant is never a casual traveler. He can't take the Staten Island Ferry without worrying that he'll have to go through another Ellis Island to get back in; and when he's worried, he makes bitter jokes and complains. As we sailed past the Statue of Liberty (with her back to us!), the smokers all lit up, and Ida cried, "Careful! One spark and we're popcorn!"

Benno and I were the only ones who defended the ship. To us, that cornmeal was stardust, that lingering meat smell attar of roses. And the *Veracruz* was our pleasure yacht, our desert island on which, like castaway children, we played endless hide and seek.

Still keeping our promise to Dalashinsky, we'd taken separate cabins. I bunked with Ida, Benno with Zalmen Hirsch, and they were as ignorant of our married state as the rest.

Like so many sarcastic people, Ida was a terrible romantic, a pushover for the unlikeliest men. Her current heartthrob was a big lummox of an assistant stagehand, one of the "luxuries" we'd left behind to keep down the cost of the tour. This lummox (why do I recall this detail from Ida's personal life which she herself has probably forgotten?) had another girlfriend and was perfectly happy to see Ida go. But Ida blamed everything on that homewrecker, Dalashinsky.

Not that Ida talked about it; she just mumbled. Sitting beside her at meals, you got a running commentary on Dalashinsky's every word. ("Ensemble?" she would hiss through clenched teeth. "I guess some people were created more ensemble than others.") You might say that Ida wasn't exactly living the part of Leah's best friend and confidante. But really, how much of a role was Gittel? All Ida had to do was make sure I didn't fall on my face onstage. And frankly, I was glad that I couldn't add to Ida's misery by confiding that *my* true love—my husband, in fact—was sleeping chaste as a lamb, three cabins down with Zalmen.

In the Yiddish theater, you couldn't go to the toilet without kissing the whole cast good-bye—and hello again when you got back. Pecks on the cheek, you understand, except for Zalmen Hirsch, who insisted on mouth to mouth, his own lips wet and wide open. He never picked on the older women, but only the girls. And what were we supposed to do? Scream? We learned to duck and weave, sidestepping his arms. Onstage, when Menasha came toward me with the marriage veil, I used my memory of those blubbery caresses for the horror in my dybbuk voice.

On board the *Veracruz*, Zalmen kidded Benno about being "in the same boat" because Anski, that louse, had written *The Dybbuk* so that neither Chonon nor Menasha ever got into Leah's pants. Like a kid who's just discovered the facts of life, Zalmen saw hanky-panky everywhere. Two strangers couldn't walk down the hall without this one "chasing" that, so occupying Zalmen with their imaginary love affairs that he never once caught me and Benno stalking each other through the corridors, the public rooms.

Across tables loaded with cold stuffed lobsters, roast lamb, pastries, and champagne, we exchanged hungry looks. And while the others were promenading the decks, too busy digesting and complaining to notice our absence, Benno and I were in one of the cabins, rocking harder than the boat. One breath of salt air and we were Tristan and Isolde, the aristocracy of secret lovers, watching those spectacular sunsets with some unsuspecting actor wedged between us like a sword. Without considering the implications, I felt that Dalashinsky was our own King Mark. So deeply did I identify with Isolde that I wasn't stealing Wagner's best line but speaking from the heart when I leaned over the railing and told Benno, "The mystery of love is greater than the mystery of death."

The only reason I could mention mysteries was that Benno had left his Kabbala books in New York. Each one weighed a ton, and we were traveling with such strict luggage limits: To save a few ounces, I even removed Mama and Papa's photo from its cardboard folder. Still I suspected that Benno's fascination with the mystical had survived the loss of his books; and like the wife who needs reassurance long after her husband's flirtation with that pretty girl at the party, I kept bringing it up. Wasn't it too bad that he wouldn't have those holy volumes in Argentina? Maybe the *Zohar* had recipes for minting pesos.

"Who's got time to study on a honeymoon?" said Benno, the only time that bourgeois word "honeymoon" ever crossed our bohemian lips. And yet that first week out did exactly what a honeymoon is supposed to do. The bride got such roses in her cheeks that even Dalashinsky noticed.

"Miss Rappoport," he told me. "The sea breeze does wonders for your coloring. My compliments. Only one thing: When we get to Buenos Aires and you're doing your makeup for the play . . . a little more white, understand? Leah wasn't so healthy."

I might have appreciated this compliment more if not for the inconvenient moment he chose to pay it: I was sneaking through the corridor to Benno's room, and Dalashinsky was blocking my way.

By then, this was a constant occurrence, impossible to ignore: I couldn't get within fifty feet of Benno without running smack into Dalashinsky—always with some "urgent" reminder, some wonder to show me which absolutely couldn't wait.

"Everything is a lesson," said Dalashinsky, whose own conversation was nonstop instruction. "Only pay attention! It all can be used. Watch how those sailors walk. Practice their voices, their laughs. . . ." I wondered how many Mexican sailors he thought I'd be playing. But later, in *Anna Christie*, I did use the rolling gait and baritone chuckle of the *Veracruz*'s crew.

Once, Dalashinsky hustled me up on deck—we were sailing through a school of dolphins. I can still see his pale hands stretched out as if to touch them; those silvery backs jumping over the waves in arcs which flashed like mirrors and were harder to look at than the sun. And I can still hear the sob in his voice as he said, "Compared to that beauty, Miss Rappoport, our art is gefilte fish!"

For one second, I almost forgot that he was a genius. I almost patted his arm and said, "There, there, sweetheart. Don't be so hard on yourself." Instead of which, I got nervous.

"When you're hungry," I said, "one piece of gefilte fish looks better than a whole dolphin." What did that mean? I slapped myself on the side of the head, not just for making a stupid joke, but also to make sure that this was really me, Dinah Rappoport, making stupid jokes with the great Leon Dalashinsky.

Dalashinsky stared at me for so long, I had to look away. Then he smiled a long-suffering smile and said, "Only in the trashiest Second Avenue theaters do actresses slap themselves on the side of the head."

Unflattering as this observation was, it still meant that Leon Dalashinsky was observing me; it took all my restraint to keep from giving myself another slap for good measure.

Of course, we'd been physically close before, sharing the stage in those intense scenes between Leah and Rabbi Azrielke. And who could be closer, you might ask, than a girl and her exorcist? But such was Dalashinsky's talent that he *became* the wonder worker of Miropol, and Dalashinsky existed only as an emotional memory of awe, respect, and a twinge of fear to be used for Leah's feelings toward her deliverer.

We'd even been on tour together, with *Tevye*, by train to Kansas City and Chicago—tight quarters, but not nearly so buddy-buddy. There and back, we rode coach, while Dalashinsky secluded himself in a private compartment. Now too he had the only single cabin, but the layout and the general informality of the *Veracruz* were great equalizers. Besides, *The Dybbuk's* success had made stars of us all, and the way I knew was that Leon Dalashinsky took me on deck at night and showed me the constellations.

When it came to the theater, our director had no race or religion; he was a true citizen of the world. But faced with the wonders of God, he turned into one of those Jews who takes you aside and tells you (he has documented proof!) that the man in the moon is Jewish. Tracing the Big Dipper, Dalashinsky explained:

When Rabbi Yehuda was imprisoned by the Romans, he was kept in the hot sun till his tongue blackened from thirst, then set before a pig trough full of ice water. Before drinking, the rabbi prayed to God to forgive him in advance for touching such *tref*—when suddenly an angel flew down with a magic dipper which avoided the sides of the trough and miraculously purified the water. When Rabbi Yehuda had his fill, the angel took the dipper and hung it up, as if those black heavens were a hook on God's kitchen wall.

Dalashinsky showed me the so-called Warrior of Masada with his club, his shield, the three stars forming his belt, and told me:

During the tragic siege, one brave Jewish soldier hooked his belt over the battlements and hung from it, suspended outside the wall. What could the Romans do but stop everything and watch? For the three days that it took the soldier to die, the Israelites inside the fort got a break. In honor of this, God slung the warrior's belt over His own starry throne.

I remember Dalashinsky saying what marvelous stories

these were! If, God willing, he lived long enough, he would definitely adapt them for the stage. And I thought, Oh, what a marvelous play it would make!

Well, he did live long enough, but such a play never appeared. Maybe he lost interest. Or maybe he forgot after a few nights in New York, where over the years you could almost watch the stars grow dimmer until they became like that vacant lot, that candy store which used to be on your corner: They're gone. The street looks different now. You forget they were ever there.

Only I don't forget. For how could I not remember the time when Leon Dalashinsky paid attention, not only to the stars and the color in my cheeks, but even to the food on my plate at breakfast?

"Miss Rappoport," he would lecture me from across the captain's table, "an artist can't survive on a bite of melba toast and a sip of hot chocolate."

The whole Yiddish Art Theater put down their coffee cups—ensemble. And afterward, like any family of grown children, they analyzed Papa's every action for hidden motives and signs of change.

"It's common sense," said Feivel, who was something of a naturopath, a great believer in citrus fruits and fresh-air hikes. "A good diet . . ."

"Since when," said Clara, who always had a practical point to stick in her husband's balloons, "do we look to Dalashinsky for common sense?"

"He's got to control everything," grumbled Ida. "Even our food."

"Not mine." Zalmen smirked. "But when a married man goes traveling, away from the wife and kids, he starts to notice what the young girls eat."

I *was* young—newly married, newly crowned Queen of the Yiddish Art Theater. With another man, I might have suspected that his attentions had something to do with my personal charm. But Dalashinsky wasn't a man to me; he was a kind of god. And no matter what you secretly think or hope, you can't seriously believe that God might have a crush on you.

I kept out of those discussions. I barely heard them. For like a broken record, my mind was replaying the end of Dalashinsky's breakfast lecture, that thrilling promise:

"When we get back to New York, Miss Rappoport, I will take you for breakfast to a little café where the owner's wife makes the most extraordinary noodle *kugel*."

For art, I stuffed myself with tomato herring, kaiser rolls and butter, scrambled *huevos* with onions and peppers. Then, with a stomach like a miniature storm at sea, I'd follow Dalashinsky on deck, where he'd urge me to develop my voice. Hadn't I heard of Rabbi Pincus the Orator, who'd gone down to the beach with stones in his mouth to outroar the breakers? The ocean wind blew my shouts back in my face. And when Dalashinsky shouted against the wind that the future of the Yiddish Art Theater depended on young talents like mine, I *did* feel like the Queen of Egypt, cruising the Nile on her barge.

Because let's face it: When the Great Man singles you out, you shine. It's not love, exactly. You don't imagine getting married or having babies with such a man, or even getting into bed. But like love, it makes life sweeter. Colors seem brighter; you notice shades you've never seen before. The most boring routines are almost fun, and your days move to a jazzy rhythm, a deedle deedle deedle in your head.

I'm sure the psychiatrists have their own explanation for this thrill of being chosen and approved. Maybe it comes from the desire to see, just once more, that look on Mama and Papa's faces when you took your first baby step. If so, it's not so bad. As desires go, it's pretty innocent—just as mine would have seemed if I hadn't, at the same time, lost my desire for Benno.

For where was Benno during all these private lessons? Waiting for me in his cabin.

One morning he got tired of waiting and, as luck would have it, came up just in time for breakfast. He took one look at the food on my plate and knew that something was fishy.

"What's got into you?" he whispered. "Since when do you eat such feasts before noon?" And Leon Dalashinsky (we had all seen Hinda scream in his face and he didn't hear) overheard.

"My dear Mr. Brownstein," he said. "Do you know what the great Olga Knipper ate every morning? A wild mushroom omelet, a whole cream cheese, a five-pound loaf of black pumpernickel, and coffee with heavy cream. And you're begrudging Miss Rappoport one lousy herring?"

It was one thing for Dalashinsky to teach us how to walk, talk, and breathe, but Benno drew the line at another man telling his wife what to eat for breakfast. It was so intimate, he said, he would almost rather have found me in Dalashinsky's bed.

"In bed?" I cried. "With Dalashinsky?" No, I insisted, everything was perfectly kosher. The director and I were so intimate we never called each other anything but Miss Rappoport and Mr. Dalashinsky.

"You and I were Miss Rappoport and Mr. Brownstein," Benno reminded me. "And we were already married."

I swore to God that I had never so much as laid a hand on Dalashinsky's arm. Fellow artists, we talked nothing but art, not one personal word. Besides, as Benno well knew, Dalashinsky wasn't my type. Too short, too pompous, too nervous, old enough to be my grandfather, except that my *zayde*, rest in peace, was a better-looking man. I liked my men strong and modest, soft-spoken, with voices like clarinets. If I'd wanted a rabbi like Dalashinsky, I would have looked in the *shul*. And I reminded Benno of those early nights of our marriage when, too tired for mystical speculation or even more love, we'd lie in bed and gossip about the cast. What, we wondered aloud, did all those women see in Dalashinsky? As if there were nothing to "see" in anyone but a strong young body and a face from forty days before birth.

Reassured by these memories, Benno would probably have believed me, except that as the weather turned hotter, I grew steadily cooler toward him; in the second week of that voyage, I found a million reasons not to meet him in his cabin. Later, I told him. After breakfast, lunch, dinner, after my bath. When we slipped through the corridors in our games of hide and seek, I turned corners and hid so that really, he couldn't find me.

When he did catch me, I tried to play our love scenes "as if" I were a woman in love, but the "magic if" eluded me. In bed with Benno, I feared that Zalmen might interrupt us. I heard footsteps in the hall. I thought: Dalashinsky. And though it wasn't that I wanted to be with Dalashinsky, I couldn't seem to forget that he might be looking for me.

Nor could I understand why this chilliness had come over me; all I could come up with was the physical fact that Benno's touch was rubbing me the wrong way. I asked myself, What good were Benno's magic spells when he couldn't even enchant his own wife?

Meanwhile, I faked seasickness, headaches. I pretended my time of month had come every day, and felt so miserable, it might just as well have been true. I'd heard that romance faded —but so fast? A corpse didn't cool so quick. I felt bitter, shocked, cheated out of infinite possibilities. For the first time, I was sorry that I hadn't shared my good fortune with Ida, for now I had no one to help me endure the bad.

"Some secret honeymoon," complained Benno. "It's even a secret from me." Again he would hint about me and Dalashinsky, and I would get indignant: I'd like to see *him* refuse individual coaching. And who exactly was he jealous of? Dalashinsky or me?

It took twenty years before Benno and I could joke about that trip. Then Benno asked, Wasn't I a little bit in love with Dalashinsky on that tour? A little little bit?

And I would answer, Absolutely not.

By then Benno could pretend to doubt me. Why else, he asked, had I changed overnight from being his mystical bride to avoiding him like the plague?

"Benno," I said. "*I* was the one with the plague. Dalashinsky was only the mildest symptom. Already I was teetering on the edge. And remember what happened later? Our problems on that boat were coming attractions, previews of worse to come. . . ."

For evidence, I brought up that night we crossed the equator.

All that day, there had been no breeze, and the motionless sea made it seem as if the earth at its widest point were too fat and lazy to turn. I'd spent the evening on deck with Dalashinsky, staring out at the water. The heat was so oppressive that for the first time in history Dalashinsky couldn't talk. Around midnight I went to my cabin, tossed and turned, then drifted into one of those restless sleeps—you think you're awake till something awakens you.

It was still black outside when I heard the sailors running through the halls, yelling and beating tin cans. Even Ida, who was sleeping the dead sleep of the heartbroken, twelve hours a night, sat up straight.

"Fire!" I said.

"All that exploding popcorn," said Ida. "What a way to go!"

We threw dresses over our nightgowns and ran up on deck, where we found the crew and passengers wearing ridiculous party hats and toasting each other with tequila and champagne. At first Feivel refused to drink, but after a while he was wiping the mouth of the tequila bottle on the sleeve of his bathrobe and tossing it back like orange juice. Only Benno and Dalashinsky —why was I so relieved to see this?—weren't wearing hats.

Dressed as King Neptune in a loincloth, a trident, and a paste-on beard, one of the sailors loped among us like a big friendly bear, dancing to the lilting waltzes a mariachi band was playing on fiddles and mandolins; at one point they attempted a syncopated Latin version of *"Rozhinkes und Mandlen."*

As we crossed zero latitude, the captain blew a long blast on the ship's whistle—and an awful thought occurred to me: Suppose Columbus was wrong, and the earth *was* flat. What if we fell off the edge?

Only when the whistle stopped did I notice that everyone was pointing at me and laughing. Because there I stood in that windless night, gripping the railings and bracing myself for our plunge.

3

BUENOS AIRES. If the name conjures up a clean, whitewashed harbor opening its arms to guide you into a gentle bay, it is conjuring up Rio de Janeiro. The approach to Buenos Aires is upstream along the Rio de la Plata, its water so rusty, so dishwater-dirty, you would think all the housewives in the city had turned out that morning to scour their pots and pans.

I remember Feivel Frumkin standing on deck and reading aloud from a guidebook which sounded as if Papa had written it. For every page of description, two pages of warnings about the con men, the "porters" who took your luggage and disappeared into the wilds of Patagonia. The port itself was so low and flat that, like a badly designed stage, it was hidden from view by a few large freighters docked in the front rows. Still, we could feel its heat and hear it hissing and banging like the radiators in Mama's flat.

"Buenos Aires," grumbled Zalmen. "Maybe the air was good five hundred years ago when they named the place. . . ."

Disembarking is like growing up: With all the pushing and baggage and rushing around, you don't know what's happening till it's over, and then (if the trip's been pleasant) you can look back and miss it the rest of your life. As we left the *Veracruz*, Dalashinsky barreled past without seeing me—his old oblivious self. Boarding at New York, Benno had never been more than one step behind me. But now he pressed forward with the others, leaving me to follow the back of his head. Already I was longing for the closeness of that ocean cruise (with all its problems!) just as I mourned my childhood in the ribbon shop, and maybe we all felt the same. Walking the plank in the opposite direction, Clara shook the captain's hand and said solemnly, "*Adios.*"

And yet from the moment we stepped on Argentinean soil, we had enough to worry about without getting nostalgic. If in the backs of our minds, we'd expected to be welcomed by another Miss Liberty with her uplifted lamp and placid green face, how disappointed we were to be met at the dock by a roly-poly gaucho in a hat trimmed with pompoms which bobbed in front of his eyes. I remember thinking: There's something wrong down here, these South American cowboys grow only half as tall as the Northern breed—when all of a sudden, the gaucho swept off his hat with a hearty "*Shalom Aleichem!*"

"I am Simon Popolescu," he said, revealing more than his name. For one thing, his accent. Every one of us in the theater could have given a course in regional accents, and this Popolescu's was textbook Rumanian. For another, his bald head framed by a semicircle of reddish hair. And finally, a gap between his front teeth which (I decided immediately) was made for lying through.

"My dear Mr. Dalashinsky, brothers, sisters, fellow artists and Jews . . ." While talking this blue streak, Popolescu shot his right hand out for emphasis, a gesture which reminded me of someone dealing cards. And frankly, his whole conversation suggested the patter cardsharps use to distract you while aces are vanishing up their sleeves. When Popolescu stepped forward to take Dalashinsky's valise, I bit my tongue to keep from yelling, "Watch out! Don't give it to him! Or at least demand a receipt!" Hadn't our head-in-the-clouds director heard the warnings in Feivel's book?

Apparently not. Dalashinsky surrendered his suitcase willingly, partly because he needed another free hand to accept the enormous stack of theater tickets Popolescu was pressing on him.

"Thank you," said Dalashinsky. "I'm flattered that you think we have so many friends in Buenos Aires. But really, we can

only use so many complimentary passes. A dozen, maybe. . . ."
We looked at each other. What dozen? None of us, Dalashinsky included, knew one single soul in all Argentina.
"Complimentary?" said Popolescu. "Do you think this is Second Avenue, where they can afford to give tickets away? With all due respect, Mr. Dalashinsky, this is Argentina, where the climate for Jews is so bad, we can't even grow our own actors. We must import them like caviar, and like caviar, we pay by the ounce. We've shipped in companies from London, Warsaw, Bessarabia; it isn't cheap. With travel expenses alone, we must fill the house every night to break even. Like it or not, we're a strictly nonprofit concern, and everyone pitches in. It's customary here for actors to sell tickets door to door. We divide the city up like a side of beef, and for you, Mr. Dalashinsky, the choicest cut."

In the horrified silence which followed, we studied Dalashinsky's back. He was taking the shallow *luftpauses*, which, he had taught us, fill the lungs for a monologue—or a roar. But (what a lesson in restraint!) he exhaled in one rush and spoke very softly.

"Excuse me, Mr. Popolescu. Do we look to you like old ladies hawking chances on the Vilderbester Society raffle? We're artists, my dear Popolescu, not Boy Scouts."

Popolescu put his gaucho hat back on and said, "Excuse *me*, but it goes with the job. The best chefs also know how to wash a dish."

Not us, I could have told him. If business and salesmanship were the dishwashing part of our profession, then the Yiddish Art Theater left egg all over the plates, and Dalashinsky especially didn't know scouring powder from sponge. Of us all, only Feivel had the wherewithal to read a contract, to look, as it were, for the grains of kasha stuck under the rim of the pan. And it was Feivel, with his job of getting us moving before the dog lifted its leg, who said, "Ladies and gentlemen, back on the boat!"

Dalashinsky didn't budge except to place one hand on Popolescu's shoulder. With the other, he was brushing the pompoms to one side like a mother smoothing hair back from her baby's brow.

"My dearest Mr. Popolescu," he said. "Let me be the first to tell you about a marvelous invention, the best thing to happen to the theater since electricity. It's known, my friend, as the box office."

From the corner of my eye, I saw Benno smirking, and I knew why. At home, Dalashinsky acted as if he'd never heard of a box office, except as some distant rumor hinting that he might or might not be able to finance his latest production scheme. Our director was making a private joke: He hated electricity and its limitations, and was always waxing nostalgic for the gaslit theaters of his boyhood in Bialystock. And finally, to Dalashinksy, casual acquaintances were playthings, sweethearts, chickadees. But strangers were never "my friend."

With nothing settled, Popolescu turned and started walking. And we, after all our talk about getting back on the boat, had no choice but to pick up our luggage and follow—rolling bow-legged through those streets which pitched under our feet like the sea.

"Welcome to the Paris of South America," said Popolescu. And though I had never been to France, I felt certain that the city of Rachel and the Divine Sarah would never allow its citizens to paint their houses aqua and lemon, the pastel pinks and blues of baby blankets. You might think that a girl who entered the theater for the colors would have been cheered by these. But while Rappoport's Trimmings was narrow and safe as a crib, every alley here seemed wider than Fifth Avenue. Crossing those dusty plazas, I felt vulnerable, exposed; worse horrors than con men could have come at us from anywhere.

As we trooped along those avenues of yucca and palm, I smelled a fragrance of gardenias so strong that I looked around for its source, then a whiff of horse manure which made me stop looking and concentrate on where I was putting my feet. This city had a statue for everything. Squares which didn't even have pavement had bronze conquistadors, mossy stallions reared back on two legs so the nannies could park their baby strollers in the shade of those menacing front hooves.

I remember the most tempting fried-food smell which hit us several blocks before we got to a stand selling some kind of fritters.

"Pork knishes," explained Popolescu. And those two words proved, once and for all: We really were on the other side of the world.

"What?" we cried, half in disbelief and half because we weren't sure we'd heard. This Buenos Aires made New York sound like the reading room in a public library. Every oxcart, every carriage, every bicycle had a horn, and like geese, everyone honked. Shouting over the racket, Dalashinsky, Feivel, and Popolescu argued all the way to the hotel. Still yelling, Feivel had collected our passports and was signing the register when Popolescu conceded: Out of the goodness of his heart, and respect for the Leon Dalashinsky Art Theater, the Teatro Colonial would establish a box office, strictly on a trial basis.

"Watch," Dalashinsky told Popolescu. "History will justify me."

The Zona Azura Hotel was an instant migraine of turquoise paint, inside and out. The first bad sign was the outhouse in the courtyard, so thickly hung with green lizards that I mistook it at first for a grape arbor. The second was the dumbwaiter of an elevator which wheezed and dangled over the first floor before summoning the strength to go up. The third—and most telling —was our bellhop, a scrawny twelve-year-old who appeared to be in constant pain; only when he set down our baggage did we realize that his agony was the strain of being unable to scratch.

If I wrote a guidebook, my first sentence would be: Watch out for hotels where the bellhop scratches. But how could I write guidebooks, when I have learned that one man's fleabag is another man's Ritz? This I know from Dalashinsky's memoirs, which state categorically that the Ritz wasn't good enough for the Yiddish Art Theater.

Ida and I shared a tiny turquoise cell with two cots, two moth-eaten blankets, no pillows, a giant crucifix, and a billion mosquitoes. I burrowed under my blanket to escape them. And what did I find crawling there?

"Jesus." Ida clasped her hands and extended them towards the crucifix. "Make me stop itching."

The walls were so thin we could hear the others in their rooms, slapping and cursing the bedbugs. I wondered how Dalashinsky was planning to use this. Then I thought about Benno, and was glad that we were apart. If one last drop of passion still ran in our veins, those bloodsuckers would have drunk it for breakfast.

If so, they would have been the only ones who got breakfast which, our bellhop informed us, the Zona Azura didn't serve, thus driving a grumpy and disheveled Yiddish Art Theater out into what passed there for daylight.

Natty Kauffman, a sweet little *feigele* who was playing a half dozen minor roles, was wearing an eye patch, which he lifted to show us both lids swollen shut from an insect bite. But he took the patch off when we got to the first place which seemed like it might serve coffee, the kind of café which makes even actors sink down in their collars and cut the pirate act.

The Café El Rastro was wall-to-wall racketeer—sailors, smugglers, white slavers of every nationality but only one sex. Ida, Clara, and I were the only girls in the place. With all the huddling, the hushed discussions, every table looked like a crapshoot. But these hoodlums were too serious for dice, too busy making deals.

In an open kitchen, a cook with a drippy nose was brewing what looked like tea in what looked like a dirty sock. Not that it mattered: I took only one sip. Dying of thirst, I couldn't have put that cup to my lips again, not even if Rabbi Yehuda's angel had come down with the magic dipper. I didn't expect a sugar cube to sip through in a civilized way; but neither did I expect the sugar bowl to be an ant farm mapped with the tunnels and byways of an insect civilization.

No one could eat, but no one (and these were the big gourmets who'd squawked that the *Veracruz*'s anisette-flavored dem-

itasse was poison) made a peep. Feivel paid the bill and re-
corded the outrageous sum in a notebook, then we set off with
such joyous expressions that, as our little procession passed,
you could actually see people looking around for the coffin.

Our spirits lifted when we spotted the theater: Popolescu had
kept his promise. From two blocks away we could see the new,
still-unpainted kiosk with its narrow window and a huge sign
saying THEATER TICKETS in Yiddish, Spanish, and English. And
what could have warmed an actor's heart more than the sight of
a hundred people already milling around beneath the marquee?

"You see?" said Dalashinsky. "Down here in the tropics, history works fast."

We were almost at the theater when I heard Zalmen whisper
to Feivel, "Well, I'll be damned if these Buenos Aires ladies don't
look like a busy night on Allen and Delancey."

And Feivel said, "Solly, what's wrong with your eyesight?
These ladies make Allen Street girls look like the kind of prizes
you bring home for dinner at Mama's."

Up close, a blind man (unless he also had no nose) could
have told that these weren't ladies. The women on Allen Street
made lewd remarks when men walked by, but these Buenos
Aires girls let their perfume do the talking. Allen Street ladies
dressed like the rest of us, with maybe a little less at the hem and
neck; here they ran around in their underwear—frilly, old-fash-
ioned bodices with necklines down to the waist. On Allen Street
they dyed their hair, smoked, spat, and did other things ladies
don't do; here they lounged around with their hands behind
their heads, their elbows out, lifting masses of ringlets (oiled
like frying pans and long enough to sit on), displaying the
points of their breasts and the curls in their armpits. And the
makeup was out of this world! With all his Expressionist craziness, Dalashinsky would never have let us walk onstage in war
paint like that.

Like the crooks at the Café El Rastro, these women were an
international crew: Germans, Italians, Irish, Swedes, the off-
spring of every imaginable mixed marriage. Given that it was a
Yiddish theater, the majority of Jewish girls was no surprise.

The shock was that they were the ones who glared at us just as Rachel's neighbors must have eyed Abraham's servant: What were we doing at *their* well?

Suddenly I got light-headed. Before each step, I felt for the ground as if I were going downstairs in the dark. I had the strangest notion (almost a hallucination) that we had missed the theater completely and stumbled into a market for the buying and selling of tropical birds. The ladies' dresses were as showy as parrot feathers; the gossip, in a dozen fractured languages, sounded like the yammering of cockatoos. And the musky blend of perfume, hair oil, and sweat smelled, in my agitated state, like a bird cage.

I remember passing a bunch of pimps—what else could they have been in those snappy panamas, those nasty malacca canes suggesting hidden switchblades, those pointy shoes so brightly polished that they could look at their feet and adjust the tilt of their hats? From the way they were leaning together, passing something around, I naturally assumed: dirty pictures. I couldn't resist a peek—and what did I see? A miniature pearl-handled pistol, like a toy. It was difficult but not impossible to imagine it shooting real bullets.

My first thought was: Get me out of here! Tomorrow night I'll be playing to a houseful of gangsters armed to the teeth. Suppose some hothead decides he doesn't like the show? Poor Mama and Papa, now they'll really have reason to cry!

In my fantasies, I was traveling back to New York as a bullet-riddled corpse, crated and stacked with the sides of beef on the *Veracruz*. This daydream was so vivid I actually heard someone slide back the hatch and enter the hold—when suddenly a pointy shoe speared my foot and I thought, Thank God, I'm alive!

The grating sound had come from the box-office window, opening for business, and the shoe belonged to one of the pimps who were charging it like the Light Brigade. Squabbling like friends grabbing the check at a restaurant, they mobbed forward; each one insisted on buying tickets not just for his neighbor, but for his neighbor's girls. All in fun, at first, but then someone shoved, someone snarled; half of them were still having fun and the others were ready to punch it out.

In New York in those days, celebrities got a wide berth. When people started recognizing me from *The Dybbuk*, I felt them giving me extra space on the street. But there, on the other side of the world, fans trampled right over the stars they were paying to see. What would have been a full-scale riot back home, complete with police and reporters too, was simply the way these Argentineans bought tickets.

At the time, though, I wasn't making fancy comparisons. I was concentrating on breathing.

"Benno!" I "projected" for all I was worth. "Dalashinsky! Come save me!"

And where was my mystical bridegroom? My spiritual father? Neither Benno nor Dalashinsky was looking for me. Instead they were following Popolescu, who had bobbed up like a cork on that human sea. And it was Popolescu who fished us out of that crowd and stuffed us, one by one, through the stage door.

"*Mazel tov*," he was saying. "This box-office idea is pure genius."

Dust, old upholstery, mildew, perfume, disinfectant—if I closed my eyes and sniffed, it was Stuyvesant Place. What did it matter that the Teatro Colonial was so badly designed, if a midget sat in front of you, you couldn't see? What did we care about acoustics which muffled sound like eiderdown quilts? Even there, so far from home, that musty theater smell worked better than opium. We closed our eyes and sniffed.

Drugged, we located our dressing rooms. Crates were pried open; our sets, props, and costumes appeared like long-lost friends. That they'd weathered that leaky shrimp boat in perfect shape seemed like a good sign.

"The trip to America should have been so smooth," said Clara. "I'd still have Mama's wedding china."

Not until we'd regrouped onstage did I contemplate the empty house and remember the crowd outside. Talk about pearls before swine! Tomorrow night the cream of the Yiddish theater would be playing to the dregs. We all must have had the same thought—Dalashinsky voiced it. He took a deep breath, sighed wearily and said, "When Yiddish drama first came to the New York stage, the rabbis made an awful stink. To those poor, tradition-bound old geezers, theaters and bordellos were one and the same, and a theater ticket was an instant passport to degradation.

"At the risk of sounding immodest, I have always considered myself an imaginative man. Whole plays pop up in my head like mushrooms after a rain. Even so, I could never imagine how a theater could be like a whorehouse—never, that is, till now."

"Yes." Popolescu was stalling. "Well . . ." He took a breath (if Dalashinsky could sigh, so could he) and drew himself up to his full five-five.

"Let me explain," he said, and launched into the speech he obviously gave everyone—touring companies, local rabbis, respectable citizens, maybe City Hall. After so much rehearsal, his explanation was so polished, so logical, impassioned, dripping with good intentions—if I hadn't known, I'd have thought it was Ibsen.

The gist of it was that prostitutes and theater people were one big happy family.

We girls were the first to get this gist and the first to get itchy. For this, you must understand, was a sensitive point. Things haven't changed so drastically, don't be fooled; but in those days, *no one* believed that an actress could be an honest woman, married for life to one man. Rumors involved us in daily scandals, adultery and worse. We denied till the cows came home, but that didn't stop the Suffolk Street rabbi from denouncing us from his pulpit, intoning our names from the playbill like the seder list of plagues. As artists, we were theoretically invulnerable to such barbs; but it stung when no one would tell us exactly what the Suffolk Street rabbi said. And though Mama and Papa never doubted my virtue, their fear of my being hurt by nasty gossip helped reinforce their opposition to my life in art.

Now Popolescu was implying the same thing in different words. And the proof of his eloquence was that we let him talk.

"Since the dawn of time," he was saying, "prostitution has flourished in the temple of art and vice versa. In classical Greece, in the theater of Sophocles and Euripides, what do you think those boys were selling at intermission? Lemonade?"

Who knows how the mind works? What crossed mine at that moment was that Leon Dalashinsky had met his Hinda selling lemonade at Stuyvesant Place. I glanced at Dalashinsky, but he was giving Popolescu his famous total attention. The thought of Hinda and the fact that I was the only one thinking it gave me the tiniest twinge of guilt, as if Hinda's husband and I had really done something on that boat. By the time it wore off, Popolescu had worked his way through a thousand years of theatrical history.

"What about Shakespeare? You think men took their *wives* to see *Romeo and Juliet*? To hear Falstaff's filthy jokes? And what do you think the King of England bought from Nell Gwynne? Oranges?

"Soon after"—Popolescu lowered his voice—"the Puritans severed this vital connection, cut the very umbilical cord of art. And the baby was never the same. Only in one place"—he was practically shouting now—"has this golden tradition survived. And where is that? Argentina!"

"Don't flatter yourself," said Zalmen. "I could take you to a half dozen Bowery music halls where it's still going strong."

"I wish your attitude surprised me," Popolescu said. "But it doesn't. Artists and prostitutes have always been an embarrassment to their families. And in most families, I've noticed, the black sheep don't talk to each other either. When in fact. . . . Let me tell you a story:

"A few years ago we imported a company from Paris. To put it mildly, this was no Dalashinsky Art Theater. These were entertainers, and what I had in mind was honest trash, dancing, singing the sentimental old favorites. Ophelia has to go mad?

Fine, I say, so long as she does it to the tune of *"Rozhinkes und Mandlen."* But those French are such snobs. Missionaries to the yokels, they were bringing us a Yiddish translation of Racine! " 'Messieurs,' I said, 'this is not the Sorbonne.' But what could I do with Jews who claimed they'd never heard *"Rozhinkes und Mandlen"*? And of all the troupes who have ever played here, they were the most indignant to learn that the opening night crowd would be, as I explained to you, *tref.*

"Well, even God can't see a snob without wanting to rub his nose in it. Two lines into her biggest scene, the Jewish Phèdre got a stomachache, some tourist complaint. Ever since Bernhardt, the French have nearly killed themselves outsuffering each other, but this girl was really in pain. They lopped ten minutes off the second act and were just about to call it a night—"

"No understudy?" said Dalashinsky.

"What can I tell you?" Popolescu shrugged. "But at that point, a 'lady' "—he hooked quotation marks in the air around lady—"came up from the audience and offered to do Phèdre so they could finish out the show. Now take one guess who this lady was."

"Lola Montez," said Zalmen.

"Close," said Popolescu. "Mamie Rifkin-Ramirez."

"I couldn't have guessed in a million years," said Ida.

It took Popolescu a while to believe that we didn't recognize the name. "You've heard, of course, of The Aviator?"

"Earhart?" said Feivel.

"No," said Popolescu. "Engelhart! You haven't? It's incredible, don't you have newspapers? Half the streets in Buenos Aires are named after him: Calle Engelhart, Engelhart Park, the Boulevard Engelhart. . . . Well, never mind. It's a different story, it happened later. I was telling you how Mamie Ramirez volunteered to play Phèdre.

"The Frenchmen almost died. So I gave them a choice: Give the lady a chance or pay for your own tickets home. They unwound that poor actress's toga so fast that she spun—and put it on our Mamie.

"Now, I'm no critic. But take my word. If it wasn't Racine, Racine should only have written such Yiddish. No, don't take my word—ask anyone. Or better yet, count the curtain calls. The stamping almost turned the balcony into a mezzanine. Between bows, the director was offering his 'find' a free trip to Paris and a lifetime contract.

" 'Why travel so far,' said Mamie, 'to do the same work?' "

Benno was raising his eyebrows and nodding to show Popolescu that we knew he was pulling a fast one. For Dalashinsky had drummed it into us: In the theater, there were no "naturals." Talent, of course, the essential gift. But then came years of work. You didn't just wrap a *schmatte* around yourself and do Phèdre.

"How did she do it?" said Benno, and I liked it that he asked. Not so long before, Benno would have recognized Popolescu's story as a parable about a downpour of emanations and a lucky rain barrel.

"That's what everyone wondered," replied Popolescu. "And guess what our little Phèdre said? 'Ask any "working girl" in the audience,' she said. 'Our job is nine-tenths acting.' "

It's astounding how many dignified, sophisticated people will fake a laugh in response to an off-color story, especially if the joke's on them. There was Popolescu, suggesting that every streetwalker could do our job better than we did. And there we were, chuckling like traveling salesmen. Only Dalashinsky, our integrity, refused to crack a smile.

"Children," he said, "this Argentina is truly a marvelous place. Here the prostitutes spout Racine off the top of their heads, and the pimps write Shakespeare's sonnets in their spare time. But really, Mr. Popolescu, *shouldn't* we be giving tickets away? Family passes? What bothers me is that our brothers and sisters out there are paying to get in. . . ."

"All right," said Popolescu. "We're all grown-ups. Let's put our cards on the table. The girls are big business here. Import-export, and perfectly legal. It's nothing to boast about, but it's not *my* line of work. I wouldn't want my sons to go into it. I thank God that I don't have daughters—"

No sooner had Popolescu said the magic word than I thought of Mama and Papa, and of the evening when Benno and I went over to tell them about Dalashinsky's travel plans.

"It's the other side of the world!" wailed Mama, the real Sarah Bernhardt. She put one hand to her forehead and sank down into a chair. "I'm fainting!" On the pretext of getting her water, Papa dragged me into the kitchen.

"Buenos Aires," he hissed. (Papa was a fastidious man, and what hurt was that, in his terror for me, he sprayed the air with spit and didn't care.) "Better you should play the Black Hole of Calcutta. Argentina is where girls go to disappear. It's the international capital of the white slave trade, and Buenos Aires is one big auction block. If you must go, Dinele, please don't eat anything. Don't drink. They slip something into your food and soon you're in Shanghai or worse, in the harem of some fat greasy Turk with a passion for Jewish girls."

At that age, I was the bravest I'd ever be, but nervous enough about traveling so that this Turk was easier to imagine than an old age rummaging through garbage.

Meanwhile, I hadn't eaten one bite in Argentina, I hadn't drunk . . . but what about that tea at the Café El Rastro? Was one sip enough? The fact was, I *did* feel woozy. I could almost hear myself telling the Turk, "You can't do this to me, I'm the Queen of the Yiddish Art Theater. . . ." Down here, so far away from Mama and Papa—if I went under, who would pull me up? Not Benno, not Dalashinsky, and certainly not Popolescu, who (even as I thought these terrible thoughts) was droning on.

"It pays the rent, so we make do. For a while, we had two separate theaters, two *shuls*—one for the meat trade, one for the cream. But ask any housewife what it's like with two sets of dishes: double trouble, and someone's always mixing it up. We compromised: one theater, two separate sections—until the rabbi's wife heard from some quack that social diseases could be caught through the air.

"'Rebbitzin,' I said, 'if that were true, all Buenos Aires would be one running sore.' But when women get something in their heads, an earthquake can't dislodge it. We compromised again. One night kosher, the next night *tref*. And in between we wash the theater down with disinfectant."

"Children," said Dalashinsky. "This really is the opposite side of the world, if the *tref* gets opening night."

"Know why?" said Popolescu. "The actors prefer it. The greatest stars have told me that easy livers make a warmer first-night crowd. For who could better understand a drama of high passion than people whose business is love? And tell me, Mr. Dalashinsky, in how many places are there riots to buy tickets?"

There was a silence. Then Dalashinsky said, "In New York too we have riots."

On Second Avenue, I thought, but not on Stuyvesant Place, where the Art Theater crowd queued up in orderly lines. The fact that Dalashinsky had felt challenged enough to borrow from Second Avenue made me jump to his defense.

"Since when is a riot so great?" I said. "I'm black and blue to the knees from those pointy shoes—and that was getting off easy."

"Ah, the prima donna," said Popolescu, and I knew that I was feeling the backhand of his card-dealing style. "They're trampling each other to see her—and she's complaining."

"We have no prima donnas," said Dalashinsky, but it felt less like a defense than another betrayal, a reprimand for having spoken out of turn. "We work as an ensemble."

Then suddenly his whole face relaxed, and I could tell that just saying the word "ensemble" had reminded him of our identity, our purpose. We had come to Buenos Aires to create art, not to bicker with Popolescu about the sex life of his audience.

"Enough," said Dalashinsky. "Who are we to go against an ancient tradition? It's only a five-night engagement, not our entire careers. Besides, we've all played to lower forms of life than pimps and prostitutes—critics, for example. Just promise me one thing, Mr. Popolescu. Promise that this audience won't be doing its business while we're doing ours. As long as we're onstage, we must have total silence, attention, respect. . . ."

"That goes without saying," said Popolescu. "Take my word. The theater will be so quiet, you'll be able to hear the fleas bite."

By the time we left the Teatro Colonial, it was early afternoon. The box office was shut, the crowd dispersed. Streets were deserted, shutters drawn against the midday heat. In just a few hours, Buenos Aires seemed to have been devastated, as if by war. Yet only in the plazas had this battle left corpses: peasants sleeping in the shadow of their donkeys, who were sleeping, in turn, in the shade of those giant bronze hooves.

It was lucky that things moved fast down there since no one stayed awake very long. And after the long walk back to the Zona Azura, we too were ready for a siesta. We sat in the lobby, snoozing like old folks after a meal, until, one by one, we made ourselves get up and go to our rooms.

When I opened my door, a dozen lizards froze on the wall, then skittered toward the ceiling. I let them get settled, and was just climbing into bed when Ida came in, carrying a newspaper. I grabbed for it.

"What good is this?" I whined, cranky from heat and disappointment. "Between us, the only Spanish we know is *café con leche.*"

"It's not for reading," she said. "It's for fanning ourselves and swatting bugs." She divided the paper in half and we lay there, fanning like mad in the hopes of creating unfavorable conditions for mosquito landings. Then Ida said, "Dinah," in a strangled voice, and before I could ask what was wrong, she'd turned gray as newsprint, clapped the paper over her mouth, and run out the door.

I knew what was wrong. Ida's color was its own diagnosis. And selfish or not, my first reaction was that Ida hadn't eaten or drunk any more than I had. So maybe the rebbitzin was right, maybe you could catch diseases through the air. And maybe the white slavers' drugs could work the same way. Oh, Papa (I sent him a desperate postcard in my mind), come look for me in the fleshpots of Istanbul!

At that moment, someone knocked on my door, and I had no

doubt that it was the Turk himself—or anyway, one of his henchmen. Instead of calling for help (I was too afraid that no one would come), I sat like a statue. Nothing, I decided, was worse than watching a doorknob turn when you haven't said "Come in."

What a relief to see Benno! It made my knees knock harder than the danger itself and also made me see what I'd overlooked on the *Veracruz*. Namely, my mate from forty days before birth. Apparently, Benno was thinking the same; he locked the door behind him.

One key click, and I was miserable.

"Don't lock it," I said. "Ida . . ."

"I passed Ida." Benno puffed out his cheeks like a chipmunk. "She didn't stop to say hello. From the looks of it, she'll be gone for a while."

And that gave Benno the right to lock *my* door? I felt a little shiver of annoyance. Since then, I have learned that such shivers come and go without permanent damage to love or even passion. But it was so new to Benno and me that it shook me like a fever which shot right up when Benno sat down on the edge of my bed and started stroking my forehead, smoothing back the stuck-on hair.

Two weeks before, that touch would have sprung me like a jack-in-the-box into Benno's arms. But now it bothered me like another mosquito; I brushed his fingers away. Two weeks before, the challenge of sneaking around would have thrilled me; now discovery seemed like another inconvenience.

"Somebody might come in," I said. "You'd better go. Anyhow, it's the middle of the afternoon, for God's sake. Broad daylight."

This finally was what made Benno's jaw drop, and now he let go of *me* like a hot potato.

My Benno was a most extraordinary man. In forty-four years of marriage, he never once used the past to accuse or compare me—not even then, when our history was so short and sweet. And why state the obvious? In the past, we had always preferred the light for love, even if moths flew in.

In forty-four years, Benno never asked twice; he had pride. He was already retreating, but not fast enough for me.

"Benno," I said, "I didn't feel those strong arms around me this morning when the pimps of Buenos Aires were stomping on my head."

So this was what I was holding against him! I jumped at this almost logical explanation, then jumped back, horrified to be looking for things to hold against him.

"Dinah," said Benno. "No one was stomping on your head. Besides, you're a city girl. That crowd this morning was no worse than the rush-hour El."

"You wish," I said. "You wish the rush-hour El meant perfume and naked armpits and parrots to buy and sell. . . ."

"Parrots?" said Benno. "Armpits?"

Another man might have started a shouting match. But Benno was halfway out the door. I knew him; he would have liked to leave me laughing. But not even Benno—that sparkling Trigorinstein, that brilliant Chonon—could have made his exit line sound funny to me.

"Excuse me, lady," he said. "I was looking for my wife."

4

WHAT WENT WITHOUT SAYING is that Popolescu lied through the space between his teeth. He had promised that the Teatro Colonial would get quiet. But when the houselights dimmed and the footlights came up, the buying and selling really took off.

Peeking through the curtain, we were dazzled by the flash of diamonds and gold teeth in the first row, then pelted by the spray of assorted fruit pits which those juvenile delinquents were spitting from the balcony. The yipping and yapping was worse than a parrot market as the girls showed off their new dresses, the pimps showed off their new girls. From the volume of business, you'd have thought that the ladies in our audience were the last available females on earth.

From the wings, we were singing in chorus the opening chant: "Why has the soul fallen from the heights to the depths? In the fall is the start of the ascension." And from the mezzanine we heard, "Escondida! Escondidele! What did you *do* to your hair?" Onstage, the professional students were boasting about their miracle-working rabbis, and a man's voice came from the dress circle, shouting, "Sixteen? She was sixteen when my grandmother was sixteen!"

Only Yiddish actors could have hung a curtain up in front of a whorehouse and played like it was a *shul*. This in itself was madness—but not what was driving me crazy. Two seconds before my entrance, I knew that we should have had a rehearsal instead of a nap.

A lot had changed since the last time I'd played Leah, the

main thing being my feelings for Benno. Since the *Veracruz*, I no longer felt like Benno's predestined mate, one-half of our orange soul. Overnight, I had turned into one-half of a married couple with problems.

Ida and Clara walked me out into the middle of a new set of undercurrents. I wasn't supposed to meet Chonon's eyes, but Benno's face fascinated me, like a photo of someone I used to know; I could have stared at it forever.

That night I had to act. If everything could be used, I used everything. For a blush, I embarrassed myself with details from our honeymoon. I concentrated on the story of the husband and wife lighting up their room and hoped that it would make me glow. As I danced with the beggars, the thought of Mama watching me on opening night was my shame, my debasement. Visiting the cemetery to invite her dead grandmother to her wedding, my Leah imagined that Mama would die in New York without ever getting the chance to dance at mine.

And, oh, did I have a tragic sense! The tragedy was that my hot love affair with Benno was all in the past, though a long lukewarm life stretched before us.

My biggest problem was suppressing the thought that Leah and Chonon were lucky to die before their passion cooled, before the honeymoon even began. Yet this too I overcame. Of course, training helped, and also the power of the ensemble. Benno, I could tell, had enough "emotional memories" to last a lifetime. For Chonon's sense of powerlessness, he had only to recall those herring breakfasts on the *Veracruz*; for disappointment, those afternoons spent waiting for me in his cabin.

By the end of scene one, I'd managed to act myself out of my skin. Dinah Rappoport was someplace else, likewise Dinah Brownstein. As Leah Sender, I stood onstage like a vacant dwelling with an unlocked door and windows wide open for anything to fly in. From what seemed like miles away, I heard a woman yelling, "Be quiet!" A man answered, "In the grave, you'll have quiet!" But the sound in my ears was the whoosh of wind gusting through an empty house.

All went smoothly until the last part of the second act, my big scene. Chonon was gone forever (so I thought), and my father was marrying me off to Menasha. The only thing which came effortlessly all evening was nausea at the prospect of sharing a marriage bed with Zalmen Hirsch, and as he held the veil toward me, it was instinct to push him away.

"You are not my bridegroom!" I'd given the line so many times it practically gave itself. Right on cue I fainted—not one of those phony swan dives from the old Yiddish stage, but a "genuine" Dalashinsky faint, which we practiced with twenty-pound weights on our knees. As the cast rallied around to pick me up, I tightened my throat muscles in preparation for my dybbuk voice and ran through the lines in my head.

"You buried me!" were my dybbuk's first words. "And now I have returned to my destined bride and will not leave her!"

But that was not what came out of my mouth.

The voice was as grisly as my "regular" dybbuk's, a dead man's voice—but not Chonon's. This one, I could tell, had died at a younger age and a higher temperature. And whereas Chonon's dybbuk could answer questions and make relative sense, this restless spirit had me talking nonsense straight out of Benno's books.

"Inside the clouds," I said, "the air drips with diamonds."

At the time, this was total gibberish to me, and only later, when Feivel Frumkin translated, did I discover that my words had any meaning at all.

Onstage, I had been speaking Spanish.

I have heard that the mental hospitals are filled with people who spend the whole day saying, "I am not a *meshugana*." And yet, in telling this story, I feel that I cannot say this often enough.

I don't dribble food on my blouse, nor do I wear garish makeup. I don't get lost two blocks from home or hide my glasses in the fridge. My watch is always wound; I keep appointments on time. Okay, I hear voices; I can't feel sorry for myself without hearing Benno play "Hearts and Flowers" on an imaginary violin, but I know that he isn't there. On any psychological test I would score ninety-eight percent normal. And frankly, it seems crazy to *me* that I, as a girl of twenty-two, stood on the stage of the Teatro Colonial and talked in someone else's voice.

They say that the two things which deteriorate fastest with time are the memory and the teeth. But I refuse to believe that memories crumble like molars. They're more like gifts which each passing year wraps up in another layer of tissue; you can poke around, feel the shapes, almost guess what's inside.

Yet through all that wrapping, I can see that my dybbuk's first appearance wasn't so very different from little incidents which happen every day: the excuses, the insincere compliments, the well-meant white lies, the countless occasions when your mouth acts independently from your brain and you hear yourself saying something you don't mean at all.

My so-called possession seemed no more extraordinary than that—except that I was talking nonsense about diamond-dripping clouds. Nonsense or not, the audience (so someone was listening!) appreciated my attempt at Spanish and responded with the kind of applause you hear when comedians tell jokes about somebody's hometown.

Fortunately, half the cast was holding me up. One less pair of hands would have dropped me flat. They were staring at me with their mouths open so wide, I could count the fillings in Zalmen's teeth.

"What's the big idea?" whispered Clara.

At that point the script called for a commotion; what we had onstage was bedlam. Everyone babbled at once, then fell silent and looked at Natty Kauffman, who in this scene was playing the Messenger.

"The bride is possessed by a dybbuk," he said. That line was the curtain-closer, but before it could close, Zalmen committed the sin of sins and ad-libbed:

"You're telling us?"

Never was I happier to see the back of a curtain or sorrier to recall that we were doing the next act without intermission. We had less than three minutes to change the set from Leah's village to Rabbi Azrielke's study. At the thought of Azrielke, we thought Dalashinsky—and froze.

Dalashinsky would be furious. Zalmen had monkeyed with Anski's sacred text, but I had mauled it like a gorilla. If Zalmen and I weren't fired on the spot, we'd be working for free in Buenos Aires, Montevideo, and who knew how long in New York. We'd lose our salaries, but the whole cast would pay.

No one moved for fear of running into Dalashinsky. Personally, it was easier for me to worry about him than about the fact that I'd just said a line—in a voice—from nowhere. And where *was* he? If I hadn't been so worried, I would have remembered that he was backstage praying to God.

Like the rest of us, Dalashinsky was the sort of Jew who went to *shul* for funerals, weddings, high holy days, and once in a blue moon on *shabes*. But in preparation for playing a miracle worker, Dalashinsky had found God. I was troubled at first, that he was "using" religion like a sailor's chuckle. But I told myself, God's been used worse. Why should it bother God if someone *davens* in his dressing room? Every night, before his third-act entrance, Dalashinsky bobbed and bowed through every prayer he knew and made up new ones for good luck. And when the curtain rose on Rabbi Azrielke blessing the bread, God really did seem closer than the orchestra pit.

Maybe God was pleased—He certainly spared *my* skin that night. As soon as Dalashinsky took his seat center stage, we understood that he had been lost in prayer and had no idea about my "ad-libbing." The hope that the night might still be saved gave us strength to scurry around with props and flats, working double speed to make up for lost time.

Hard work is the best cure for troubles, and that evening, as I set the Rabbi of Miropol's table and ran for the platter of cardboard *challah*, this medicine took less than a minute to work. For extra reassurance, I reminded myself that, as Dalashinsky said, we were vessels open to the sky. If frogs had been known to fall down with the rain, what was so strange about a few words of Spanish?

By curtain time I was panting shallow breaths which made me light-headed, light-hearted too. I had perfect confidence in my ability to pit my dybbuk against Rabbi Azrielke, get exorcised, become Leah again, and die on cue in the final scene. But as I stood in the wings, listening to Rabbi Azrielke's story about the Baal Shem Tov, I sensed that my troubles weren't over. This story, as told by Anski and delivered by Dalashinsky, was as follows:

Once (and again I am taking liberties with Anski's sacred text), a troupe of acrobats visited the town of Medziboh. Their star was a young man who stretched a rope between the river-banks and, balancing two parasols, skipped back and forth over the gorge below.

In the crowd which turned out to behold this miracle was the Baal Shem Tov.

Now the Baal Shem was not exactly a regular circus-goer, and when his disciples asked what he was doing there, he said: "If only that tightrope walker had developed his soul as fully as his body! What deep abysses he could cross on the thin rope of life!"

The first dozen times I'd heard this speech, I'd understood that it was a lesson in how to live. I'd felt inspired and (how to describe it?) *springy*, as if my own soul had been tightened a notch. After that, I made myself forget about content and listen to Dalashinsky's technique, his swells and pauses, the almost subliminal sigh he put into the Baal Shem's regret.

There followed a period when I couldn't help hearing the story as a kind of personal reproach: Newly married, Benno and I were so deeply engrossed in the physical, I feared that we would have bodies tight enough to walk across—and loose souls which flapped like sheets in the wind. Yet then, given the choice, I would rather have walked that tightrope with Benno than crossed the abyss of life with the Baal Shem Tov.

Now, watching from the wings of the Teatro Colonial, it sad-dened me to recall how I'd worried about nothing. Once again, my only thought was Dalashinsky! How beautifully Dalashin-sky tells a story! And somehow this scared me more than any-thing.

Suddenly I was afraid that the "magic if" would elude me, that I would go out there and see not Rabbi Azrielke, but

Dalashinsky, the same Dalashinsky who'd told me those beautiful stories at night on the *Veracruz*. . . .

These thoughts were what possessed me as Clara and Ida led me onstage.

I have said that the presence of God felt close in this scene. But it wasn't all Dalashinsky's doing. The set made its own contribution. The Rabbi of Miropol's study was furnished with a simple table, a chair, *challah*, a wine cup, candlesticks. Commissioned from the Essex Street Expressionists, the flats had been painted to resemble the interior of a ramshackle hut, mud and wattle, every beam and slat tilted at a different crazy angle. Everything slanted toward heaven, and maybe that was what gave you the feeling that Someone was watching.

I had always admired the conception, but that night I truly appreciated its achievement. For as soon as I walked onstage, the "magic if" was as tangible as the silver candlesticks on Rabbi Azrielke's table. And I was Leah Sender, meeting the wonder worker of Miropol.

"Sit down!" commanded Rabbi Azrielke.

I sat.

"Dybbuk, who are you?" he said.

My line was "Rabbi of Miropol, you know who I am." I took a deep breath, tightened my throat, opened my mouth—and nothing came out.

"Tell us your name? Who are you?" The rabbi came so close that I could smell greasepaint and mothballs. This nearness was supposed to drive my dybbuk wild. But I didn't feel frantic, nor did I have the slightest urge to curse the wonder worker of Miropol.

My one desire was to crawl off somewhere and go to sleep. And how did I keep myself awake?

"*Mi novia*," I sang. "*Mi corazón, mi amor.*"

I recognized my "new" dybbuk's voice, younger and shakier than Chonon's. But what a time and place to discover that your dybbuk is tone-deaf! At that moment I should have been giving the most moving speech of the play, my dybbuk's cry of loneliness from the numberless worlds he must travel in search of a spot to rest. And I was singing trashy love songs in Spanish! Without knowing the language, I could tell that the lyrics were one long list of endearments. The tune (what little I managed to carry) was something I must have picked up from that pickup mariachi band on the boat. But why in all the numberless worlds was I singing it now?

For the first time that night, the house got quiet. The pimps stopped haggling and leaned forward in their seats. A few sang along on the chorus, and when I finished, they stood up and cheered. Something grazed my knee; a hail of tinny coins was bouncing off the stage.

Well, that broke our unbroken line; so much for our sense of illusion. In one horrible flash I realized that Rabbi Azrielke *was* Leon Dalashinsky, and I thought, Look who this dybbuk of mine has been serenading!

It was an open secret that Dalashinsky sprayed drops in his eyes to make them red. But no drops could have achieved the effect I was privileged to see that night. The whites of his eyes were positively black; his eyes were all pupil.

"Enough!" he hissed at Feivel. "Curtain!"

The curtain came down. The clapping got three times as loud. Apparently, our fans didn't care about an unexorcised dybbuk, a scene cut off in mid-sentence, a whole act hacked from the end of the play. If they were authors, they would have concluded every drama with a popular love song, *"Mi corazón, mi amor."*

"Encore!" they shouted.

"No encores," said Dalashinsky, who was grabbing my wrist so hard it hurt, and dragging me backstage. As we flew hand in hand through the wings, the others trailed behind. I remember passing the candles, shrouds, and horns we were supposed to have used in the exorcism scene and feeling as if those objects were reproving me, the way a dress you bought on impulse and never wore will accuse you from the closet.

Dalashinsky's dressing room *was* the size of a closet on Stuyvesant Place, but the whole Art Theater piled in. Despite the crowding, I found myself sitting in the center of a circle, the position Leah should have been taking for the exorcism. I was out of breath, but I had to talk before the others got started.

"Feivel." I had to know. "What did I say out there?"

"The song you can translate yourself," said Feivel. "Sweetheart, honey, darling. But the rest was something about the insides of the clouds dripping diamonds."

I caught Benno's eye. I didn't want him to say what he was going to say.

"Kabbala." He said it anyway. "Pure Kabbala."

Meanwhile, Dalashinsky couldn't have staged a better ruckus. Each one had to ask, "Dinah, what happened? What were you doing?"

"Don't ask *me*," I said. "I don't understand."

The only one who didn't care about understanding was Dalashinsky, who hadn't even heard about the clouds and diamonds, but only my Spanish love ditty—and that was enough. From the horror on his face, you'd have thought that I'd tortured a baby onstage and drunk its blood.

"Miss Rappoport," he said. "I'm afraid you've got the wrong company. And definitely the wrong play. Pardon me, but we're doing *The Dybbuk*. Just because this is Argentina doesn't make it *Carmen*."

"Pardon *me*." In my instinct for self-defense, I came as close as any of us would ever come to imitating Dalashinsky to his face. "I didn't think I was doing *Carmen*. I didn't think, period. You're the one who's always talking about open rain barrels. . . ." My little speech about frogs falling down with the rain convinced no one, and only succeeded in undermining my own rickety courage.

Nor did it help my case when Popolescu skipped in, pumping his clasped hands over his head. He was dressed like a minstrel-show player in top hat and tails, white gloves, and, for all practical purposes, blackface; under the freckles, his skin was the grapey color of *kiddush* wine.

"Congratulations!" he was saying. "They went crazy for it." He looked around specially for me, then said, "That song at the end was a brilliant touch."

"It wasn't in the script," I said, wondering why I was explaining to Popolescu, who hadn't even asked. "Something got into me. . . ."

"Ha-ha," said Popolescu. "A dybbuk."

Ha-ha. I felt like telling him that this joke had already nipped my career in the bud and would probably do the same for our Argentinean tour. I didn't feel like telling him—and didn't have to. Someone knocked on the door.

"Go away," said Feivel. Another knock.

"Vamoose," yelled Zalmen, and the doorknob turned.

It occurred to me that this was a great day for doorknobs turning no matter what you said. Then I stopped thinking and only looked.

For there in the doorway stood a young woman who looked exactly like me.

5

WELL, NOT EXACTLY.

Like superstitiousness, vanity wasn't a family trait. Mama never had a decent mirror in the house, and Benno too could go weeks without combing his hair. But making up as Leah, half an hour at the mirror every night, had taught me what I looked like—and the differences between me and that girl in the doorway jumped right out.

Her nose was a tiny bit straighter, her braids an inch longer; her chin and forehead shone, oily like mine would have been if I didn't take care. Otherwise, she was my carbon copy, another parakeet with big cocker-spaniel eyes. For an evening at the theater, she wore as much kohl and mascara as Leah possessed by a dybbuk. Even the white dress was similar, though mine was part wedding gown, part shroud, and hers was one of those frilly corset affairs. . . .

All right. If she wasn't my mirror image, she could have passed for my long-lost twin. Nor was it one of those resemblances which strike some people and others can't quite see. This one hit the whole cast like a truck; the accident victims stopped breathing.

Later, when Benno gave up Kabbala for real literature, he'd bring me Gogol, Poe, Dostoyevsky—stories in which characters met their doubles. But these meetings were nothing like mine. These characters were always men, half batty to begin with, the kind who'd run after their doubles, shouting, "Who are you? What do you want from me?" Me, I stood motionless. Though maybe I would have acted differently if I'd met my double in one of those lonely hotel rooms, those foggy St. Petersburg bridges which writers so like.

I've never read one word about meeting your double in the company of your family and friends, nor one eyewitness description. So let me be the first to record that "electrified" isn't the word; the whole room buzzes. What it did in my case was to double my credibility. Seeing two of me made the cast take me twice as seriously; on the threshold of their subconsciousnessess, they were beginning to understand that I hadn't been fooling around on that stage, ad-libbing for the hell of it.

"Mamie!" cried Popolescu. "What a coincidence!"

A coincidence, that's what it was—so obvious, we had to laugh. In the midst of it, I was paying attention to how a whole roomful of people can laugh without easing the tension one iota. The laughter stopped cold when we realized that Popolescu meant something beyond our coincidental looks.

"This is Mamie Ramirez," he said. "The volunteer Phèdre I was telling you about this morning." Then he focused on me:

"*Now* I know who you remind me of."

Like Popolescu's, every head was swiveling. Only Mamie's and mine were fixed on each other. For a while I had to suppress the sheepish smile you might exchange with a woman wearing your identical hat. But this urge disappeared as it dawned on me: Beneath the similar feathers, this Mamie was a much tougher bird. She was staring as if *I* were the double and she the character about to chase after me, yelling what did I want?

"Why did you do it?" She spoke Yiddish in a voice I recognized (and this was before tape recorders) as close to my own. Her question could have had a dozen meanings. My answer to all of them was, "I don't know."

"Why were you talking and singing in Paco's voice?"

"Paco who?"

"Paco Engelhart," said Mamie, as if I'd asked, Leonardo who?

So, my dybbuk's name. No wonder Chonon's dybbuk refused

to identify itself to Rabbi Azrielke. Theoretically, a name only gives so much information, but when it's your dybbuk's. . . . Even sitting down, I felt faint. What brought me around was Popolescu saying:

"Pincus Engelhart. The Aviator."

"Oh, yes, you mentioned," said Natty. "The hero. . . ."

"You knew, then." Mamie was accusing me.

"I didn't."

"Then how could you do him so perfectly? He never sang unless he thought no one was listening."

The sad tone beneath Mamie's accusations made me feel the tragic sense of losing your predestined mate. I was all set to start apologizing when Popolescu, who seemed to be making a specialty of the obvious, said, "Mamie and Engelhart were great friends."

"Great friends," said Mamie. "We were secretly married."

God in heaven, said a voice in my head, and this voice was definitely my own. I couldn't look at Benno or Dalashinsky, so I concentrated on watching the jaws drop. The Yiddish Art Theater hadn't seen melodrama like this since Alba Springer slammed her braided wig onto the stage.

"Why would I imitate your husband?" I said. "I don't know his singing voice, I don't even know Spanish. Something came over me. . . ."

"A dybbuk!" cried Popolescu. "Like I said. What's that line the Messenger has in your play? 'Dybbuks are restless souls with unfinished business.' Well, who could have more unfinished business than a kid who goes up in an airplane one day and never comes down?"

"He was always talking about dybbuks." Mamie seemed to have finally caught the chills which had been making the rest of us shiver for the last ten minutes. "When we first met, he was playing around with alchemy, Kabbala, the Zohar. . . ."

This time I had to check Benno, who was looking at me with his teeth bared in a grimace meaning, What have we got ourselves into? Two weeks before, that monkey grin would have cheered and comforted me, excluded the rest of the world. But now I stared into those chattering teeth and thought, It's your fault, you and your mumbo jumbo.

"That line about the diamonds and clouds was a message in code," said Mamie. "And the meaning of it was that he did it all for me."

"Of course he did it for you," said Popolescu. "Everybody knows that. No one names streets after a guy just for doing a couple of flips and falling into the water—not unless he does it for love."

"That's what makes a hero down here?" said Feivel. "Imagine our mayor renaming Broadway after a kid who's nose-dived just to impress some girl."

"But, oh, what a wonderful story!" said Ida, who, like so many cynics, could be counted on to drool at the scent of anything romantic.

Mamie shrugged and rolled her eyes, but somehow I made her look back at me.

"Why?" I said. It was one of those questions which, I'd learned from Hinda, are better not asked. But it wasn't quite like asking whose names Dalashinsky called in his sleep. Now I was the one who'd talked, so to speak, in her sleep. And when you find yourself talking in someone else's voice, you're curious for details.

Maybe you're just as curious when this dybbuk is the restless spirit of someone you've loved—which was why Mamie went so far back and out of her way to explain:

"Paco used to say that we come into this world with our minds made up. Forty days before birth, an angel pinches our plump little cheek and we're born loving fat people. Or taps our wrist, and our heart beats for skin and bones. Some love boys, some girls, and some (God only knows where the angel's touched them) love both—but only at that age when you can't quite tell the difference. Down here this age comes early and lasts about as long as an ice cube; and so, like a taste for iced coffee, this passion is complicated and expensive to indulge.

"It was my good luck (if you could call it that) to stay at this stage years longer than most. At that in-between age, you can enter a room with a thousand men and pick out that one with a preference for the in-between. You know you won't have to do much except sit on his lap; it's not a lover he wants, but some kind of elegant puppy to cuddle and stroke. The worst thing he'll ask you to do is tell him how you got started in such a career. As if his pesos and presents entitled him to your life story. As if your life story was that you'd spent it waiting for him to ask. So you make up a different story each time, until you can't remember which one is true."

"If you ever knew," said Dalashinsky.

Had smiles sold like ribbons, by the inch, Mamie's wouldn't have brought in a nickel. But I envied her freedom to give hers to Dalashinsky. He wasn't a god to her, but simply a man who had paid her the compliment of his total attention; and she could thank him with as big or as little a smile as she liked.

"If you ever knew," she agreed. "Not that these gentlemen cared. The thinnest stories satisfied them. Afterward, I could sit on their laps and stare at the wall while they imagined that I was speechless with love for them. As I said when that Frenchman asked how I'd made up Phèdre, 'Our job is nine-tenths acting.' And men never know what's real."

You might think that the men in the room would have taken offense at this. But it was Clara and Ida and I who cringed. In the old neighborhood, in the bosom of the family, you heard remarks about "men." But we were too sophisticated, too modern to lump our male fellow artists together. Somehow, though, Mamie's tone had made us feel involved, exposed, more closely implicated than all Popolescu's babble about the sisterhood of prostitution and art.

"For some people, this in-between stage lasts a lifetime," she was saying. "But I wasn't one of them."

"This we can see for ourselves," interrupted Zalmen.

"As soon as I felt myself growing out of this childish stage, I slid off those laps and threw myself into children's games: Hide and seek. Catch me if you can. My greatest thrill was leaving my gentlemen waiting on street corners while I ran off to the Café Flora.

"This café, where the bright lights of the Buenos Aires underworld went to twinkle, was done up like a pimp's dream of heaven—beveled mirrors, crystal beads, flocked wallpaper of the same color as the cloying cherry brandy which for some reason was the gangsters' favorite drink. In the house band were the kind of musicians who flattered themselves that every fiddler is an outlaw, and played their hearts out for their brothers in crime as if at a family party. There were tables ringing the dance floor, and after so many pillowy laps, how good it felt to sit on those hard wooden chairs and wait to be asked to dance!"

"The tango," said Popolescu.

"What else?" said Natty.

What else. In the variety shows which Dalashinsky sent us to as homework, the most popular number that season was a novelty tune called "Far Away in Honolulu, They've Got the Tango Craze." And this, as far as we knew, was no exaggeration. Every road show had its tango couple, its Raoul and Maria tricked out like an apache and his moll. On the Bowery, Wally's Tango Follies drew sell-out crowds. Even at the Jewish ballrooms they played tangos, and though I would have liked to join in, I couldn't. Just being at those ballrooms meant that we were up to date, but those snapping heads and interlocked wrists were a little too modern for unmarried Jewish girls. And so when the tango music came up, the floor emptied except for smooth middle-aged couples who practiced at home, those neat plump ladies with their pomaded husbands and graceful little feet.

"The Flora had been named for a former madam who died at eighty-eight, on the dance floor, slumping to the beat so that her young partner tangoed through two more verses without suspecting till the music stopped. What better namesake for a place where they did what was called the dance of love and death—inspired, if you believe the story, by the frenzy of the black widow spider devouring her mate."

"Good God," said Zalmen. "I hope not."

"But how many men," said Mamie, "can dance like a black widow spider?"

"More than you'd think," said Natty.

"Not one," said Mamie. "Not unless they're dancing with the woman they were born to tango with. One night a boy appeared across the room, walked toward me, and asked me to dance—"

"A boy appeared across the room," sneered Ida. "Just like in fairy tales."

"Not just in fairy tales," said Dalashinsky. "In great drama, *Romeo and Juliet*. In literature, Balzac, Tolstoy, *Anna Karenina*. And why do so many love stories begin this way? Because in life, it happens."

I wondered what Dalashinsky knew about this, outside of books. Then I thought of myself, watching Benno-Trigorinstein from the second balcony, and suddenly I understood why this particular dybbuk might have chosen me: He too was the type who fell in love across rooms.

"Before the music began, I had just enough time to see that this boy was also growing out of that in-between age. The band struck up *"La Paloma"*; we crossed the floor. And all at once, I thought, This *is* the dance of love and death. Though maybe I was fooling myself. For how could I have been doing the dance of love and death and still have caught the exact moment when the people around us stopped talking and put down their drinks?"

"This could play Second Avenue!" said Feivel. "They meet across a crowded room. They dance and the whole world watches."

"This also happens," said Dalashinsky, his voice so hushed with reverence for Mamie's sense of truth that once again I felt jealous. "The world does watch."

"When *"La Paloma"* ended, the band swung into another tango. At every table, snapping fingers: Waiter, another drink. Ordinarily, two dances were nothing to me. But after the second with Paco, I couldn't breathe. It was too noisy to talk, and like two little bats in a tunnel, we flew on instinct straight for the fresh night air.

"We zigzagged through the city at a fast pace which felt like our tango—every turn smoother than any we could have rehearsed. Neither of us seemed to be leading, but Paco must have been. We stopped at a fancy apartment house on the Calle Barcelona and he took out a set of keys.

" 'Shush,' he said. 'There's people sleeping.' "

"What people? I wondered. Only Queen Victoria could have slept in a palace like that. Every surface which couldn't be carved was upholstered in satin or velvet; stuffed, fringed, or embroidered or all three at once. The air was as musty and thick as the rugs. But if the rest of the flat was designed for a dowager empress, Paco's room was pure Scheherazade, an Arabian dream of pillows and canopies, paisley and polished brass.

" 'Who owns this place?' I said.

" 'Some old English guy,' said Paco, in such a way that I knew how hurt this Englishman would be to hear Paco call him old. Instead of being shocked, I thought, Hooray! He makes his living like I do!"

"A young boy living so," wailed Clara. "What kind of country is this?"

"When Paco finally patted his thigh and said, 'Come here,' I sat too fast and bruised my tailbone on his knee. For sitting on laps was something we'd both learned to laugh at. We were half scared to death that the other would laugh."

Either Mamie had forgotten us—or she *was* a natural. For she really seemed to be talking to herself as she smiled a bit wistfully and said, "We *didn't* laugh. Anyhow, not until later."

She paused. And though Dalashinsky had taught us a million pauses, we'd never seen one which contained in ten seconds of silence a whole night of love.

"The next morning, when Paco and I went out for breakfast, the café owner sent over two platters of eggs and meat on the house. It wasn't a purely romantic gesture; he knew we were good for business. For there was something about us which made people want what we had. Even the customers who'd already eaten ordered *huevos* and *carne asada*. And that meal was our first taste of the fact that strangers would feed us just for being in love."

"In my experience," said Ida, "the world hates lovers. They're so jealous, they won't give them the time of day."

The obvious (and unmentionable) was that Ida and her lumpy stagehands were a different breed of cat from Mamie and her tango boy. Even Popolescu did Ida the kindness of ignoring her, and Mamie went on:

"We were the Café Flora's star attraction. For dancing, we got free *empanadas* and all the cherry brandy we could drink. We began getting invitations to parties where artists voulunteered to paint us and poets stared at us like chimps in the zoo. Stuck together like Siamese twins, we inched up through the society of fashionable hostesses who vied for the privilege of having me sit on Paco's lap at their teas. And afterward, when they counted teaspoons missing, they fired the new maid and refused to believe that their sterling might have wound up in Paco's jacket.

"For Paco was the kind of boy who couldn't get through the day without a little spit in society's eye. To hear him boast, there was nothing but murder which he hadn't tried. He'd drunk the rawest gaucho bootleg, smoked the nastiest cigars, rolled sailors, and shoplifted from the most exclusive shops. From the Indians, he'd gotten powders which made his head go off like a firecracker. He'd cat-burgled, second-storied, lived off women and men. Drugs, drink, prostitution, what was left? Black magic? Why not? He was an amateur magician."

"Rabbits out of hats?" I was hoping against hope.

"Messiahs out of hats was more like it. He claimed he could summon spirits, materialize exotic flowers from distant soils. Like Rumplestiltskin, he knew spells to turn straw into gold; but unlike that girl in the story, I wasn't dumb enough to ask him to show me how.

"And yet with all this witchcraft and crime, the cruelest thing he did was to take me to live openly in his room: If the Englishman didn't like it, let him throw us out. Some chance! At our footsteps, he ran like a roach. In all that time I only saw him twice, the first time late one night, when he knocked, then entered our room. He wasn't old, but middle-aged, not much different from most of the men who paid me to sit on their laps.

" 'We're busy,' said Paco. Thank God we were dressed and talking. As he hesitated momentarily before leaving, I was struck by the Englishman's pallor, his skin so floury that I half expected the tears running down his face to turn into paste.

"There's nothing like seeing your sweetheart be mean to someone else to make you appreciate how kind he's being to you; nothing like an outlaw boyfriend to make you feel dangerous. And vain? I must be pretty, I decided, if this beauty had liked me (he finally admitted) ever since he'd seen me onstage doing Phèdre!

"Like teenagers playing grown-up, we pretended we'd had no childhoods. According to the rules of our game, the most innocent questions (where did you grow up? what did your father do?) were out of bounds. And so it took me ages to find out that my wild gangster lover was none other than Engelhart the dentist's son."

"*The* dentist is right," said Popolescu. "The biggest in Buenos Aires. When this man first immigrated from Vienna, he was hailed as the Messiah practically...."

"Another girl," said Mamie, "might have thought that this Messiah's son was just working overtime to live down his background. A girl like me who sat on laps from necessity might have thought twice about this rich boy who did it for the luxury of being bad. But for me, it was simply a wonderful coincidence that Paco and I were both Jewish, proof that we'd come from the same neighborhood in heaven where the angels had gone around matchmaking, forty days before birth."

"Where did you get this forty days business?" asked Feivel. "From our play?"

"From Paco. When it came out that we were both Jewish, he confessed: All his magic spells were Kabbala. And he planned to go way beyond alchemy and exotic flowers. He would concentrate emanations, hasten the Messiah, climb up into heaven and unravel the curtain of Paradise."

The whole cast must have thought, Chonon's very words. Only Benno and I knew: Benno's too. No one knew what to say until finally Clara took it on herself to break the uncomfortable hush. "What a life for two Jewish children! Tango dancing, liquor, black magic, and laying around in bed!"

"Meanwhile," Mamie went on, "we were common garden-variety lovebirds. We necked on the beach at night. We went window-shopping. We stared into each other's eyes and picked fights about nothing. We assumed we would be madly in love forever, and the silliest thing: We stood outside the jewelry store and picked out wedding rings."

As an Artiste, a sophisticate, I could hardly believe that I was involved with the kind of dybbuk who'd take his girlfriend to window-shop rings. Benno and I would have died first. And apparently (though for different reasons, I guess) this didn't sit well with the rest of the group.

"Frankly," said Dalashinsky, "it goes against my sense of character to hear that two such hard-boiled eggs—"

"Everyone does it," said Mamie. "Here in Buenos Aires it's the favorite sport. Soccer's only on weekends, likewise bullfights and *shul*. But every day, mothers can pick out rings for their baby daughters in diapers. Later, when the match is made, the jeweler's is the first place they run; before the wedding, they'll make twenty trips, with every aunt and third cousin dragged in for consultation. It's one of the only places a proper young couple can go while the chaperones turn their heads. After all, what can happen in a jewelry shop window?

"The answer is: plenty. It was there, I'm almost ashamed to admit, that Paco said, 'Let's get married.' We rushed to City Hall, where a vendor sold rings of shiny wire which came unwound two minutes after the ceremony. And it was only a few weeks later, in front of that same window, that our troubles began.

"One afternoon I gazed past the tiers and cases into the store and saw a giant hippopotamus of a man waving come in."

An image of that hippo flashed through my mind, and I thought, How the beckoning of one heavy arm can knock things down so low. Seconds before, we'd been hearing about two soul mates betrothed in heaven. And now it was the story of an older man and two kids. Right then I decided to stop speculating about why this dybbuk had chosen to speak through me. I sensed parallels between Mamie's story and Leah's and my own which I wouldn't have touched with a ten-foot pole.

"Against my own judgment, I steered Paco into the store. The fat man approached us and said, 'Can I help you?' You could almost hear the necks creaking as every head turned to watch a millionaire wait like a salesclerk on two ragamuffins in off the street. For my hippo, as it turned out, was a diamond-mine owner, a real-estate magnate, the famous Don Eduardo Feigenbaum."

"Please." Popolescu looked nervous. "No names."

But I was glad she'd said it. Because when you're talking about a triangle, you can't keep calling one point "the hippo." Fat or not, things are never so simple.

"I sensed that Don Eduardo had just at that moment (late in life, it's worse) discovered his taste for the in-between. And it was mostly to test this hunch that I said, 'We're looking for a wedding ring.'

"Had Don Eduardo been a porcupine, spines would have stood straight up. What man can help bristling when he wants you for his own? He didn't want me to marry Paco, didn't want me to know him. He told us to sit down, and I wasn't surprised when the tray he brought out from the back contained not one single ring.

"Against that black velvet lining, that twelve-inch square of nighttime sky, thousands of tiny diamonds glittered like stars. My eyes lit up; I could feel it. If I'd closed them, light would have leaked out from under my lashes.

" 'Put out your hand,' said Don Eduardo. He took a big pinch of diamonds and, like a cook salting a stew, let them dribble into my hand. Their coolness made me shiver.

"Meanwhile, Paco was rummaging thorugh his clothes, drop-ping keys, running through all the tricks he used as distractions while teaspoons vanished into his coat. But before he could pocket my diamonds, Feigenbaum told me, 'Go ahead. Keep them.' That took the wind out of Paco's sails.

" 'Let's get going,' he said.

"Another girl might have wasted everyone's time by politely refusing, but I was used to extravagant gifts. I knotted the diamonds so tightly in my shawl, salt couldn't have poured through. Then Paco and I got going.

"Outside, he said, 'What did we get?' Ordinarily, this was what I said after the tea parties, the signal for him to bring out the sterling, our haul. But now I cradled that tied-up lump of shawl in my hand and said nothing.

"The first bad sign was that I waited till Paco was out of the room before slipping the diamonds into a matchbox which I hid in a drawer. The second was what happened when he came back:

"Until that afternoon, I hadn't been able to go to bed with him without thinking that we were hastening the Messiah. And now I was wishing that *he* would hurry up and go to sleep so that I could sneak back to the jeweler's."

Shot through the heart, I couldn't have flinched harder. I thought, Just like *I* hurried Benno on the *Veracruz*. That's how it is when you first start to go wrong in love; the most casual remark sounds like a personal indictment.

"When Don Eduardo saw me, he couldn't hide his surprise; his idea of an encouraging smile made me want to die. He took me into the back room and unlocked a safe. Again he brought out a velvet-lined tray, but this one contained a solitary blue-white diamond, cut like a pyramid with facets like steps. Touching it wasn't enough for me. I wanted to climb it, to crawl inside.

" 'The Star of Brazil,' whispered Don Eduardo. His breath came fast, unpleasantly moist as he told me some crazy story about going on an expedition as a young man to Minas Gueras, where he found the Indians playing poker with precious gems.

" 'The Star was the blue chip,' he said.

"I reached for it. He grabbed my hand. His palm felt fatter and softer than all the laps I'd sat in put together. I was thinking of Paco's hard brown hands—and wanting that diamond badly enough to let Don Eduardo hold mine.

" 'Meet me at'—he gave me an address—'tomorrow at four.'

"The next afternoon, I led poor Paco to believe that we were putting real pressure on the Messiah to hurry up. By four, he was dead to the world, and I was exploring the apartment which was obviously not Don Eduardo's house. Designed for business and quick stays (a big parlor, a tiny kitchen), it was still larger and more luxurious than all but the richest family homes.

" 'Where's the diamond?' I said.

"Don Eduardo smiled, then raised his arms slightly and held them away from his sides.

" 'I've got it on me somewhere,' he said. 'Find it.'

"I never had a papa to tease me, or an invitation to go through a man's pockets. My instinct was: Watch out. The odd invitations are just starting. But with Don Eduardo, his outside jacket pocket was as far as it ever went. I found the Star of Brazil in the darkness of the woolly lining, brushed off the crumbs of lint and tobacco, rubbed it against my skirt. Then Don Eduardo poured two glasses of sherry and motioned for me to sit down. Not on his lap, you understand; on the couch.

" 'Where do you live?' he said.

" 'On the Calle Barcelona.' I felt no need to volunteer details about Paco and the Englishman.

" 'My wife's dressmaker lives on the Calle Barcelona.' And bingo! Within three sentences, Don Eduardo had mentioned his wife three times. For almost an hour, he told me stories about all the cute tricks his two grown children had played as babies."

"Like what?" said our cynical Ida, the only one of us who would actually request stories about someone's cute babies.

"I don't remember. I wasn't listening. What I do recall is that somehow he made it clear: If I wanted another diamond, I could come back the next afternoon.

"The next day, the same routine. Again I went through Don Eduardo's pockets. The only difference was the reddish teardrop-shaped diamond. Don Eduardo told new stories, just as boring as the day before's. He liked to boast about the business deals he'd pulled off, the people from all walks of life who valued his opinion more than gold. But most of all he loved anecdotes which cast his work in a romantic light, as if being a millionaire required the combined talents of a Michelangelo and a Napoleon.

"One, I recall, concerned his *estancias* in Patagonia, which he'd visited right after giving his gauchos a huge Christmas bonus. The men were so grateful, they'd roasted a whole steer in his honor. That blackened meat, said Don Eduardo, was the best *tref* he ever tasted."

"Now this strains *my* sense of truth," said Zalmen. "Strains, did I say? It gives it a hernia to hear that a man would pay a fortune in diamonds just to talk about what he ate for dinner in Patagonia."

"The most intimate it ever got," said Mamie, "was after I'd been there a few times, Don Eduardo mentioned that he and his wife had honeymooned in Mar del Plata. And when I asked him what the resort was like, he sighed and said, 'We never went out.' I sensed that this was the moment to bring certain things into the open, and I asked him, What was he paying me for?

"'With all my travels, my successes, my brilliant coups,' he said, 'the greatest pleasures of my life so far were those moments when I rediscovered the world—saw things as if for the first time—through my children's eyes. When I'd return from trips with trinkets hidden on me and let my children look for them, I felt that I was truly understanding the purpose of pockets. Now they're grown up; it's checks they want, not trinkets. Only recently, with you looking for your diamonds, do I remember why pockets were invented. When I saw your eyes light up in my store, I knew. If I told you my stories, I could still believe that they'd actually happened to me.'

"I was more than flattered; I was moved. And besides, if Don Eduardo was in it for the wonder of things, so was I. I would have felt worse about deceiving Paco if I hadn't cared so for the gems. I couldn't stop thinking about them, touching them, staring. . . . In other words, it was love. I'd heard of women marrying for money, but never of a secret affair with diamonds. What I did know, though, is that there's no such thing as a secret affair. Love changes you, and it was only a matter of time till Paco noticed the change.

"One afternoon, I came home from Don Eduardo's to find Paco sitting up in bed.

" 'Well,' he said. 'What did we get?'

" 'We?' I said. In that one word: adultery. And I felt guilty enough to reach for the diamond in my purse—the Splendor of Surinam, a thirty-carat natural wonder, oval and smooth as an egg. Paco hefted the diamond in his hand, then tossed it up and caught it.

" 'So?' he said. 'So what?'

"I was trying to recall Don Eduardo's story, which had traced this diamond through five generations and halfway around the world when Paco said, " 'This diamond is nothing. With the power of the holy name, I can double it and make new diamonds from sand.'

"Oh, I was so relieved! Why had I wasted time worrying that my passion for diamonds might conflict with my love for Paco? If Paco was telling the truth, no conflict existed. If he could make diamonds, I didn't need Don Eduardo, but could spend my afternoons in bed with him. And so I got stupid, like that girl in the fairy tale.

" 'Go on,' I said. 'Show me.'

"What was in Paco's mind? What did he expect to accomplish with that sand and vinegar, rosewater, bleach, thermometers, metal trays? In those days, I think, we half believed that anything we wanted badly enough would happen, especially with a thousand years of Kabbala behind us to give things a little push.

"Back in our room, Paco mixed the magic elements in a photographer's pan while reading long lists of angels' names from his books. 'Give me the diamond,' he said, and with a new burst of double-talk about ascending to heaven and lifting the veil, slipped the Splendor of Surinam into that sludgy mess.

" 'The last ingredient,' he said, 'is night.'

But in the morning, the diamond was no bigger, only dirtier, covered with an oily gray scum. Later, I'd find out how easily this film rubbed off. But at the time I could only scream, 'Idiot! You ruined it!' And my only desire was to find a bigger, more beautiful stone to replace the one he'd 'ruined.'

"I got dressed and went out. Don Eduardo's apartment was empty. The jewelry store was closed. I was feeling so sorry for myself, I made a detour past the Café Flora. I knew the place would be deserted, with chairs upended on the tables. I peeked through a dusty window; inside, nothing moved but a steady stream of motes. Suddenly I imagined myself an old woman, haunting the ruin of a café where a boy named Paco and I used to dance. . . ."

Mamie sighed theatrically, then said, "When Engelhart the dentist first came to Buenos Aires, his chair was *the* place to be—and I went. He pronounced my teeth in perfect shape except for one, he said, which might give me trouble later on. Afterward, I'd gotten into the habit of probing it with my tongue to see if it hurt yet. So in that same way, I stood in front of the Café Flora, imagining that I had lost Engelhart's son. But when I got back to the Englishman's apartment, I discovered how different probing was from a full-blown toothache.

"The diamond was still in its silty bath, but Paco was gone. Searching the flat, I nearly tripped over the Englishman's feet. He was sitting in the living room, crying. Twice I'd seen him, both times in tears, and I understood that this was his glory, that his whole association with Paco had been preparation for this tearful day. For he was one of the most pitiful of all: Forty days before birth, the angel does something to make them cry. Knowing that such types could usually be counted on for the most embarrassing statements, I cringed in advance, and the Englishman didn't disappoint me.

" 'Well,' he said through his tears, 'we're in the same boat.'

"Instantly all my sorrow turned to rage at being left so at sea that this pasty crybaby could think we were in the same boat. I collected my things and resumed my old life, except that now I didn't have to sit on laps, but only on Don Eduardo's couch. Rather than give Don Eduardo the satisfaction of hearing me admit that Paco and I were no longer together, I let him find out through the grapevine—the same one which kept me informed of my secret husband's every move.

"The first thing I heard was that he'd returned to his parents' home on December Street. Then I got word that he was spending his days at the airport."

"An airport?" said Feivel, with new respect. "In Buenos Aires?"

"The rumor was that his parents were so overjoyed to have him back, they'd bought him a Luna Two Twenty-one." Mamie tossed this off with the casual pride which certain girls take in knowing car makes and years, the names and numbers of machinery. "By this time, I'd sold one of Feigenbaum's diamonds for a fraction of its value—but enough for me to leave the Englishman's and rent a place of my own. Still, the fact that I sold it at all must have meant that the diamonds' stock was falling and Paco's was back on the rise.

"One afternoon, I hid in a clump of trees by the airport and waited for him to arrive. Mostly the planes were yellow, red, gunmetal gray; Paco's was a pale blue which on sunny days would blend into the sky.

"In those goggles he looked like some kind of flying bug, but when he took off and began slowly circling the trees, I shivered just as I'd done when he first patted his leg and said, 'Come here'; the same shiver as the first time I'd touched Don Eduardo's diamonds. That I wasn't scared in the least for him moved me like the confidence I used to have that he would make me happy. When he landed, my knees were wobbly, but I made myself run over so close that the propeller wind practically blew me over.

"Jumping down, Paco nearly stepped on my shoulder—but didn't seem surprised to see me. He looked at me, then right past me. In my nervousness, I knew that I would say something stupid. And how smart can you be when you're competing with the engines of a Luna?

" 'Hey!' I shouted. 'Can you take me up?'

"Paco pointed to the cockpit, hardly big enough for one.

" 'Where?' he shouted, and what could I say?

"The next place I saw his face was on the front of the daily paper, beneath a headline: 'Aviator Plans Flight Across Andes.' This route had never been tried, but that wasn't the big news, which was: In honor of his historic attempt, Don Pincus Engelhart would give a demonstration of flying technique at the harbor, that Saturday at two.

"Other cities, I've heard, have street singers, dancing bears, jugglers, artists who draw on the pavement with colored chalk. But here in Buenos Aires no one gives anything away, least of all entertainment. So the promise of a free circus—an air circus—excited us more than it might have in a more generous place.

"By Saturday, the afternoon had taken on all the trappings and pomp of a national holiday. At one-thirty, the whole population turned out on the rooftops, the beaches and piers. The horn honking stopped; there was scarcely any talk. At five after two we heard a faint buzz, which got louder and louder until we saw Paco's plane, barely visible against that blue sky, banked low over the harbor.

"The Luna did two easy figure-eights and pulled out of the final loop with its nose aimed straight up. Within a few seconds, it had vanished, but we still heard the engine noise.

"The noise quit. We held our breath. The plane spiraled down in tight circles, like something dangling on a string. And when it leveled out, the whole city said, 'Ah.' Once more it stalled, but now we were prepared. It twirled once, twice, three, four times, then plunged into the water with a hollow boom like a drumbeat.

"Perhaps if the plane had caught fire, there might have been screams. But this tragedy had no color, no violence, no sound. A wreck would have given us focus, someplace to run. But we could only stare helplessly at the sea, the sky.

"The first to move were the journalists. Within the hour, a special edition had Paco's face bannered across the front: 'Hero Dies in Aerial Show.' And by morning he *was* a hero. Every politician had something to say about youth, courage, patriotism, the frontiers of technology. Streets and babies were named after him; landlords fought to have their blocks rechristened. No ground could be broken, no ship launched without invoking his name.

"Just as I had been a secret wife, I became a secret celebrity, so famous as the dead hero's girlfriend that Don Eduardo got anxious and began to avoid the apartment. I didn't miss him. My love affair with diamonds was over.

"Had Paco and I been openly married, I would have been forced to grieve publicly, the little widow in black. I was glad to be spared. For had I been forced to give speeches, I knew what I would have said: 'That fool! What was he trying to prove?' I was still angry at him, even beyond death . . . until tonight. . . ." Now Mamie was looking at me.

"When you spoke in his voice and sang like him, I knew that he was talking to me. Only I would have understood about the diamonds. And he was telling me that he'd flown up there to unravel the curtain of heaven—beyond which are more diamonds than in all Don Eduardo's mines."

I wondered how much sense this was making to anyone but Benno and me. Apparently, not much. As intense as this Mamie was, as odd the coincidence of our resemblance, still: What do most people care about decoding messages from restless souls? Around me, I could feel the discomfort which comes when strangers have told you more about their lives than you want to know. Ensemble, the Yiddish Art Theater was ready for Mamie's big scene to end. I alone had millions of questions. But Benno spoke before I could begin.

"I'm sorry," he said. "It's a tragic story. But there's one thing I want to know. Popolescu here told us about your Phèdre. He claimed that you were offered a lifetime contract. It's obvious from the way you spoke tonight that you have talent. So my question is, Why did you refuse?"

I should have been happy. For here this young woman had been transmitting communiqués from homeless souls beyond the curtain of heaven—and my Benno, the great Kabbalist, was changing the subject. Instead I felt jealous, and suddenly frightened that Benno might fall in love with my double. Why not? She looked just like me, the same attraction would have been there—but without our painful history, that confusion in the hotel room and with Dalashinsky on the boat.

"Simple." Mamie smiled back and I fumed. How upset could

she be about this aviator if she was already flirting with Benno? "I'd met enough rich old husbands. As soon as I saw Phèdre's situation—the young wife, the handsome stepson—I knew how things would turn out. I volunteered to see if I could do it and if it would be fun. I could, and it was—so much fun that only at the very end did I ask myself, What for? That story had made me miserable, and as I looked into the audience, I realized that they felt rotten too. That was when I decided: Better to sit on laps. Better, if necessary, to walk the streets. Let Popolescu say what he likes about his so-called sisterhood, but I say whores are better. Because unlike theatergoers, a prostitute's customers leave feeling better than they did when they came!"

Ensemble again, the whole cast was taken aback to hear themselves ranked one step lower than whores. I alone wasn't surprised or offended. On the contrary, I was gratified. For wasn't Mamie's statement just a more extreme way of expressing my own doubts about the value of making Mama and Papa hear voices from the grave?

All at once I felt an affinity for Mamie which went beyond our similar looks. It's only natural, that sudden sympathy for someone who's just said something you've secretly believed. It seemed somehow as if we'd known each other for much longer than one evening, so intimately that now there was no need to speak.

Mamie shook my hand. I kissed her on both cheeks. She turned her back, opened the door, and was gone.

6

ONE THING I'LL SAY for my dybbuk, he let me sleep. Back at the
Zona Azura, Ida tucked me in and I slept as if those bedbugs
were biting somebody else. Through it all I heard knocks on the
door, Benno then Dalashinsky, Dalashinsky then Benno, asking,
"How is she?"

"Hush," said Ida. "Asleep." And those muffled conversations
made me feel cozy, like being sick as a child with Mama and
Papa whispering over my bed.

I slept through the night and most of the following day. It
was nearly dusk when I opened my eyes and saw Benno.

"Rip van Winkele," he said. "It's enough. Everyone's at the
theater already."

I woke up restored, with a heart full of love for the whole
world, especially Benno; for a few blessed moments I forgot
that there was ever anything wrong. Hungry enough to brave
my first sample of Argentinean cuisine, I polished off a plate of
rice, beans, some sort of turnover—pork blintzes, I'm sure.
Only on the other side of the world would they have called that
food, but from the way I gobbled it up, you'd have thought that
it was Mama's cabbage *kuchen*, or the sweet tea and toast of our
wedding breakfast. The important thing was, once again I was
sharing a meal in peace with my Benno. And not in my wildest
fantasies could I have imagined that the stringy, beaten-down
hotel waiter (one old man for the whole dining room) was
waiting to shanghai me to the white slaver's den.

When we arrived at the theater, the entire cast insisted on

shaking my hand, wishing me good luck and good health, as if I'd just come out of the hospital. Likewise, they looked at me extra hard to see if the doctors had gotten it all.

My color must have reassured them; at the mirror, I needed double the usual white. Even so, the makeup went on like icing on a cake—always a good sign. I felt not just cured but (and I knocked on wood) immune to dybbuks and whatever else might fall down with the rain.

At seven, I peeked through the curtain and saw the house filling up with a whole different crowd.

"See?" Popolescu was saying. "I promised. How many pimps can one town have? The first night we pack the place with trash. After that, your wife and kids can eat off the floor."

"Listen to that racket," said Feivel. "Those wives and kids are louder than the pimps."

From backstage we could hear every wife in the audience with her ten screaming kids and her *tante* in the balcony shouting down the latest gossip. From behind the curtain, we could smell every item in their picnic hampers. For in crossing the Equator, we seemed to have traveled back in time. And now, across the footlights of the Teatro Colonial, the "old" Yiddish audience was unpacking its pastrami sandwiches.

These were the people who'd smacked their lips when Thomashefsky chewed the scenery, who'd mourned each of Adler's thousand deaths. When "Hearts and Flowers" was the Yiddish theater's national anthem, these patriots sang along. This wasn't the Art Theater crowd, those college professors and dentists' wives who sat on their gloves and thought only of what intelligent comments to make at intermission. These were the hungry hearts, real people longing to be entertained and moved. And their bedlam was music to my ears.

That night I fell in love with my audience, and, like a woman in love, I gave everything. How could they not respond? Even as we sang the opening chant, I could sense our listeners wanting to believe in that rising and falling soul. And as I made my entrance, I felt them rooting for true love, for mates betrothed forty days before birth.

This time, meeting Chonon was easy. Benno and I looked, we looked away; it was almost as if we were newly in love, as if all that trouble with Dalashinsky had never happened. I wasn't the same person who'd sung silly love songs in someone else's Spanish. I hadn't yet met my double. I felt as if our lives were being given back to us—together with the fear that they would be taken away again.

Every word came out with a built-in heartache, and the audience went wild. Three lines into my part, I was already getting free advice from an old lady in the front row.

"Go to him, darling," she shouted. "Otherwise you'll regret it through this life and the next."

"Good evening, Chonon," I said, while a young mother up front was holding her squalling baby up and saying,

"Look, *kindele*. When you meet your match made in heaven, this is how it will be!"

It stopped the play, but not the baby. The caterwauling went on and so did we. It was a wonder anyone heard; we couldn't hear ourselves. But every distraction—every rattling program, every whiff of garlic, every tubercular cough—inspired me to work harder. That night's performance was a full head and shoulders above Great Art; that night was love.

When Chonon died, the audience wailed as if every heart out there had lost its predestined mate. When Zalmen came toward me with the marriage veil, he got hooted and hissed like a melodrama villain. You'd have thought that there was no one in the house but women who'd been married off for money.

"You are not my bridegroom," I said, and a hundred different voices chorused, "That's right, *maydele*. You tell him."

I ran through my preparations, filled my lungs, and constricted my throat for Chonon's dybbuk to squeeze through. I opened my mouth, but the dybbuk who spoke through it was not Chonon of Brinnits, but Paco of Buenos Aires.

I don't even know what to call it. An attack? A fit? Possession? None of these apply. Whatever it was, the fact that I now knew my dybbuk's name didn't make it any easier. For if the previous night's episode had been as casual and unconscious as an insincere compliment, this was more physical—like hiccups, sneezes, but more violent; something torn from the heart.

"Mama warned me!" I heard myself shout. "Marriage isn't the tango!"

This time, at least, it was Yiddish. But for all the bearing this outburst had on Anski's text, I could have been speaking Chinese. I couldn't look at the cast, and luckily my dybbuk had swiveled me around to face the house, where I saw:

They were eating it up. Just as the old Second Avenue crowd had relished jokes about Moscowitz and Lupowitz's restaurant, so these people savored my reference to their national dance. Had this been Stuyvesant Place, where all the dentists' wives had read the play thirty times, I would have been tsk-tsked off the stage. But this was the kind of audience which had egged Thomashefsky on to stop in the middle of *Shylock* and lecture extemporaneously on the four great sufferings of the Jews. One: the destruction of the temple. Two: the diaspora. Three: the sweatshops. And four: the freshness of the fish at Moscowitz and Lupowitz.

Besides, that marriage wasn't the tango was something most of them had learned from bitter experience. They applauded my wisdom for almost a minute, thus giving me a chance to regain my self-possession, so to speak, and motion to the rest of the cast, I'm Dinah again. It's all right. Go on.

We went on—four lines and we'd finished the scene. The curtain came down, but no one could move for staring at me.

"Let's go," I told them. "Maybe Rome wasn't built in a day, but we've got exactly two minutes to set up the wonder worker's study."

I knew from the night before: Activity would help. We positioned the candlesticks, goblets, *challah*, the table and chair. Then Dalashinsky entered, straight from God. Even Moses coming down from Mount Sinai must have stumbled over a few rocks. But Dalashinsky walked on air. That night, though, this air seemed heavier than usual and we could tell: Dalashinsky wasn't so high in the clouds. This time he knew what I'd done.

Still he said nothing and it wasn't till the curtain rose that I understood: He was working doubly hard as if to atone for my sin against the sacred text.

In some ways Rabbi Azrielke's part was the juiciest in the play, and that night Dalashinsky wrung it dry. As he told the story about the Baal Shem and the acrobat, his body stretched taut as a tightrope. And when he reached the Baal Shem's lament about the loose souls and tight bodies, the rope uncoiled—and collapsed. Watching from the wings, I thought, Look at that man act!

When it came time for my entrance, Ida and Clara grabbed me—not like two loving friends, but like policemen dragging a criminal off to jail. Maybe they thought that finger marks on my arm might make an upstart dybbuk behave. From center stage, Rabbi Azrielke looked straight through me, and in a commanding bass with a double vibrato said, "Dybbuk, who are you?"

I took a deep breath and felt the whole cast doing the same. And right in the midst of that tragic scene, they actually grinned with relief when they heard my dybbuk voice, gritty and raw, Benno and Chonon lost beyond death: "Rabbi of Miropol, you know who I am!"

So another thing in my dybbuk's favor. He (and here, to be perfectly clear, I mean The Aviator's dybbuk) was well behaved. He'd said his piece; he kept quiet. And frankly, I couldn't blame him for not wanting to share the stage with Leon Dalashinsky, who was playing his most brilliant Rabbi Azrielke so far, storming at my dybbuk as if its very existence were an insult to his faith in the goodness of God. He battled my poor restless spirit through that scene and the next and then—not a minute too soon—declared the necessity of an exorcism.

The whole house went black, and this was all that was needed to set the babies off. Full-grown women cried, "Mama!" In the darkness, the only visible thing was the procession of lit candles, emerging one by one from the wings.

"Fire!" yelled some joker, but no one paid attention, and even the children got quiet as the lights came up on the *minyan* with their black candles, shofars, and shrouds. The first shofar blew one long eerie note.

"*Tante* Rosa!" cried a woman in the mezzanine. "Are you scared?"

As if it were a wrestling match, they cheered Rabbi Azrielke and booed the dybbuk. And when the stubborn spirit finally agreed to leave Leah's body, they whistled through their teeth and threw their caps in the air.

But wait. When the audience found out that, dybbuk or no dybbuk, I was still going to be married to Menasha, we almost had a riot on our hands. All during that last tender love dialogue between Leah and the ghost of her dead Chonon, the ladies kept shrieking, "Go to him! It's your last chance! Go to him now!"

I fainted, a slow Dalashinsky dissolve from the knees. The curtain fell before people had gotten it through their heads that Leah was dead. First came shocked silence, then a few sobs. We could have done the play all over again in the time it took them to recover and start to applaud.

That evening, the curtain calls meant even more to me than they had on the opening night on Stuyvesant Place. I wanted the bravos to go on forever, partly because I loved this audience so and partly because I feared what was waiting for me backstage.

The whole cast was gathered in my dressing room. And as I walked in they pounced on me—though only, thank heaven, with words.

"Aha!" said Zalmen. "The prima donna!"

"Last night was ridiculous," said Feivel. "But this is absurd."

I looked to Benno to defend me, but Benno was looking away.

"This can't go on," said Dalashinsky. "I can't take any more. To have come this far so some ingenue can improvise"—he spat out the dirty word—"like some trashy Thomashefsky."

"The Thomashefskys were artists of a sort," murmured Feivel, daring this treason just as firemen, in extremis, might use dynamite to put out a blaze.

"I wasn't improvising," I said. "I didn't know what I was saying. Like last night, it wasn't me."

In reply, I got silence. Finally Benno said, "Maybe it *is* a dybbuk." Later, Benno would explain that this possibility was beginning to appeal to him as an explanation for our troubles, the last three weeks of problems: Better a dybbuk than a shipboard crush on Dalashinsky. "It wouldn't be the strangest chapter in the history of Yiddish theater."

We looked at him. What could be stranger?

"If artists of Anski's stature chose to write about dybbuks," continued Benno, "maybe it's like Dalashinsky says: It happens. And it stands to reason that this aviator. . . . As Anski makes clear, the souls who come back are always the ones who died young, with unfinished business. . . ."

"Brilliant diagnosis," said Dalashinsky. "And what do you suggest, doctor? An exorcism?"

Benno shrugged.

"Mr. Brownstein," said Dalashinsky. "She's nutty—and you're nuttier. You both need your heads examined. You know which rabbi we should call in? Rabbi Sigmund Freud."

Well trained, we laughed at Dalashinsky's bad joke—laughed and worried at the same time. For we knew that things must have been in pretty sad shape if Dalashinsky was calling in Freud.

Dalashinsky's position was that we artists owed Freud a measure of respect for having been the first to explore that magical place, the threshold of the subconscious. But that was as far as it went, and beyond that, Freud was not to be taken seriously. How idiotic to imagine that one's whole life might be blighted by a glimpse of Mama and Papa doing what everyone did! An artist's soul, said Dalashinsky, was as lush as a tropical garden in which analysts, like inept gardeners, would prune every hedge to fit the mold; such clipping would mean spiritual disaster.

Yet such was my faith in our director that when another knock interrupted our discussion, that second night backstage at the Teatro Colonial, I half expected to see the Viennese professor with his neat goatee and cigar.

"If it's Popolescu, get rid of him," said Feivel.

"Popolescu?" said Zalmen. "It's that girl again, Dinah's twin."

But this knock was too tentative to have come from either Popolescu or Mamie—two hesitant little taps of the kind which automatically arouse your sympathy for whoever is knocking. Naturally, the most sympathetic was Ida.

"Come in," she said, and inch by inch, the door opened.

Well, you could have knocked me over with a feather. For there in the doorway stood a woman dressed in black, a short middle-aged lady who so closely resembled Mama that my knees went weak. Within a few seconds, though, I realized: It wasn't Mama. For the way you first know your mother's face is not by how she looks, but by how she looks at you. And the fish eye this woman was giving me couldn't have been less like Mama's warm browns.

"It's not enough"—she was talking to me, very icy and controlled—"that you wrecked his life, dragging him to tango parlors and such. But after all that's happened, to stand up and imitate his voice. I warned him about you, and even you knew I was right!"

Natty Kauffman, who maintained his dexterity even in the knottiest social situations, was the first to unravel this one.

"Madame," he said. "This isn't the girl you think. This is Dinah Rappoport, one of our actresses, who just happens to resemble—"

"Then it's worse." Now, as she stared at me, she wasn't seeing Mamie, but Dinah—and it *was* worse. "You had no reason to imitate my son except pure malice."

"Great," said Zalmen. "First the wife, then the mother—we've practically met this dybbuk's whole family."

"Dybbuk?" said the woman.

"Mrs. Engelhart," I announced in a noble voice which swelled to a pitch which Sarah Bernhardt herself might have thought to tone down. "Your son has returned as a dybbuk."

Briefly I wondered why the spirit of this tough tango-dancer/ gangster/aviator should come back to tell the world that his mama was right. Then it occurred to me that this woman must once have been beautiful, and that her face, regarding him with love, was the first thing he'd ever seen. In recognition of that, and to comfort her, he'd come back to say what boys who die young must die thinking their mamas want to hear: You told me so. You were right.

It made me give this woman her due. And as so often happens when you give people their due, the weight of it is just too much and they crumble in front of your eyes.

When the woman began to cry, I thought, This isn't theater to her. Life won't give her another son. And though I caught Clara (who got all the grieving mother parts) watching clinically, the rest of us were so paralyzed with sympathy, no one moved toward her or offered so much as a hankie. It was up to her to compose herself, which she finally did, saying:

"Even in his rebellious stage, when we so rarely saw him, my Paco came to tell me he'd married that girl. Like a real Jewish son, he told Mama—*after* the deed was done. Too late, I warned him that marriage wasn't the tango. But he couldn't hear; he had tango music playing in his head, twenty-four hours a day. Soon enough he found out for himself and came home. We were so happy to have him back—of course my husband bought him that airplane. We'd have bought him the moon and stars if he'd told us they were for sale.

"But the first time he returned from the airport, I only wished he'd stayed with the girl. It wasn't my fear that he'd be hurt, though (how could I help it?) that too. It was the look in his eyes, a thousand times more in love than on the day he'd announced his marriage. Right then I knew: My own son was one of the worst.

"Forty days before birth, an angel's tapped them—not with its fingers, but with some sort of magic wand. And they're born loving something—an object, an idea, what does it matter?— more than they can ever love flesh and blood. That's how my son was about flying. To his ears, engine noise was sweeter than the tango. From then on, he was more lost to us than in all that time he'd run like a mouse with the garbage of Buenos Aires.

"In the Bible, Abraham is a hero for taking his son up the mountain; Isaac a hero for going. But I always thanked God that it wasn't my family, and I wondered how that story would have sounded from Sarah's point of view. For everyone who climbs that mountain because he hears something calling, there's usually a sacrifice bloodier than anything Abraham was prepared to do. And almost always, there's a Sarah waiting down below. That was where my son left me; left the girl too. While to strangers—the people of Buenos Aires—he's a bigger hero than Abraham and Isaac combined."

So, I thought, a new perspective on my dybbuk. The night before, I'd imagined that this spirit had chosen to enter me because I too fell in love across rooms. But this new light cast shadows which troubled me more. Before I could fully consider this, Popolescu came flying into the room.

"Fantastic!" he was shouting. "You were a smash! That tango bit was the best thing yet. We're sold out for three nights, the rest of the run—"

We followed his exit with our eyes, but my dybbuk's mother never took hers off me.

"You're just like my son," she said. "No wonder you can imitate his voice. You're a pretty girl, already you could have a family, three lovely children. But you don't, so there must be something you want more. What is it? Money? Fame? Applause?"

"Art," I replied, and couldn't help sneaking a look at Dalashinsky.

"Art!" She snorted. "Art can't put its arms around you in the middle of the night. When you're old and sick, art won't tuck the blankets around your chin and bring you a cup of tea. If I were your mother, I'd tell you, 'Forget about art. Love's more important. Find a husband, have kids.' "

At this point, I could have said, I *do* have a husband. Instead of which, I kept quiet. We'd promised Dalashinsky not to ruin everything; I only wondered what was left to ruin.

"Otherwise," she concluded, "otherwise your Mama and Papa will go to their graves without ever having had the chance to dance at their daughter's wedding!"

This was all I needed to hear. I began to cry—softly at first, then harder. At this, my dybbuk's mother seemed satisfied, as if somehow she'd made me pay for her son's going up in that plane.

"Good evening," she said. Since that timid entrance, she'd picked up steam. On her way out, she gave the door a healthy slam.

Zalmen whistled, and Natty said, "With a mother like that. . . ."

His voice died out. My sniffling was the only sound in the dressing room. Why shouldn't I cry? I was miserable.

Now I *knew* why this dybbuk had picked me to possess: We both had cold hearts. Like Sarah at the foot of the mountain, Benno would suffer for my sake. And while I was up there making sacrifices for art, he'd get tired of waiting and leave. Meanwhile, Mama and Papa would go danceless into their graves while I did loop-the-loops in the clouds. If only I could change—but I couldn't. The angel had tapped me with its icy wand. These ugly truths weighed on me, and when they got as heavy as I could stand, I shrugged and said, "If we don't get out of Buenos Aires in twenty-four hours, I'm killing myself!"

"Dinele!" said Benno, and even in my suicidal state, I realized that this was the first time he'd called me Dinele in front of the cast.

"Dinah, don't say it," said Clara. "Don't even think it."

I was as shocked as anyone. For a life-loving girl like myself, to threaten suicide was totally out of character. But in real life, I've noticed, it's not so unusual for people to act out of character. I'd said it—and I meant it.

Moreover, I knew exactly what I would do. I'd go down to the docks and throw myself into the river. Even if someone saw me, the current would keep them from trying to change my mind. I thought of an illustration in Benno's Shakespeare, the drowned Ophelia floating downstream with water lilies in her hair.

Benno would grieve for a while. I couldn't stand to think about Mama and Papa getting the news. But they'd recover, and in the end it would be kinder than more years of mistreatment from me. The cast would feel sorry in an abstract sort of way, Dalashinsky irritated by the bother of finding another Leah. And Art wouldn't miss me at all. Suicide had been done before, by better artists than me.

"I'll do it," I promised. "I swear it on Mama's and Papa's heads!"

As they all stared at me, I was studying Dalashinsky, the only one of them who knew enough about acting to understand that this was for real.

"Children," said Dalashinsky. "Miss Rappoport is not the kind of girl to swear lightly on her Mama's and Papa's heads."

7

FIFTY-SOME YEARS LATER, I saw the movie *One Flew Over the Cuckoo's Nest* on television, and quite honestly, I was skeptical. If only it were true that a little nerve and team spirit could make the *meshugana* sane. The only scene which convinced me was the one in which the cuckoos escape from the ward and go fishing. The freedom, the mischief, the thrill of getting away with it make them seem normal—no goofier, from a distance, than some slightly tipsy conventioneers.

Seeing this, I became crazier and forgot that Benno wasn't there.

"Benno!" I said out loud. "That's how we must have looked leaving Buenos Aires!"

For that cuckoo fishing trip had taken me fifty years back and reminded me: There's nothing like a little escapade to delude a lunatic into feeling healthy.

All through that South American trip, I was as cuckoo as they come. But as we stole out of Buenos Aires under cover of darkness, I felt fine. It wasn't only the challenge, the edge of danger, but also the logistics. Worm on the hook, line in the water, don't rock the boat, no time to think about problems.

Just to plan our escape took an all-night meeting, which Feivel called to order with an outline of our situation:

"The first problem is, our contract with Popolescu has no escape clause to cover a three-night shortening of the run."

"So he'll sue us," said Zalmen.

"Let him try," said Ida,

"All right," said Feivel. Was this parliamentary procedure? "Problem two: We've got tickets paid in full on a boat to Montevideo which isn't scheduled to leave till next Friday."

"Exchange them, Feivele," said Clara. "Book us on a shrimp boat. It won't be the first time."

"A leaky washtub," I said. "I'll swim, I don't care. I was planning to do that anyway."

This settled it more conclusively than a full discussion and a vote. For what were technical problems compared to the difficulties of keeping a suicide watch till we sailed? And then what?

No one mentioned the problem of forfeiting every cent we'd made for the two shows in Buenos Aires. And for this I could thank the fact that I wasn't the girl who cried wolf. I was no Alba Springer, no hysterical, palm-reading prima donna flinging her wig onstage. I was Dinah Rappoport, the young woman with the head on her shoulders. And now that this sensible head had spoken in someone else's voice, conjured up her own double, and threatened suicide, they were paying attention.

Maybe the others were bored anyway, itchy and bug-bitten at the Zona Azura. Also they knew that what happened in Buenos Aires would mean nothing one way or the other for their careers. Whatever the reason, the Yiddish Art Theater had never had less trouble reaching a consensus.

At seven the next evening, we'd sneak out like thieves in the night. Immediately we lowered our voices and started plotting our elopement as if Popolescu were Juliet's father. We joked about him pursuing us with a battalion of pimps. But really, what would he have done? There was no need for such overacting, except that the others must have hoped that, as I said before: A little caper might work better than fifty shock treatments.

At dawn Feivel went out to reconnoiter and came back with the information that we could get a ferry straight across the Rio de la Plata that evening; from there we could catch another boat to Montevideo. The trip would take a day longer than the direct boat, but we'd reach Montevideo in time for our engagement.

The last problem—and this was the big one—was luggage; not ours, but our play's. We carried shabby valises, weighed in by the ounce, but *The Dybbuk* traveled in style. Those marvelous sets commissioned from the Essex Street Expressionists. That wedding canopy hand-embroidered by the ladies' auxiliary of the Leon Dalashinsky Fan Club. Those silver candlesticks Dalashinsky had carried all the way from his mama in Bialystock and which, he claimed, meant home to him, meant *shabes*; those candlesticks which were the essence of his Rabbi Azrielke and the subject of a million lectures on how a prop could be drawn on for its emotional memories.

Even if we could crate it all up and sneak it out of the theater behind Popolescu's back, how could we get it on and off two ferries?

"No problem," said Dalashinsky. "Leave everything—except maybe the candlesticks. We'll simplify. We'll play Montevideo the way Goldfaden toured the bars and beer gardens of Bessarabia, doing *Hamlet* with nothing more than a lantern, two swords, and a sheet. We'll send an apologetic letter to Popolescu, explaining. We'll ask him to send our things on to New York."

"Good luck," said Zalmen. "Don't hold your breath."

"Leon," said Feivel, "it's ridiculous. Your mama's candlesticks alone weigh fifty pounds, we'll need a derrick to lift them."

"Then drop them!" said Dalashinsky. "Such is the life of an artist! From time to time everything must be given away, unloaded so the soul can float free like a message in a bottle. Read the life of Tolstoy. He was always giving the shirt off his back, the roof over his children's heads. When we get back to Stuyvesant Place, we'll begin anew, creating from scratch. A whole new production for which I already have ideas!"

Feivel's idea was that we should take what we could. And so that day, we each made three trips to the Teatro Colonial, on progressively feebler pretexts. The men filled their pockets with makeup jars and false beards. In my dressing room, I put Leah's wedding gown under my street dress and tucked the hem up in the waistband of my petticoat. Poor Ida went to the trouble of tying the cardboard *challah* up in her shawl; back at the Zona Azura, Feivel yelled, "Dumb head! In Montevideo, we can find a real one!"

At seven (what better time to sneak out than the hour when everyone's waiting for you at the theater?) we left the Zona Azura one by one without paying our bill. ("They should pay *us* for feeding their bedbugs," said Natty.) The plan, if anyone asked, was to say that our suitcases were full of costumes which we were taking to the theater. But no one asked, and even the bellhop waved and seemed relieved that he didn't have to stop scratching. As those turquoise doors swung behind me, I felt simply wonderful, without a thought for my dybbuk, my double, my icebox of a heart.

By prearrangement, we assembled in a small park a few blocks from the hotel. And there we were, the Yiddish Art Theater on tour with less equipment than a dog act—not even a dog! But when something's breathing down your neck, you don't need equipment to jump; fortunately, we were jumping in the same direction.

The truth was that a dybbuk was chasing us out of Argentina. But instead of truth, we talked platitudes: A change of scene would do me good. A new place, a new beginning. When the show's a flop and you know it, get out before the reviews.

In the fading twilight, we headed by smell for the harbor. Aiming only as far as the nearest light, we made our way from the flickering streetlamps to the smoky lanterns at the fritter stands. Meanwhile the plazas were filling with pedestrians: respectable families strolling clockwise with their marriageable daughters; counterclockwise, the parents of eligible sons; while in the shadows, pressed against the bases of the equestrian statues, the less-than-respectable sweethearts embraced.

When I caught up to Benno, he whispered, "Dinele, be calm. Everything will be hunky-dory. Five hundred miles is an awfully long way for a dybbuk to travel."

I *was* calm—goofy, almost. Still, I had no faith in the hunky-doryness of it all. If a dybbuk could jump into a person, what was to prevent it from hopping wherever it pleased? For a soul without even a body to lug from one place to another, what could be easier than traveling?

But as we boarded the ferry, which sailed immediately as if it had been waiting just for us, I truly believed that every slosh meant that much more water between me and my Buenos Aires dybbuk. And from the way I stared back over the bow at the port receding behind us, you would have thought that the Rio de la Plata was the Red Sea crashing down on the Egyptians.

Two minutes out, it became clear that we weren't the honored guests on that boat, but rather, the last straw. Weighed down, we rode so low that we could have trailed our hands in the river—not that we would have touched that brackish mess. Anyway, who cared? The very same hard-to-please travelers who'd grumbled nonstop on the *Veracruz* now seemed quite delighted to sit on the floor of that open tub, those planks glued together with what looked like bird droppings.

Luckily, the construction was hard to see—every inch of deck space was covered by Indian women with babies attached up and down their bodies like sunflower heads on a stalk; chickens, goats, burros loaded with blankets and pots, farmers more heavily laden than their burros. Any self-respecting Argentinean—even a mental hospital escapee—would have drowned himself before setting foot on that crate. But we'd come from halfway around the world, and like those tourists who travel in search of departures from everyday life, we loved every uncomfortable minute.

"Look at the stars!" cried Dalashinsky. For the benefit of the peons and their burros, he told the whole story of the Warrior of Masada. And I was in such a good mood, I only minded a little that he was telling it the exact same way he'd told it to me.

Surrounded by a crowd of children, Benno was doing coin tricks, a talent I'd never suspected he had. Not to be outdone, Zalmen and Natty mugged funny faces. Miming like a deafmute, Ida was complimenting the mothers on their beauty of their babies. The women pulled their shawls tighter over their children's faces and kept on chewing and spitting over the side of the boat in a stream of froth which trailed us like an extra wake.

At one point, a chicken ran across my foot. I jumped, then looked up to see fifty grinning mouths and teeth you could have counted on the fingers of one hand. One Indian woman gave me a start—I'd seen enough doubles on this trip. And though she wasn't my twin, if I'd darkened my skin and knocked out half my teeth, we could have passed for sisters.

By this time, the mosquito netting which had shrouded part of the boat was rolled up. The deck was strung with tiny blinking lights. In one corner, some men had fashioned woven mats into a canopy under which they played cards; the full moon cast slatted shadows down through the thatching.

It wasn't a big boat, but with the constantly shifting population of children and babies, I managed to get separated from my friends. For a while, I felt as alone as you can only be in a crowded foreign place. And just when I was starting to feel lost, Benno found me.

He guided me to an empty spot on a bench and we squeezed into a place hardly big enough for one. Somehow that crowd—with its noise, its colors, its distractions—gave us more privacy than a cabin on the *Veracruz*, and Benno felt free to put his arms around me.

"Dinah," he said. "You'll see now. Everything will be fine." Squashed against his chest, I believed him and drifted off.

In some ways, that night reminded me of the first sweet nights of our marriage. I slept and yet I was conscious of being asleep; I let the boat rock me and tasted the salt in the air. Sleeping unafraid in the midst of wild Indians, I could dream that I was a much braver girl than I was.

Benno woke me for a spectacular sunrise. Pink and orange I'd seen, but purple and green? We separated just as the cast began to regroup, for it seemed as if the restful night had made more room on the boat. Roosters were crowing, but the children still slept, and in the relative quiet I heard Dalashinsky say, "Ah, Feivel. If we could only find a lighting man to do colors like this, I would write *The Burning of Moscow*."

Soon after, we smelled land. Land? It was garbage, seaweed, and petroleum. Nevertheless, the entire Yiddish Art Theater burst into applause, while the Indians stared at us as if we really were escaped mental patients.

As the mob swept us along the pier and onto Uruguayan soil, I understood for the first time why certain emotional travelers might want to kneel down and kiss it. I wondered if this was how Mama and Papa had felt on Ellis Island, until I remembered, it wasn't. On Ellis Island, they'd worried from the minute they got there till the minute they left. And there we were in that godforsaken dump of a fishing port, bouncing on our heels without a care in the world.

Our good cheer survived Feivel's bad news. "The boat for Montevideo stops here every ten days. And we've just missed it by an hour!"

"Feivel!" Clara jumped on him the way tourist couples will go at each other in foreign places. "What kind of way is this to travel?"

We quieted her and Feivel went on. If we wanted to arrive on schedule we had two choices. He'd already found someone to rent us pack mules for a two-day caravan along the coast. Or we could take a four-day train ride along two sides of a triangle, inland to Mercedes, then out to sea again at the capital.

"We could walk quicker," said Benno. "I vote for the burros."

His was the only vote they got. No one could imagine our great director with saddle sores, and I myself didn't like the idea of being hoisted like a feed sack onto a donkey's back. Even after sleeping all night in Benno's arms, I could look him straight in the eye and say, "I vote for the train."

"I second," said Clara.

"We've got the time," said Ida. "Why rush? Why not have the comfort—and the adventure?"

Were these the same crybabies who'd whined about exploding like popcorn on the *Veracruz*? I barely recognized these passionate travelers, who practically ran to the train station and over a dozen sets of half-rotted tracks, overgown with scrub palm and primeval vines; Darwin could have written another book on what grew between those ties.

Meanwhile two birds were circling overhead, some species so prehistoric, they made the vegetation look like Versailles. Their wingspread was enormous, and suddenly I understood why people told stories about eagles carrying off babies. I was trying hard not to think about Paco Engelhart's flight. And only now, picturing them in my mind, do I recognize what I refused to see at the time: buzzards, circling God knows what.

On one wall of the station was a pockmarked schedule, which Feivel managed to read. The train would arrive in six hours. We dragged our luggage into the shade, sat down on it, and waited.

Later, when I would find myself in airports where everyone ran (with escalators and even conveyor belts to run underneath your running), I knew that these were for business, not travel. To me, one of travel's greatest pleasures is wasted time. In certain moods, nothing's pleasanter than a delay. There's nothing you have to—or *can*—do. Most likely, nothing bad or good will happen to you. The pressures of your life fall away, and yet this idleness is finite; at some point, the train will come.

I wasn't the only one to feel this peace. We were all of us happy as clams—steamed ones, that is, but no one complained of the heat. The big event of the afternoon was a visit from three little girls selling packets of slightly rancid chips. Kissing his fingertips, Zalmen pronounced them superior to the potato pancakes at Moscowitz and Lupowitz.

Ordinarily, this would have gotten a knowing laugh. The fry cook at Moscowitz and Lupowitz was known as The Poisoner. But our mouths were too full for a chuckle; we hadn't eaten all day. As we sat in the shadows of that Uruguayan afternoon, the songbirds made sweeter music than a teatime string quartet at the Plaza, and those greasy fries tasted better than truly superior *latkes*.

Two hours late, the train pulled in, rattling so hard that we felt it before we heard it. Those last two hours of expecting it every minute had made the time drag, but that only made us welcome it more. The engine shone like a freshly blacked stove, with its name in red letters: THE QUEEN VICTORIA.

"Hail Britannia!" cried Zalmen.

Though I'd read in the papers what Britain had done to the poorer parts of the world, I was glad to see signs in that jungle that England had been there before. Soon the train had pulled into the station, where it snorted and steamed like a prize Hereford bull.

According to the schedule, there was no place else that train could have been going. Still, you don't want to board something that powerful without asking. Feivel found the conductor—a pink-faced, barrel-chested old man—and tried out his Spanish with no success. Then Feivel turned to me and said, "If only that dybbuk of yours were here to do some interpreting."

When Feivel's German got no more action than his Spanish, he said, "Is this the train for Montevideo?"

And better English than Feivel's, though with maybe a trace of a Cockney accent, the conductor replied, "Yes, sir. Arriving Montevideo Station on Tuesday, fifteen hundred hours. That's nine hundred Greenwich."

"Children," said Dalashinsky. "Pay attention to how beautifully this man speaks." And just as this beautiful English cheered Dalashinsky, I was encouraged to hear that even on the other side of the world, they were counting Greenwich time.

The conductor patted the train as if it *were* a bull's flanks and said, "Only the British could have built this line. And only the British can run it."

Only the British could have divided that backwoods trolley into classes. And only an Englishman could have made the minute class distinctions dividing our raggle-taggle bunch from the salt of the earth with their chickens and pigs. And so for the first and only time we rode, as Dalashinsky would later claim, first class.

Our coach was fitted with wainscoting, dark red plush, windows clear as wineglasses, built to withstand, at the very worst, a foggy day in London. Already the coastal heat had gone to work. The plush was bald and pink with spots of mange; termites had chewed away at the gilded window sashes, leaving piles of shiny sawdust on the sills.

But what did a little seediness matter when, at six the next morning, the conductor rolled in a clattering cart of teapots, cups, tiny plates, and tinier cucumber sandwiches with the crusts cut off?

That morning the landscape stayed flat; another swamp like Argentina. I snoozed on and off till a sudden drop in temperature woke me; we were traveling through the woods. The forest floor was perfectly clean, as if it had been swept, and carpeted with needles. The pines were evenly spaced, and so tall they seemed to meet at the top like railroad tracks in the distance where the dappled light shone through.

We were having an early supper of roast beef, Yorkshire pudding, runny custard with berries when the train stopped, backed up, took a deep breath, and charged full speed uphill. A snail could have beaten us up those gentle slopes. We climbed all evening; half that time, we seemed to be slipping back down to the bottom, but we never worried. Years afterward, I was putting away Hannele's stuffed bears when I thought of the Cuchilla Grande and of the night we crossed those furry brown hills while I slept like Hannah cuddled up with her teddy.

In the morning, I found myself semi-sprawled in a semi-upright seat. Beside me, Ida was snoring.

"Ida!" I said. "Wake up! This Uruguay is purple!"

Many years later, Benno and I were vacationing in the Catskills in August when we saw what the local folk called loosestrife. I remember asking a desk clerk, who waved his hand at the view and said, "The most beautiful weed in the world." Beautiful, I wanted to say, but not the most. In the Catskills, this loosestrife grew mostly in patches. But the hills of Uruguay were brighter, and from the top of the Cuchilla Grande, the country was solid purple to the horizon and for thousands of miles on either side.

Next I woke Benno, and trying very hard to be casual, said, "Look. The other side of the world is purple."

And where was Dalashinsky? I didn't have to look. I did look, though, and saw him off by himself at the far end of the coach, gazing soulfully out the window. I knew what he was thinking, and I could almost hear him say, "Compared to that beauty, Miss Rappoport, our art is crabgrass!"

It cheered me that I didn't want to hear him say it. But I did feel that same desire to put my arm around his shoulders and tell him not to be so hard on himself.

From time to time towns appeared like islands in that purple sea. I recall a sign, COLONIA SUIZA, printed in Gothic letters. At the station, a crowd of the oddest children (some Indian, some blue-eyed blond, some mixed) jumped up and down, reaching into our windows with cuckoo clocks, all chiming at once.

"Next they'll be yodeling," said Natty.

"Don't laugh," said Zalmen. "At least our Dinah isn't the only cuckoo out here."

This so-called joke goaded Benno into parting with a handful of coins in return for a miniature monstrosity of a Swiss chalet, with a mechanical girl and boy who emerged from two separate doors, polkaed over each other's feet, then disappeared when the cuckoo stopped. Bowing deeply from the waist, Benno presented it to me.

"Mr. Brownstein," I said. "Thank you."

Later, when I cross-examined my memory for some evidence that something was going on between me and Dalashinsky, I dimly remembered a split-second flash of jealousy on Dalashinsky's face.

"Artists," he said, "have a natural sense of time."

The implication was that dilettantes had clocks, and it hurt me, just as it hurt to overhear Clara whispering to Feivel, "Cuckoos for the cuckoo." But I wasn't so hurt that I didn't have to fight the urge to throw my arms around Benno's neck and kiss him. I was wondering where we would put the clock when we got back home. The bedroom, I decided, and immediately began imagining what we would do there while those mechanical children danced. Instead of trumpeting ram's horns, the cockadoodling of a clockwork bird would announce the Messiah's arrival.

Of all my wild fantasies on that trip, this one would come closest to the truth. Yet not even I could have imagined that a clock from the wilderness of Uruguay would last sixty years, and that even today, every hour on the hour, my poor neighbors would hear the call of that cuckoo from the purple plains.

8

As THE *Queen Victoria* CHUGGED through the suburbs of Montevideo, a gang of boys ran alongside, mincing and smirking like big kids racing a toddler. Let them beat us, I wasn't insulted. I liked going slow enough to see that these healthy boys could have run very fast. Their racecourse was a smooth dirt road with none of the suspicious puddles which had covered Argentina. Beyond it were whitewashed houses, each one with a window box and more flowers than Jacob Adler's whole funeral.

Normally the railroad tracks aren't a city's showplace, but you could have shown off the ones in Montevideo to anyone. For if Buenos Aires had been a shadowy lady of the evening, Montevideo was a housewife, unafraid of the strongest sun, saying, "Come in. Look around. My house has no cobwebby corners." I was braced for turquoise and baby-sweater pastels, but the downtown was the comforting gray-brown of New York. The tracks skirted plazas planted with bougainvillea and geraniums.

Montevideo Station was modern, bright, antiseptically clean. Dignified redcaps threaded their way among families kissing hello and good-bye. What could have been less threatening? And who could have been less like Popolescu than the gentleman who came out of that crowd to meet us? In one second flat, we knew that this one would never ask us to sell tickets; nor, for that matter, would he offer to carry Dalashinsky's valise.

From this perspective, I would rather see Popolescu; looking back, I already miss him. But when you're the Yiddish Art

Theater, on tour in South America with no equipment and a possible dybbuk, you want someone who acts like he knows what day it is. This man gave the appearance of a college professor or perhaps a banker in a homburg, a three-piece suit, a watch chain, and a perfect beard. His Yiddish was right on the German border, but what he said made it clear that he was venturing into uncharted lands.

"Leon Dalashinsky, I presume."

Inwardly, we groaned. Dalashinsky said, "Correct."

As the stranger stuck his hand out to shake Dalashinsky's, I thought: Only a rabbi would have such clean nails. And just at that instant, he said, "I'm Rabbi Rupert Schmuckler."

Only Zalmen, our six-year-old, giggled, though frankly I was tempted.

"I didn't know how many cabs to hire," said Rabbi Schmuckler. "I do hope you're not too exhausted to walk. Come with me. . . ." This was the last he mentioned us for some time; from then on, it was all Rabbi Schmuckler. Two blocks from the station, we knew his whole résumé: ordination by the chief rabbi of Cologne, postdoctoral studies in theology at Heidelberg, a record so impressive (or at least Rabbi Schmuckler was so impressed) that even Dalashinsky paid attention. Nothing could have been more obvious, but for the sake of conversation, Clara said, "Rabbi, I take it that your congregation is Reform?"

As if an Orthodox rabbi would have turned out to greet the Yiddish Art Theater! When Rabbi Schmuckler nodded, Zalmen leered and said, "I also am reformed." Without missing a step, the rabbi turned to give Zalmen a peculiar look, while in an effort to change the subject, Feivel pointed to a pleasant-looking doorway with a brass nameplate and a silver mezzuzah.

"Is this the Jewish section?"

"There is no Jewish section," said the rabbi with great pride, as if assimilation were his idea. Which brought him to the subject of his ideas: to tend the flame of Jewish culture, to lay, stone by stone, the foundation of international Jewry, to build the Third Temple of Jewish Life—in Uruguay! To this man, Jewish life meant something like a season ticket to the opera;

listening to him, you might have thought that the Yiddish Art Theater was Rabbi Rupert Schmuckler's idea. Indeed, the rabbi was so full of noble intentions that we were on the front steps of our hotel before he informed us of the two catastrophic occurrences which, needless to say, hadn't been his idea.

Number one: He had just received a telegram from the Teatro Moise in Rio canceling our engagement there. ("They can't say it in print," he explained. "But you know. Political unrest, the usual anti-Semitism.") Thus Montevideo had become the last stop on our tour.

All right, I thought, the sooner we'll be home.

And number two: Ten days ago, the Yiddish Theater of Montevideo had burned to the ground.

A less Reformed rabbi might have thanked God that no one was hurt and shrugged at the impossibility of understanding His will. Rabbi Schmuckler blamed the Montevideo fire department.

"Two buckets, a mule, and a wagon," he said. "What can you expect?"

Not to worry, he told us. Because of their commitment to art, he and his wife had decided to open their home. In order that his congregation might not be deprived, we were invited to play our entire three-night engagement—to smaller crowds, of course—in the rabbi's own living room.

"Thank you," said Dalashinsky.

Because the rabbi had been so unforthcoming with the true facts of our situation, we felt no need to volunteer the information that we had left Buenos Aires on the lam from a theater manager and a dybbuk. But maybe that was why we accepted the rabbi's offer so readily. In the back of my mind, I was hoping: If by any chance my dybbuk had followed us from Argentina, perhaps it might still think twice before invading a rabbi's front parlor. I was foolish to hope that the Schmucklers would inhibit it when, night after night, my restless spirit had made itself comfortable at the wonder worker of Miropol's.

Rabbi Schmuckler had booked us rooms at the Occidental Hotel. Accidental, we joked, but no. Every detail there was on purpose. The manager let Feivel check us in and waved the rest of us into the care of bellhops who led us down well-lit corridors and then, two by two, into bedrooms with carpet thick enough to sleep on. But why would you, when every double bed was wide enough for a family, and every room had two of them, with blankets neatly turned down over sheets so white that Mama could have slept on them without fear?

Ida and I had hardly settled in when a bright-eyed little chambermaid knocked and asked if we wanted to send out laundry. We put on our robes and sent everything.

"This is paradise," I heard Ida say; though I, in the other bed, might already have been dreaming.

For breakfast, the dining room offered as many choices as the *Veracruz*, but now we were on solid ground; without the rocking, I relished the same foods I'd choked down on the boat for Dalashinsky's sake. I was finishing my tea when Benno leaned across Zalmen, who was sitting between us, and in the overly casual tone of a man who expects to be turned down, said, "Miss Rappoport, would you like to take a walk?"

Maybe it was the breakfast, or the clean sheets, the good night's sleep, or the general hopefulness we'd all felt since arriving in Montevideo, but for whatever reason, I gave none of the excuses which had come so naturally on the *Veracruz* and in Buenos Aires.

"Yes," I said, and was just as surprised as Benno.

"Ah-ha-ha," said Zalmen. "Could something be starting up between Chonon and our little Leah?"

Later, I would return from our travels with a memory of every stone in Venice, every organ grinder in Amsterdam. But I can't tell you one sight we passed on that walk through Montevideo, nor one sound we heard. In fact, my memory is of unnatural quiet, our not saying a word.

If I had been Benno, I would have been talking a mile a minute, demanding to know what was happening. What was this business with Spanish-speaking dybbuks and Dalashinsky? Where was I when he was waiting for me in his cabin? But Benno had instincts, intuitions, the sense to know: Sometimes when you don't know what's happening, it's better to wait and pretend that nothing is.

Any mention of our problems would have put the whole Yiddish Art Theater between us. And on that walk, we didn't want company. The silence, the tension, and the care we took not to touch made it more uncomfortable—but also a lot more exciting—than walking beside a stranger.

What I remember best is that we walked in one direction, then turned and were almost back at the hotel when Benno stopped and grabbed my hand. We looked, we looked away—then he pulled me into a hallway and kissed me. And though my feet were on Uruguayan soil, my soul was in bed on Fourteenth Street; for those few seconds, I had no thoughts of dybbuks or Dalashinsky.

By that evening, when our company arrived at Rabbi Schmuckler's house, I would have loved anything, and I fell head over heels for the elegance. Every crystal in the chandelier reflected security and good taste. The folding chairs looked fit for a musicale at the Guggenheims', as did the sideboard arrayed with samovars of coffee and tea, platters of Napoleons, and bowls of bright Jaffa oranges. A uniformed maid took our hats as a horde of ladies—all chattering at once, discussing great moments in Yiddish theater as if they'd witnessed every one from the first row at Stuyvesant Place—descended on Dalashinsky.

If Yiddish culture were a flame, Rabbi Schmuckler's crowd stopped one step short of pyromania. Feivel didn't even have to clear his throat, he just gulped—they took their seats and got quiet. Then Dalashinsky stepped out to discover that there, on the other side of the world, they gave standing ovations at the *start* of the play.

He waited for silence, then said, "Ladies and gentlemen. Though tragedy is the highest art, there is nothing in art to compare with the real-life tragedies like the burning of the Yiddish Theater of Montevideo. Out of respect for that disaster, and with gratitude for your rabbi's gracious offer, we've agreed to perform in his home. Inspired by this new set of limitations, I have designed a new *Dybbuk* without equipment or sets, with only the simplest costumes and props, and with whatever lighting has been provided by the rebbitzin. . . ."

Where was Dalashinsky's sense of truth? Did he expect them to believe that, on hearing about the fire, we'd chucked all our scenery into Montevideo harbor? Surely Rabbi Schmuckler would recall that we'd arrived empty-handed—or was he too busy enjoying the fruits of his latest idea?

"Tonight," said Dalashinsky, "we stand before you like virgins. Having never done it before, we must ask you to meet us halfway."

Halfway? No sooner had we opened out mouths for the chant than those flame tenders were halfway down our throats. The reverence was so thick, you could have cut it like pumpernickel. And when an audience looks up to you so, you can't help feeling taller. Those people knew Anski, so Anski was what we would give them. For those culture lovers, we were culture itself. Had they come to see an ensemble? We practically said each other's lines.

Rising to the challenge of no sets and no props, we became pure illusion. Who needed a Torah when I could embrace the air and imagine that it was Benno's back, that afternoon in the doorway? Those pasteboard tombstones seemed like excess baggage now as I stared at the figures in Rabbi Schmuckler's Persian carpet and saw Leah's grandmother's grave. And for all my jokes about ensembles, there was magic in working together. . . .

Even so, as the crucial wedding scene approached, you could feel the tension building. What marvelous actors, our audience must have thought. But we knew better. I could sense the others' anxiety, and behind it the question: Had we made a mistake? Basically, these were good people—a little cerebral, pretentious, but what was the crime in that? What had they done to deserve our taking the chance of introducing a dybbuk into their midst? Not any dybbuk, but the spirit of a boy who would have stolen the silverware from the rebbitzin's buffet. What would he care about the decorum befitting a rabbi's home? Provoked, he might say anything!

Despite our misgivings, the wedding canopy went up, and my heart went out to the ladies of the Dalashinsky Fan Club, whose handiwork had been left in Buenos Aires. Now in its place, we were using Clara's paisley shawl.

Zalmen lumbered toward me with the marriage veil, which I identified as one of his own grayish handkerchiefs. I prepared my dybbuk voice, got as far as "I have come—"

And burst into tears.

My memory of those tears is so clear, I could start crying now. I remember how my mind skipped from one tragedy to another, casting everything in the dimmest light—and that I was weeping for all the best reasons.

I was crying first of all for myself, for being the kind of woman who climbs mountains while her family grieves down below. This led to morbid thoughts of Mama's and Papa's death. I'd still have Benno, knock on wood, and with him a future of misunderstandings and reconciliations, more Dalashinskys followed by more alleyway kisses. Apart, together, apart, together —we'd play our marriage out like loves me, loves me not. But the joke was that the game always finished: apart. At least Anski believed in an afterlife, two souls embracing beyond the curtain of heaven. But Benno and I would be lucky to wind up side by side in the ground.

I was I, not my dybbuk, crying; of this I was reasonably sure. A tough dybbuk like mine would never have weakened in front of that crew. But I couldn't help feeling that he was helping me along. A normal person can only weep for so long, but I could have gone on forever.

Though my misery transcended me *and* my dybbuk, I remained inside myself enough to think, Better I should have sung love songs in Spanish! No monotone could be worse than my sobs.

Yet like those hungry hearts in Buenos Aires, Rabbi

Schmuckler's circle ate it up. This, they assumed, was my brilliant interpretation of a woman possessed; eventually I would dry my eyes and get back to the sacred text. Only real culture lovers could have mistrusted their own perceptions and convinced themselves for so long that my histrionics were part of the play. And only Dalashinskyites would have let me go on while they stood back and made mental notes on hysteria.

Once again the Yiddish Art Theater came through, consoling me with much the same sympathy they'd shown my dybbuk's mother. No one lifted a finger, not even Clara and Ida, who were supposed to be holding me up.

Later, Benno would claim that they were thunderstruck by the most awesome crying they'd ever seen. John Barrymore, said Benno, could bring a catch to your throat. Bernhardt's tears could make your lower lip tremble.

"But your tears that night made us want to cry the way a seasick person can make you want to throw up."

"Benno," I said. "Thank you very much." Actually, I don't remember any of them looking tearful, but rather, watching me as if I were juggling eggs. I must have been a pitiful sight, mascara dripping and blossoming into black flowers on my china-white cheeks. In that skimpy shred of a wedding gown, those braids. . . . Fragile? I was already broken. No wonder nobody would touch.

Through my tears, I noticed that our audience was finally growing uneasy. I looked from one confused face to another until I found Rabbi Schmuckler's and saw that he was having the only heartfelt reaction in the room.

He couldn't have been more horrified. All he wanted was for us to vanish, and I was a little surprised. You'd think that grief would be a rabbi's stock in trade. Funerals, broken marriages, dashed hopes—what else did he hear about? He saw tears every day. Yet I could hardly blame him. This wasn't what he'd bargained for, poor man. He'd opened his home for a civilized evening of Yiddish Art and gotten this wailing barbarian!

The rabbi's wife was the only one whose training came through. Though she looked more like a baroness than a rebbitzin, maybe she *was* the spiritual mother of that congregation. The first to react, she startled the way mothers will turn toward the sound of crying, long after their own babies are grown. And then she did just what Mama would have done. She ran to the sideboard, filled a cup from the samovar, and rushed it toward me as if it were a water bucket and I a fire.

So much for the illusion that all this was part of the play! I drank the unsweetened tea in one swallow and in doing so, burned my tongue—the pain was a fresh source of tears. By now Feivel was gently shouldering me back against the grand piano which stood where the wings should have been. Like a proper guest, I looked for a doily on which to put down my cup while Dalashinsky took center stage.

"Ladies and gentlemen." His voice was grave. "Miss Rappoport hasn't been well. Our tour's been an awful strain on this child who should still be in school, this chickadee no bigger or stronger than the ones in your own nests. . . ."

"I'm twenty-two!" I wanted to shout. But Dalashinsky was playing the seducer and I couldn't interrupt. Not that it would have mattered. Resentful at having been cheated out of their Anski, the audience was immune to his charms.

"You could bet they wouldn't allow this on Stuyvesant Place," someone muttered, and in that one line we heard all the secret inadequacies of provincials who boost their town as the hub of the world.

"I'm sorry too," said Rabbi Schmuckler, though no one else had apologized. Under the neat beard, his lips seemed to be drawing thinner with every word. "It's been a thought-provoking performance, what there was of it. . . ." Though desperate for us to leave, he just couldn't restrain himself from giving a review. "Perhaps a few month's rest. . . . If there's anything I can do. . . ." He mumbled these last words, because in fact, he wanted us to disappear without asking him to do anything.

For such an oblivious fellow, Dalashinsky was quick to take the hint.

"Thank you," he said. "Good evening."

At this, my fellow actors began propelling me out of there.

As those genteel faces flowed by, I lip-read: *Buenas noches, Guten Abend, Shalom.* I couldn't hear, and I felt as if I were floating downstream on my back while the rabbi's guests called to me from the shore.

Crying gave the nighttime city a rainy shimmer which made me suspect I'd been wrong about Montevideo. Everything looked slightly oily, even the young parents, the babies in their strollers. I looked at those damp baby ringlets and thought, Someday they'll straighten, turn gray, whiten, and keep growing in the grave. In the plazas, the floodlit plantings looked wilted, black, with that sour geranium smell. And those lovers smooching on the bench? They'd soon betray each other in ways I didn't want to know. Beside the treachery of Montevideo, Buenos Aires seemed in retrospect like a harmless dirty joke.

The doorman at the Occidental took one look at us and whistled for coffee. Another believer in the healing powers of caffeine. But I knew that no nice hot drink on earth would save me.

That night Ida came the closest she would come in real life to her stage role; that is, my crutch from the lobby as far as our room. She was helping me into bed when we heard a knock on the door.

"On this trip," I said, "nobody knocks with good news."

"Dinah," Ida said soothingly, "it's the laundry."

The same bright little maid now grinned like a cretin till Ida came up with a big enough tip. After she left, I understood why she thought she deserved it: She'd washed so enthusiastically that all our buttons were cracked. Never before or since have I been the sort of woman who cries over laundry. But when the knock came again, seconds later, I felt that my furious weeping might have summoned her back.

But this time, it wasn't the maid. It was Benno, carrying the maid's rag in one hand and, in the other, both shoes and a small tin of polish.

One thing my Benno couldn't do was whistle. Maybe because he could do everything else, he was excessively embarrassed by this inability, which he confessed to me (we'd overheard a stranger whistling *The Dybbuk*'s opening chant) only when I asked.

"It's a good thing," he'd said, "that Chonon isn't much of a whistler."

Yet that night in Montevideo, Benno must have been feeling the need to whistle so badly, he pretended. Pursing his lips and humming spared him from having to say one word to me or Ida. Without a good-evening or even a nod, Benno sat down on the edge of my bed and started blacking his shoes.

To this day I'm not sure what he had in mind. Until that moment I'd seen no evidence that he knew what shoe polish was. His own oxfords were broken in, scuffed and stained from winters without galoshes. Conveniently, he tended to play characters like Chonon and Trigorinstein, whose feet never quite touched the ground. Nor did it seem logical that Benno had taken up shoe polishing as one of those mindless activities which work so well as distractions. If that were true, he could have stayed in his own room, where certainly it would have been easier to distract himself from my crying.

Right or wrong, I've decided that Benno was doing it for me, to show me that my troubles weren't as serious as I thought. And the proof of this was that my own husband could sit there calmly, whistling that phony whistle and buffing his shoes.

Well, it worked. Florence Nightingale sponging my forehead couldn't have calmed me more than Benno's spit shine. Until he stopped whistling and started to sing.

Have I mentioned that Benno sang beautifully? If his speaking voice was a clarinet, his singing was a saxophone, my favorite. And, oh, how he could sing and act at the same time! That evening, for example, he had both me and Ida convinced that he'd forgotten us and was singing to himself.

> *"With your little head like a little apple*
> *Your little nose like a little rabbit's*
> *Your little behind to the families,*
> *Dance . . ."*

I thought, Benno's mama sang him that song. First I imagined Benno as a toddler, delighting the relatives with his dance. Then I tried to imagine all the times he'd sung this song to himself since then. Suddenly my brain got crowded with grown men crooning to themselves like little boys as they washed their hands and faces, tied their ties, and polished their shoes. I remembered my dybbuk's love song, overheard by Mamie, and I wondered, Had he worn shiny tango shoes? I considered men like Don Eduardo, rich men who had their shoes sent out and never sang. Could their women love them as much? I thought of all the men who'd ever hummed baby songs to themselves, believing that no one was listening. And I wept for each one.

Maybe this was the craziest I got, speculating about the singing and shoe-polishing habits of strangers when what I should have been doing was thanking God that I wasn't having these hysterics in New York, where some knowledgeable physician might have suggested a few weeks' observation at Bellevue.

I was lucky it happened in Montevideo, where no one would consider leaving me in a loony bin thousands of miles from home. Nor did this alternative occur to the hotel doctor who was finally brought in. Couldn't that well-run hotel have done better than that seedy, unshaven quack whose bedside manner made me instantly suspicious that the initials on his doctor's bag weren't his?

He shone a light at me, but instead of peering into my eyes, gazed blankly at the surface, then blinked.

"D.O.A.," I said.

"How?" The doctor wiggled his fingers, as if trying to pluck translations out of the air.

"In English," I said, "that means dead on arrival."

"Ha-ha!" The doctor's shiny suit made an odd crinkly noise as he laughed. "A sense of humor! Good sign!" Then he turned to the others and said, "She's not crazy, just overworked. Everything normal."

Was this the state of Uruguayan diagnosis, that jokes about

death meant the patient was well? Before leaving, he prescribed
paregoric; perhaps he'd been taught that every tourist needed a
dose. By chance, he'd brought along a bottle, which he sold to us
for a small fortune. I took a big gulp, and as the camphor
burned a path toward my stomach, I imagined that the opium
was already making we weepy.

By now, Benno had his shoes on; he and the others drifted
into the corridor for consultation. Even Ida tried to escape, but
Feivel pushed her back, saying, "Stay with her." Shamefaced,
Ida returned to her post on the other bed.

"Dinah," she said, as if no one had asked me before, "what's
wrong?"

"Everything," I said. "Anything."

All night, I could hear the cast buzzing outside, but now it
wasn't like listening to Mama and Papa when I was sick as a
child; I fantasized being dead in my coffin while my mourners
debated the best route to the cemetery. Nor did it revive me
much to hear, the next morning, that Feivel had found us a
direct boat back to New York, the *S.S. Copenhagen*, leaving
Sunday from Montevideo harbor.

"What day is it today?" I asked. Imagine my not knowing.

"Thursday," said Ida.

Of all things, I thought: Tomorrow night will be Dalashinsky's first sabbath without his mama's candlesticks. He'll be miserable, he'll know whom to blame. He'll curse me every miserable
shabes of his life. If I went down in Yiddish theater history at
all, it would be as a saboteur.

I was sorry for my crimes against art and the trouble I'd
caused my friends. In my craziness, I focused on the loss of
Dalashinsky's candlesticks. I wanted to apologize, to find some
tactful way of asking if he missed them. But despite our starry
conversations, our high-flown talk, I knew I could never ask
Dalashinsky such a personal question. Whereas he could tell me
what to eat for breakfast!

And for all my regret over Dalashinsky's loss, I realized that I
would feel sorrier still if I couldn't lose my dybbuk, if it fol-

lowed me back to Attorney Street and one day, out of nowhere, started haranguing Mama and Papa in Spanish. Suppose I couldn't stop crying? What then about Benno? Not in City Hall nor in any of our private ceremonies had he agreed to live as man and wife and dybbuk. Was this what I was running back to New York for?

You'd think I would have been overjoyed to be going home. When in fact what was making me cry was the fear of going home before I'd stopped crying.

What's odd is that the whole cast seemed to feel the same dread. Odd, but not surprising. It's instinct, I think, to want everything settled before you go. I know what Freud called this instinct. To him, every trip to the grocery was a practice death; to him, it was the joke about ladies wearing clean underwear in case they got hit by a truck. But I think it's more complicated, connected somehow to the longing for order and harmony—and to the compulsion which makes quarreling lovers linger, long after the last word's been said, listening for that one word which will make it all better.

Dalashinsky must have known the feeling; he used it in his famous pauses. His hesitation after denouncing Desdemona was the most moving moment in his Othello. And so once again Dalashinsky voiced the dreads and desires of us all as he led the cast back into my room and said, "I fear for every one of us unless Miss Rappoport pipes down before we leave Montevideo."

And Feivel, whose job it was to find rational reasons for Dalashinsky's instincts, said, "We'll never get her through customs. The emigration man will see those tears and suspect us of kidnaping her. They'll check our Jewish noses, the Argentine stamps on our passports and conclude: white slavers!"

Feivel, what were you saying? Did you really think that the nosiest customs man would care if some nutty actress left town? Didn't you realize that men who work on piers and train stations see more tears every day than gravediggers? Feivel knew, but he was desperate for some clear explanation for our murky

apprehensions. And what could be more understandable than
that immigrants might be worried about emigration?

"If only this were New York." Clara sighed. "You know people, Feivel. In the Traveler's Aid. She could faint all over the
luggage and we'd still pass customs." How worried Clara must
have been, to be praising her husband's connections!

"It's Montevideo," said Feivel, "where we've never exchanged two words with anyone but Rabbi Schmuckler."

The name created a silence around itself, in which I thought,
This whole customs business is Feivel's excuse to call for help
on the one man we've exchanged two words with in Montevideo.

Only actors could have played out that charade of sending
Feivel to ask Rabbi Schmuckler if he knew anyone at customs.
What unnerved me, though, was the suddenness with which the
young lions of the Yiddish theater had turned sheepish enough
to seek Rabbi Schmuckler's assistance.

After Feivel had been gone two hours, Benno and Dalashinsky went after him. An hour later, all three returned with the
rabbi in tow.

"See?" Feivel pointed at me. "She hasn't stopped since last
night. It's not that she's crying any harder. It's just that she's still
doing it."

"Does this happen often?" asked the rabbi, his voice so
syrupy with false concern that I suspected his wife had reminded
him of how young I was and begged him to be nice. Most likely
too, the culture lovers had informed him that it was a prima
donna's prerogative to go nuts from time to time.

"Not in my troupe," said Dalashinsky.

"I should hope not." For his part, Rabbi Schmuckler couldn't
understand why professional actors couldn't act like professionals; rabbis didn't interrupt bar mitzvahs to start communing
with God.

In the face of his contempt, our fear of the customs officials
seemed suddenly contemptible, and we were shamed into
dropping the pretense that this was our real worry.

"Listen," said Feivel. "There must be a better doctor in
Montevideo than that greasy clown the hotel sent up. Somebody

with training. . . ." Knowing Feivel, he meant some sort of homeopath, a spotless old man with a satchel of natural extracts.

But Rabbi Schmuckler had a different somebody in mind when he visibly brightened and said, "We have a psychoanalyst! Here in Montevideo! A certificatee of the Institute in Vienna and a student of Dr. Freud's!" Rabbi Schmuckler announced these qualifications with enormous satisfaction, as if not only psychoanalysis but modern medicine itself were his idea, and concluded with the additional credential which, even to this blue-ribbon product of the enlightenment, was the ultimate recommendation. "Dr. Zweivel," he whispered, "is Jewish."

No wonder Rabbi Schmuckler was proud! His congregation was absolutely up to the minute! What classier way for him to show off those matchmaking skills which were the best part of his job, finding lawyers for the accused, electricians for the builders, specialists for the sick. A modern rabbi's friendship with the internist matters more than his good relations with God. And what could be nobler than a match between modern science and modern art?

Meanwhile, he wanted to make sure we knew that art was marrying up. "I can't promise that Dr. Zweivel will see you. He's awfully busy, and generally he doesn't handle emergencies unless they're part of the ongoing long-term—"

"I see," said Feivel, a little nastily, I thought. "Still, I can't believe he would pass up this once-in-a-lifetime chance to dig around in the brain of an artist, a member of the Leon Dalashinsky ensemble. Suggest it to him. I'm sure he'll make an exception."

"As a matter of fact," said Rabbi Schmuckler, "Dr. Zweivel had tickets for tomorrow night's performance. . . . Perhaps it *might* be possible to set something up. I'll go see him this afternoon and hopefully, make an appointment for early tomorrow morning."

Ordinarily, I could tell, this rabbi was the kind who acts as if he can't arrange a trip to the bathroom without twenty-four hours' notice. And now he was so excited, he was running.

Unaccustomed to his own speed, he seemed put out that we didn't respond faster. But good manners go hand in hand with enlightenment, so Rabbi Schmuckler waited politely while I too waited for Dalashinsky to put a stop to this talk of analysts. Honestly, Dalashinsky would demand, did Rabbi Schmuckler seriously believe that I was crying in a Montevideo hotel room because, twenty years ago, I'd accidentally seen Papa pissing?

At least he didn't say *that.* Still, it bothered me that he said nothing, not one word of protest when Feivel said, "Why not? It's certainly worth a try."

Hadn't Dalashinsky warned us about how unspoiled we were, how pure the water in those rain barrels? And now my best friends were inviting Viennese gardeners in to muck it up.

"Friends! Benno, where are you?" I yelled—but only inside my own brain. For though I could weep shamelessly all day and night, the very idea of yelling made me queasy with embarrassment. I'd lost my mind, apparently, but not my social sense.

Rabbi Schmuckler, of course, had no way of knowing that my manners, unlike my dybbuk's, could be trusted. He was edging toward the door, mumbling about getting in touch with us when he'd reached Dr. Zweivel, when suddenly Benno cried:

"Rabbi, wait! This is may not be your ordinary case of overwork and nerves. We have reason to suspect that there are unusual circumstances at work here, complications which you should probably bring to the attention of this doctor."

"Such as?"

So quietly that you couldn't have made out the words unless you knew them, Natty whispered his line from the play:

"The bride is possessed by a dybbuk."

"Pardon?" said Rabbi Schmuckler.

"Rabbi," said Benno, "this may be one of those crazy situations when life imitates art."

"Please." Rabbi Schmuckler waved impatiently. "No riddles."

"It would take hours to tell you every detail," said Benno. "But briefly: A whole series of odd coincidences befell us in Buenos Aires. Onstage at the Teatro Colonial, Miss Rappoport began talking Spanish, a language she doesn't know, making references to actual events she'd never heard of. Later that same night, Miss Rappoport's double materialized out of the crowd and visited us backstage. I know this sounds insane, but from the evidence (and there's more), it seems that Miss Rappoport may actually have been temporarily possessed by a dybbuk. Before leaving Buenos Aires, this basically sensible girl threatened suicide . . . and now these hysterical tears. . . ."

Later, when Benno played Sherlock Horowitz in *The Hound of the Catskillvilles*, his restrained pacing, his orderly and persuasive summary of the facts of the case reminded me of that night at the Hotel Occidental. But saying the butler did it must have been easier than telling an enlightened rabbi to blame it on a dybbuk. And whereas Sherlock's summary brought the culprit to his knees and the audience to its feet, Benno's failed to convince Rabbi Schmuckler, whose good manners exploded through his thin lips in a raspberry of disbelief.

"You're not serious," he said.

"I am," said Benno. "Consider. For more than a thousand years, the most profound Jewish thinkers have theorized that the universe is composed of countless invisible emanations; then science discovers the atom. Who can say with certainty that the soul isn't constituted of atoms which don't necessarily disappear with the body?"

For the benefit of this educated rabbi, my mystical Benno was all academic, as if Kabbala were a course he'd taken in college. Even so, Rabbi Schmuckler was of a different school.

"Come now. This is Montevideo, 1922. Not the ghetto of Prague in the fifteenth century."

"What kind of rabbi are you?" interrupted Clara. "What do you do when you get to those parts of the Torah about Noah's Ark, Jacob's wrestling with the angel, the crossing of the Red Sea . . . ?"

"Metaphors," said Rabbi Schmuckler.

"Aha!" Dalashinsky held up his hand. "Since you understand metaphors so well, Rabbi Schmuckler, let me offer you another:

"When you go before your congregation, rabbi, I'd bet that you know exactly what you're going to say. The Torah doesn't change from morning to evening, and I daresay your wife prints your sermons out for you on neat little cards. But when we actors stand up in front of an audience, we're like vacant houses, rain barrels without lids—open to anything. And though we too have our sacred texts, we never know precisely how we'll deliver them or what, as it were, will speak through us."

So. Dalashinsky was defending me. I'd savaged his sacred text and he was pretending that bestiality was part of our job. Consumed with guilt, I sat hunched over, my arms wrapped around myself, rocking back and forth like a back-ward schizophrenic. And yet if prizes were being given for crazy behavior, Rabbi Schmuckler's was inappropriate enough to have won the gold medal.

The great Dalashinsky had just revealed to him the secrets at the very core of our art. And the rabbi was chuckling and shaking his head.

"Rain barrels I can understand," he said. "I too am no stranger to the muse of inspiration. But dybbuks? That's medieval. Honestly, it's too much. Next it will be golems out of hats and angels dancing over the roofs of Montevideo. All right, I'll talk to Dr. Zweivel about the girl. . . ."

Just before closing the door, he smiled back at us and said, "Maybe I should make appointments for all of you!"

And maybe he should have.

Reader, I am like you. At this point in the story, I think, Grown men and women talking seriously about dybbuks! They should have asked the psychiatrist for a group rate!

And maybe we would have been cured, just as the promise of a doctor's appointment cured me. For you know how it is: Rabbi Schmuckler sent a message that Dr. Zweivel would see me at ten the next morning, and immediately my sobs subsided to sighs and an occasional sniffle.

I have always thought that doctors' receptionists should earn doctors' salaries because of all the recoveries brought about just by making appointments. Who has not climbed into the dentist's chair after the miracle cure has already occurred?

With that appointment under my belt, I ate a regular meal of roast chicken and potato. Afterward, I lay in bed trying to imagine myself on a psychiatrist's couch. And when I couldn't, my mind drifted pleasantly off into nothing.

Once again, I must give my dybbuk credit for letting me sleep. That good night's rest did me more good than ten years of psychoanalysis.

Toward morning, I dreamed of a herd of zebras and woke to find stripes of sunlight streaming through the venetian blinds. I went to the window and opened it. Outside, the misty street was empty except for a small boy in a clean white shirt and dark shorts, a school bag bouncing from the handlebars of his bicycle. Though he raced past very quickly, it was long enough for me to consider the possibility that this beautiful boy was riding his two-wheeler on a course which would lead eventually to the grave. And I thought: So what? Right now he's beautiful.

In other words, I wasn't exactly optimistic, but neither was I in despair. The world was a cruel place, but what other world was there?

At breakfast, I greeted the others with a brave little smile and a shrug meant to convey, Look, it's me, Dinah! Everything's fine!

"Let's forget about this psychiatrist," I said. "Now we can leave Montevideo on schedule, no problem."

Feivel eyed me skeptically. "As long as the appointment's already made, it can't hurt to go."

At this, everyone nodded, including Dalashinsky, who said, "Go, Miss Rappoport. In case you're ever called upon to play the sort of character who might see an analyst."

Instead of being insulted by their obvious lack of faith in my sanity, I was simply delighted to hear Dalashinsky refer to a future in which I'd have characters to play. Maybe my life in art wasn't over! For art, I would see a psychiatrist, I would pay attention.

It was a lovely morning for a walk, and like a gypsy clan, the whole cast insisted on accompanying me to the doctor's office. As I strolled beside Ida, we fit right in with the energetic little secretaries going to work, none of whom paid any special attention to us. Every suit loooked pressed, every buttonhole had a flower, and it seemed to me that those geranium-filled plazas were the boutonnieres of that brisk and perky office worker, Montevideo.

So positive was my state of mind that when I spotted a woman stumbling down the center of the street, taking two steps then stopping, two steps and stopping, I watched carefully. In case I ever did get to play Leah again, perhaps I could find some way to use that loony two-step. And so, as in Buenos Aires, I was so busy smelling the flowers, I nearly stepped in it.

As we approached, the woman sped up. And then, in a faster version of that awkward shuffle, she headed directly for me.

Up close she was a real madwoman—graying, scrawny, tattered, missing teeth. Her eyes were like the dog's in the tinderbox story, and they glowed straight into mine as she hissed, "El Diablo!"

"Keep walking," said Benno.

After we'd passed her, Clara said, "Even on the other side of the world they grow nuts just like in New York."

Later, I would find out how true this was. In every country, crazy people of both sexes would gravitate toward me, singling me out for personal tirades. And I would come to understand that this was no more mysterious than the fact that I *was* paying attention. For even with hopeless lunatics, interest generates interest.

But that morning in Montevideo was the first time it happened to me. And instead of recognizing it as an artistic breakthrough, the beginning of my ability to really pay that magnetic kind of attention, I interpreted it as a bad omen. That a crazy woman had seen the devil in my face seemed positive proof that my dybbuk was alive and well.

In this cruel world, there's nothing crueler than thinking that your troubles are over—and discovering that they aren't. It stung me, and once more, I couldn't help myself. I started to cry.

* * *

Rabbi Schmuckler was understandably concerned when he met us outside the psychiatrist's office and saw me still crying. For all he knew, I'd never stopped. But instead of reaching out for me (wasn't comfort something they taught in rabbinical school?), he just stood there popping his knuckles. I felt like telling him, Maybe you should have made an appointment for yourself.

By now I was quiet, though tears kept dropping, fat and shiny as oil. I couldn't stop weeping, and yet I could walk into that psychiatrist's office and think: *I* should be the psychiatrist. Because after five seconds in that waiting room, I knew more about this Dr. Zweivel than most psychiatrists know about a patient after five years of analysis. I could tell, for example, that he was married and that his wife did his decorating: curved hard furniture, lamps like bouquets of alabaster lilies, everything according to the fashion of twenty years ago, when they were newlyweds. Walking into that office, you stepped into Vienna, 1902, at the finest hour of Dr. Zweivel's life, when he was a student of Freud.

Years later, I saw photographs of Freud's office and understood how closely Berggasse 18 was the model for the Zweivels' taste: that passion for Oriental rugs, potted shrubbery, and especially those collections, the doctor's collections, displayed on mantels, tables, and altarlike shelves. The only differences were that Dr. Zweivel's Amazon of a potted palm could have gobbled up Freud's ferns, and that while Freud's *chatchkes* were African and Asian, Dr. Zweivel's were stricktly pre-Columbian.

Rabbi Schmuckler emerged from the doctor's private office with a big grin on his face, suggesting to me that he and Dr. Zweivel had been having a field day at the Yiddish Art Theater's expense. Though maybe it was just a matchmaker's pride at this coup of a wedding.

"Miss Rappoport," he said. "Dr. Zweivel will see you." He literally grabbed me and pushed me past him through the door, then shut it behind me. If I had believed in past lives, I would have thought that Rabbi Schmuckler had spent one of his as a stagehand at the Roman Colosseum.

Except that Dr. Zweivel was hardly a hungry lion. Instead, he reminded me of his office. For just as his suite would turn out to resemble Berggasse 18, so Dr. Zweivel looked like an imitation Freud. His beard was cut similarly, he wore wire-rimmed glasses; the cigar he smoked was so foul it might have been left over from the master's private stock. Only Zweivel's features weren't as clear as Freud's, and the clipped beard failed to hide the extent to which his mouth protruded over his chin, his upper lip over his lower, his nose over that, so that his whole face seemed to have dripped out from under his small, blinky eyes.

He rose from his chair, pumped my hand once, then dropped it; anyone would have felt awkward, shaking a crying woman's hand. I felt something hard against my palm and followed the downward drift of Dr. Zweivel's hand to the diamond ring on his little finger.

Conceivably, that ring could have been one of Dr. Zweivel's bar mitzvah gifts. But somehow I was sure that he'd gotten it from his wife, a woman who'd loved him like I'd loved Benno. Twenty years ago, on a cold winter night in Vienna, she'd shivered at the touch of that cool diamond ring on her shoulders.

All at once, Dr. Zweivel was no longer runner-up in the Sigmund Freud look-alike contest, but an individual with a history and a physical life. To me, that moment when strangers suddenly begin to look human is mysterious and wonderful—but like all mysteries, somewhat melancholy. My melancholia deepened as another possibility occurred to me: He'd bought the ring as a present for himself when his practice began to succeed. This evidence of secret vanity moved me much like the song Benno sang while polishing his shoes, and I reacted the same— with hysterics.

Dr. Zweivel returned to his seat. He pointed to the couch against the wall and said, "You can lie down if you wish. Or you can sit."

Later, I would learn that the slightest gesture of sympathy was prohibited by the orthodox Freudian's religion. And I would ask myself which was worse: that doctor whose coldness was an article of faith, or the actors who just sat back and studied a good cry. At the time, I knew none of this, but Dr. Zweivel's chilliness must have irritated me enough to be needling him when, pretending innocence, I said:

"I'll sit, thank you. I slept enough last night."

Or maybe I was joking in the hope that this Zweivel, like that hotel quack, would take humor as a sign that I was well. What is this strange desire to show the physician how healthy I am? Some patients enter the doctor's office and collapse, but I've always had to fight the temptation to do jumping jacks. So for this psychoanalyst, I swallowed my tears and sat up.

"Why have you come here?" asked Dr. Zweivel. "Why were you crying?"

Already I'd noticed that all his questions began like a three-year-old's, with why. After two minutes of psychiatry, I saw the whole treatment. For years this man would ask me why. And with every why and every time I couldn't answer, I'd be farther from knowing why. The prospect made me tired, but the desire to seem sane gave me energy to go on.

I was positive that Rabbi Schmuckler hadn't mentioned the word "dybbuk," and I tried to break it to Dr. Zweivel gently. I told the whole story much as I'm telling it now—without the long-term perspective, of course, but with the same emphasis on the fact that I don't believe in dybbuks. No matter how logically I told it, it was still a crazy story. And yet it seemed excessive that Dr. Zweivel should go crazy.

By the time my dybbuk's mother appeared, he looked bored —not sulky bored, but a more active form which erupted in a rash of twitches and tics. He took the cigar out of his mouth, put it back, his lips went pup-pup-pup. He pulled off his glasses, rubbed his eyes, crossed and uncrossed his legs. At several points, I stopped and just watched, doing research on fidgeting. So the telling took me longer then it might have.

"I couldn't stop crying. And now for some reason, the others don't want to take me home until they're sure I'm all right. A crazy woman in the street called me El Diablo. But now really, I'm fine. . . ."

I counted four cigar puffs before Dr. Zweivel said, "Dybbuks? You mean *dybbuks?*"

"Not dybbuks. A dybbuk."

Another silence, longer than the first. Pup-pup-pup-pup.
Then the good doctor put his spectacles back on and said, "Miss
Rappoport, you're resisting."

I almost laughed. As if I'd made this entire wild story up just
to resist *him.*

"My question," he said, "is why you think this dybbuk chose
you."

Why again. And I thought I'd explained. I couldn't make it
clearer without starting from scene one.

"Why don't you ask him?" I said.

"All right." I could see Dr. Zweivel flipping mentally through
his sacred texts for some instance of Freud's humoring a patient's delusions. "What's your dybbuk's name?"

Looking back, I understand that this was the wrong (or
maybe the right) question. For if it was the first thing the wonder worker of Miropol asked Leah, it must have been a good
one. And just as Chonon's spirit refused to identify itself to
Rabbi Azrielke, my dybbuk was hardly about to make polite
chitchat with a Montevideo Freudian.

I started to say, "Paco Engelhart." "The Aviator," I would
add, proud of my dybbuk's accomplishments. But that wasn't
what got said.

As if from halfway around the world, I heard myself speaking
Spanish.

Just as I wanted to convince the doctor of my mental stability,
so, reader, I feel the same need before you. And so I will offer
the most sensible explanation to have come to me over the
years.

Spaniards buy ribbons like everyone else; my parents must
have had Spanish customers. Maybe I'd picked the language up
unconsciously as a youngster, then buried it somewhere. And
when my mind ran away from all its confusion over my love life
and my life in art, it hid in a cave where my unconscious still

knew Spanish, and from there, like a cornered child, flung insults at its tormentors.

Well, it doesn't make much sense to me either. And at the time, I wasn't thinking half so sensibly. All I knew was that my dybbuk had followed me to Montevideo, that Dr. Zweivel plainly knew Spanish, and that he'd balled his right hand into a fist and put it behind his back.

After a while, he asked, "Why did you say that?"

"I didn't," I said. "It wasn't my voice. It was my dybbuk's. Haven't you ever said something you didn't mean, haven't words ever slipped out of your mouth . . . ?"

Dr. Zweivel persisted, "What does it mean to *you*, what you said?"

Aha! I thought. The first question that didn't begin with why. I knew then that I had him, so I said, "What does *what* mean? What did I say?"

"You said, 'Diamonds are for babies and dimwits.' "

I swallowed hard, then answered, "It doesn't mean much to me. I don't speak Spanish."

It took ten seconds for this to sink in—and ten more for Dr. Zweivel to jump up and run out of the room.

Later, I would realize how significant this must have been for him, this analytic equivalent of a surgeon chasing a patient around the operating theater with a scalpel. If he ever mentioned it, which I doubt, how he must have marveled at this erratic behavior, so inconsistent with the rest of his career. Not once would he breathe the word "dybbuk." Instead he would ask, Had his own analysis been incomplete? When in fact, five more years on the couch couldn't have touched the panic on his face as he fled me.

I could have studied that terrified look all day, yet that wasn't why I followed on Dr. Zweivel's heels. Nor was I planning to tattle on his fall from professional grace. It was just that he'd turned so purple, I had to make sure that nothing was wrong.

Physically, nothing was. On the threshold of the waiting room, his color became normal; he straightened his jacket, stopped itching, and put his hands in his pockets. Tilting his head, he smiled casually and quite charmingly as he looked the room over and somehow picked Dalashinsky out of the crowd.

"It's a funny thing," he said. "My wife and I had tickets for tomorrow night's show."

Later, I often saw doctors fawning on artists. (Once, when severe flu brought me to an emergency room in Ellenville, the attending physician heard that I'd been on the Yiddish stage; and that afternoon, amid the Chassidim and Puerto Ricans, I was guest star.) But when Dr. Zweivel gave me my first taste of it, I thought, Absolutely crazy! The hounds of hell are on my trail—and they're discussing theater tickets.

"I told them," said Rabbi Schmuckler.

"I'm sorry we won't be playing," said Feivel, the diplomat. This apology took the conversation into a silence which seemed to point at me.

"My dybbuk's still around," I said. "It spoke in the doctor's office."

"God help us," said Clara.

"What did it say?" asked Benno.

But before I could answer, Dr. Zweivel had thrown his hands in the air and was saying, "Exactly. Look, Rabbi Schmuckler, Mister Dalashinsky. I'm a busy man. This girl's in pretty rough shape, with a resistance out to here. Anyway, delusional hysteria just isn't my cup of tea. There are several excellent doctors in New York I could recommend. . . ."

"What did the dybbuk say?" repeated Benno.

This time Dr. Zweivel heard him. He watched the rest of them watching me and said, "I change my diagnosis. *Mass* delusional hysteria."

" 'Diamonds are for babies and dimwits,' " I said.

"Diamonds again," said Natty.

Once more the hand with the offending pinky ring disappeared behind Dr. Zweivel's back. Otherwise he couldn't take this seriously—and we felt awfully silly. Talking about dybbuks in the presence of these two enlightened beings felt like announcing that the world is flat to a scientific congress, and indeed, the doctor and the rabbi treated us like geographers must treat flat-earthers: They could only assume we were joking. The doctor smiled an ironic, civilized little smile and said, "Rabbi Schmuckler, aren't dybbuks your department?"

"No, no, not mine." Rabbi Schmuckler was quick to align himself with civilization. "My great-great-grandfather's, maybe."

So now Rabbi Schmuckler was hinting that we were ignorant primitives like his *zayde's zayde*. When no one could have sounded more modern, more reasonable than Benno.

"Maybe in twenty years, psychiatric research will discover that dybbuks are a particular form of hysteria, a connection established—"

Was Benno calling me a hysteric? Regardless, the hairs on the back of my neck stood up with loyalty when Rabbi Schmuckler cut off Benno's hypothesis, saying, "Maybe the sky will fall down like Chicken Little said."

At that juncture a real rabbi would have come up with some appropriate passage from Maimonides's *Guide to the Perplexed*, some illuminating tale of Rabbi Nachman's. And who was this one quoting? Chicken Little.

"The sky *is* falling," I said, and this seemed worth crying about.

With a bit of a sneer, Rabbi Schmuckler said, "Do you want to know my wife's diagnosis? My wife said, 'Poor thing. That girl should have stayed home and married a doctor.'"

I don't need to tell you what this echo of Mama and Papa did to me; even the oblivious Dalashinsky must have heard the undertones in my weeping and moaning.

In a voice so quiet that I had to pipe down, he said, "Children, what's happened to us? Am I the only one who remembers the color in Miss Rappoport's cheeks on the boat trip from New York? And now look at her!" He sighed, then continued. "Children, I take full responsibility. I am the Baron von Frankenstein of the Yiddish Art Theater."

If Dalashinsky was willing to take the blame, I was willing to give it. Next time he'd think twice before taking married women on deck to look at the constellations. . . . It took me a while to realize that Dalashinsky was taking less blame than credit, responsibilities beginning much further back than those nights on the *Veracruz.*

"I was the one who took this chickadee with her nightingale voice and tormented her till she talked like an evil spirit with a mouthful of dirt. It was I who told her, Every role is a dybbuk. Go ahead. Let them in."

Afterward, Benno would say that watching Dalashinsky take credit for driving me crazy was much more painful than seeing him give me breakfast advice. And so, with no thought for the danger that our secret marriage might be revealed, Benno stepped in to take his share of the blame.

"It's my fault. I was playing around with Kabbala. And I was too young to understand the forces involved. My fooling with those powers must have started something. I should have waited till I was forty, with a full belly and a wedding ring."

To the others, this must have sounded like conversation, but to Benno, he told me later, it marked a revelation. Because unlike me, Benno believed in other worlds, or at least suspended disbelief in the hope that his Kabbala studies might show him what, if anything, was out there. And on that morning in Dr. Zweivel's waiting room he had come to the conclusion that there *was* something, and that it was formidable; it didn't like to be dabbled in, and Benno never would, not even when he was fat and forty. Despite all my "sensible" explanations for this whole episode, Benno would insist to the end that on that South American trip, I was actually possessed by a dybbuk; otherwise, I never heard him mention spirits again, except on days when every little thing went wrong and he would jokingly blame the demons.

At the time, though, I wasn't listening for new turns in my husband's spiritual development. I was thinking, with some irritation, that he was doing an excellent job of keeping our marriage secret. And yet I was twice as irritated at Rabbi Schmuckler and Dr. Zweivel for the looks they were giving Benno.

Partly to get Benno off the hook, partly to take some credit for myself, and partly because I thought it was true, I dabbed at my eyes and said, "If it's anyone's fault, it's mine. Whoever this dybbuk is, I'm just like that aviator, flighty and selfish, leaving everything I might love in this world, running off toward the stars. . . ."

"Bravo!" Dr. Zweivel was smiling at me and nodding. "Now we're getting somewhere!"

I had just voiced my worst fears about myself. And a doctor with degrees in human nature had confirmed that we were getting somewhere. I can safely say that this was the hardest I cried in all those days of tears.

"Don't worry," said Dr. Zweivel. "Often the patient must get worse before she can get better."

"Later she can get worse," said Benno. "But isn't there anything we can do to make her better now?"

I have always wondered why, in the theater, God's messengers tend to be so down at the heel: fools, ragpickers, drifters with their solemn one-liners. Wouldn't God be just as glad to send a message with someone neat and clean, a schoolteacher perhaps, or even a bureaucrat?

And I have always believed that on that morning in Montevideo, God contacted us through Feivel Frumkin. For only Feivel truly comprehended that the hounds of hell were lifting their legs, and his stage manager's move-along instinct was what saved us.

"Go ahead and laugh," said Feivel. "But isn't there anyone in Montevideo who might know how to deal with a dybbuk?"

Isn't there anyone in Montevideo who might know how to deal with a dybbuk? Some joke! To me, two thousand years of Jewish history were contained in that question—the exile, the Diaspora, assimilation and return. Those hungry hearts would have known how to handle a dybbuk, as would the wonder worker of Miropol. But Freud? Rabbi Schmuckler? Obviously not. Such a heartbreaking question, and Feivel was inviting us to go ahead and laugh?

Only Rabbi Schmuckler and Dr. Zweivel took him up on his invitation. Not that they laughed outright, greenhorn-loud; like cultured people, they smirked and made private jokes.

As if he and the rabbi were consulting on a case, Dr. Zweivel leaned toward him and said, "There's an old Indian lady down on the Calle Riojo. One of my patients was traumatized in early childhood when his mother brought her his toenail clippings for some kind of psychic reading."

I remembered the good doctor's theater tickets for tomorrow night and wondered what this man who equated predestined unions with divination from toenails could have gotten out of Anski.

Now that the doctor had taken the first shot, the rabbi opened fire. "There's always my colleague, Rabbi Israel," he suggested, a joke so private that only Dr. Zweivel got it.

"That's right, Rabbi Israel. Why didn't I think of him?" This came with a sly smile implying that the doctor went years, thank you, without ever thinking of this Rabbi Israel.

Zalmen nodded toward the two of them and said, "A regular Bones and Jones."

"Who is this Rabbi Israel?" asked Feivel.

Ignoring him, Rabbi Schmuckler asked the psychiatrist, "Did you know that Rabbi Israel was a disciple of the Chazzer Rabbi?"

"Chazzer?" It didn't take a Yiddishist to know that *chazzer* meant pig. "Who's the Chazzer Rabbi?" Playing the interlocutor in their little vaudeville team, Dr. Zweivel seemed delighted to be allowed questions which didn't begin with why.

"A Chassid." said Rabbi Schmuckler. "A Hungarian from Budapest. He got his name from the ecstasies he went into whenever he passed a wallowing pig. And from the prayer he invented, asking God to make him as happy with his lot as a pig in mud." Rabbi Schmuckler rolled his eyes, and I thought, If he doesn't eat pork, his children will; but even for him, a holy man known for envying pigs is a little much.

"That's terrific," said Dr. Zweivel.

"I like the sound of this Chazzer Rabbi," said Clara. "A real down-to-earth guy."

"That's not our Rabbi Israel," explained Rabbi Schmuckler. "The Chazzer was his teacher. Rabbi Israel is called the Schvartze Rabbi."

"A schvartze!" moaned Ida. "Wouldn't you know it?"

"A real schvartze would be better," said Dr. Zweivel. "This one's just called that because he's so dirty."

"Suntanned, actually," said the rabbi.

"A suntanned Chassid?" said Natty. "This really is the other side of the world."

"It's crazy," said Rabbi Schmuckler. "He advises his followers to take off their hats to the sun, out of respect for the oldest of God's creations. Of course, as we know from Genesis, that's completely inaccurate."

"But he's right," said Feivel, thrilled to the bottom of his naturopathic heart. "Tell us more."

Rabbi Schmuckler perked up like a child who's just noticed that all the adult eyes are on him. You'd think that a rabbi would be used to attention, but apparently, this one had never quite suppressed his childish pleasure in being the center of it.

"One day," he began, "the Chazzer Rabbi assembled his court and told them, 'Cast your souls, like messages in bottles, on the ocean of God. Leave your baggage of vanities and ambitions on the beach.' With that, he pushed off for good; while on the shore, his disciples were already feeling the weighty tug of ambition.

"There followed the usual wrangling about who would succeed the master, and when Rabbi Israel realized that he wasn't even being considered, he took the first train out of Budapest without asking its destination; in Danzig he cast his soul on the first boat to sail. And maybe God enjoyed the message in Rabbi Israel's bottle. Because really, Montevideo isn't such a bad shore to get washed up on.

"Soon after landing, Rabbi Israel felt hungry and, recalling the Talmudic permission for traveling Jews to eat *tref* in exotic locales, went into a restaurant which turned out to be a sailors' bar."

"Oh, do we know how *that* is," said Clara.

"Two sailors bought rounds of drinks. Rabbi Israel ordered up one, then reached down for a gold coin which he'd brought from Hungary in his sock and in sign language asked if the bartender could make change—"

Just when things were starting to get interesting, Dr. Zweivel interrupted. "You certainly do know the whole story, Rabbi Schmuckler."

"There *is* a grapevine, doctor." Rabbi Schmuckler smiled modestly, and for me, this was the moment when *he* became human. I thought, He can tell stories! If only he'd stuck with all the good ones in the Torah instead of getting so refined.

Undeterred by the doctor's sarcasm, the rabbi went on.

"At the sight of that gold coin, the whole bar fell silent. Scared lest these roughnecks see him as a hundred-pound gold mine, Rabbi Israel found a Jewish stevedore to translate and proceeded to tell them a quick story about the worthlessness of gold.

" 'Gentlemen,' he said. 'Once, a follower of the Chazzer Rabbi gave him fifteen kilos of pure gold. The Chazzer took the gold, some jeweler's tools, and a lamp, then retired to his study and emerged a week later with a solid gold urinal.'

" 'Where's this?' a sailor asked Rabbi Israel. 'El Dorado?'

" ' El Do—where?' said Rabbi Israel.

"A longshoreman placed two thick elbows on the bar and said, 'In El Dorado, whole shithouses are made of gold.'

"Well, you know how some people are. They can't hear a story without thinking at every line how to top it. After two drinks, every man in Montevideo has a story about El Dorado. And that night, Rabbi Israel heard them all: infants slumbering in gilded bassinets, cooks seasoning stews with gold dust, presses printing the daily paper on sheets of gold leaf. Thirsty from lying, the sailors bought round after round—as if their money, like the currency of El Dorado, could be scraped with a fingernail from the barroom wall.

"The next morning, as soon as Rabbi Israel's hands had stopped shaking, he wrote these stories down in a letter which he mailed to the biggest gossip in Budapest. And within six months, he'd imported his own congregation of five hundred souls. You might ask, Who would want a following made up of the kind of people who would drop everything and run after El Dorado . . . ?"

"Three cheers for him!" said Feivel. "We too are always looking for cities of gold. He sounds like our man. Where can we find him?"

Looking puzzled, Rabbi Schmuckler turned toward Dr. Zweivel. I wondered how he could know what someone said to a bartender on his first night in town—and not know his address.

"The suburbs somewhere?" The downward curve of Rabbi Schmuckler's mouth drew the outer limits of downtown Montevideo.

Dr. Zweivel shrugged; he had no idea where this dirty Chassid lived.

"Try Villahermosa." The rabbi's expression betrayed his opinion that this was the lowest of the low, the dishwashing part of his job. Testing the ritual slaughterer's blade, visiting hysterical Jewish actresses, even finding specialists for the most grotesque complaints were picnics compared to this most distasteful task of recommending a good exorcist.

No one, of course, had spoken that word. But I cried at the thought of it.

9

IN THE TIME IT TOOK Feivel to locate Rabbi Israel, he could
have found El Dorado. I was glad it was Feivel who'd been so
enthusiastic about seeking out the Schvartze Rabbi since, while
we waited in the relative comfort of the Hotel Occidental, he
was out pounding the pavement. I was crying into my tea when
Feivel walked in, all sweated up, and announced that he had
found our wonder worker.

"Did you see him?" asked Benno.

"No," said Feivel. "But I know where he lives."

It was remarkable that this information had taken him all
afternoon to obtain; theoretically, the Jewish community of
Montevideo should have been a small world. Too small, said
Feivel; and when he approached, it shrank even more, closed in
on itself like the fringes of a mimosa. Though he'd tried all the
obvious places—the *mikveh*, the kosher butchers, the dairy
cafeterias—no one seemed to know Rabbi Israel. At the diamond exchange, he'd spotted a Chassid with *pais*, a fur hat,
and a Florida tan. But to him, Feivel's beardless, hatless, short-
sleeved style marked yet another species of *goy*; though Feivel
called after him in Yiddish, the Chassid ran.

Feivel canvassed the market, stall to stall, until at last he
reached the kosher egg man, who happened to be an Italian
named Tazzini.

"Who doesn't know Rabbi Israel?" cried Tazzini. "My best
friend!" Then he looked Feivel up and down and said, "The

world would be a much better place if everybody ate as many eggs as you Jews."

The truth, you understand, is that Jews eat no more eggs than anyone else. So as soon as we heard this, we knew: If Rabbi Israel had intended a personal summons, he couldn't have found one which went more directly to Feivel's naturopath soul. And maybe that was why none of us hesitated when Feivel said, "Let's get going. It's a walk."

A walk? Montevideo was jammed with carts, streetcars, taxis. Mules and chickens rode—we were supposed to walk? But after we'd been walking five minutes, we understood. The streetcars didn't run in this direction, and certainly not the taxis. In this part of town, you walked. A few minutes more and I thought, You wouldn't be in this neighborhood unless you were looking for an exorcist.

Only on the other side of the world would they have called that slum a suburb, named Villahermosa like some sort of Mexicali rose. Clearly this wasn't how the train had come in; this neighborhood couldn't have been less like those fairy-book cottages with their window boxes and trellised gates, their children healthy enough to outrun the *Queen Victoria*.

If God was so pleased with the message in Rabbi Israel's bottle, I thought, He should have beached it on Ellis Island. For truly, the hovels of Villahermosa made Attorney Street look like paradise on earth. And later, driving through the worst industrial slums, the hot baked flats of the Deep South and northern California, I would think how pleasant they were compared to Villahermosa, where the shacks were as ragged and dark as woodchuck burrows and gave off a similar smell. No greenery anywhere, not one measly palm, and what could have grown in that dust which ran for blocks at a time along high blank stucco walls, studded at the top with shards of glass? Who would want to climb anyway? You could tell what was going on inside, smell the banana-packing plants, hear the textile mills. Nor could you miss the slaughterhouses. Only a holy man, I thought, could live in a neighborhood where the very air is *tref*.

The farther we walked, the poorer it got, and just when I was thinking that I'd never seen anything like this before, Benno sidled up to me and said, "This is as far as we got yesterday."

Yesterday? Impossible! I would have noticed, I would have remembered the tired fathers who sat in the doorways and tried to rest while tangles of naked babies squirmed on them. Though I guess things look different when you're waiting for a man to drag you into a hallway and kiss you. Now I saw every detail: the markets where women squatted on the ground behind starved little pyramids—four wrinkled tomatoes, three shriveled chilis, onions no bigger than quail's eggs, everything so dry that you knew that the streams running past the houses weren't fresh spring rain. For open sewers, this neighborhood was Uruguay's answer to Venice, and we swam through while small boys in undershirts skidded around us like bugs.

Counting chilies and tomatoes took my mind off our destination and the fact that this was one show I didn't want to be star of. For extra distraction, I made nervous jokes: If Leah's exorcist had been an Expressionist's nightmare, mine was a health inspector's.

But when we turned onto the Calle Judea, the whole scene changed. The children had clothes on, long-sleeved dresses for the girls, coats, trousers and hats for the boys. Toddlers with three curls had two of them trained into *pais* in front of their ears. These children were as dark-skinned as any in Montevideo, but they were yelling at each other in Yiddish, and their noses would have fit right in on Delancey Street. And I loved it so, I stopped crying. We passed a young girl who so resembled my second cousin, I couldn't help myself. "Anneleah," I said. "Good evening!" But she shied away from me as the cast threw me nervous looks and hustled me along.

The only thing this street had in common with the rest of Villahermosa was poverty, except that the Jews had raised it to a literally higher level. The houses had been built up with every sort of construction material, one story lumped on another like layers on a cake. Were these crazy Chassidim building closer to God—or to their memories of Budapest?

A narrow, cavelike cul-de-sac, the Calle Judea ran two

blocks, then dead-ended; its sight lines drew you into a small caramel-colored cottage at the apex of the triangle. Drawn in, we didn't need Feivel's directions to know which one was Rabbi Israel's house.

By now it was almost dusk, and the street was empty but for the children and a few older girls who giggled and hid their faces as we passed. But it wasn't till we reached the modest stucco *shul* and heard the singing coming from inside that we realized where all the men were.

"Friday evening," said Feivel. "Wouldn't you know it? What a time to be paying social calls on Chassidim."

Social calls? I let it pass. I knew what Feivel meant. Imagine how disoriented we were, it was *erev shabes* and we had no idea. (Though maybe, I thought guiltily, if Dalashinsky still had his mother's candlesticks. . . .) Still, we hadn't lost our sense of things completely; we knew better than to barge in on a Sabbath service. And so we kept walking toward Rabbi Israel's home, though now, the knowledge that he wouldn't be there made us drag our feet.

"It's probably better," said Feivel, hurrying us along. "Most rebbitzins know more than the rabbis."

Meanwhile the architecture of the block was shutting out light in such a way that, as we walked along it, evening fell. The *shul* and Rabbi Israel's were the only places where lamps were lit. Feivel knocked on the rabbi's door, and when a woman cried, "Come in," we did.

Inside, the light was so dazzling that tears welled up in my eyes. El Dorado, I thought. Though in fact, it wasn't a city of gold, but of copper.

The downstairs was one big barn of a kitchen, every inch of wall space covered with copper skillets in overlapping layers, each pan polished like a new penny and reflecting the kerosene lamps. Light played constantly, winking from one pan to another, flashing so brightly it was painful to look at.

With my eyes shut, I heard Dalashinsky say, "Feivel, Feivel, what a set!"

"Forget it," said Feivel. "Where would we find a lighting man to knock himself out like this? Electricity alone would eat up the profits, and anyhow, the audience would wonder why a *tzaddik*'s house should be done up like a copper bazaar."

Oh, Feivel, I thought. For the lights, the lights! But I didn't say it.

On one side of the room, dozens of women were chopping, peeling, stirring, doing that complicated dance Mama and I used to do in the kitchen to keep out from under each other's feet. The whole place smelled of warm butter, chicken stock with dill, and, not surprisingly, a faint edge of copper polish. Clara fluttered her eyes and inhaled.

"Ah." She sighed. "If only the theater had not only sound and light, but smells. This would be the smell of home."

Twice I had been to Clara and Feivel's apartment, and what I remembered was the pungency of Feivel's health tonics and, already, a sour, old-couple smell; it depressed me that Clara's memories should be so far from the truth.

"Children," said Dalashinsky. "I have dedicated the last decade of my life to taking the smells *out* of the Yiddish theater!"

A woman approached us, stumbling not unlike the *meshugana* who'd seen El Diablo in my face. I cowered behind the others until I realized that her problem wasn't derangement, but children, one in her arms and two more dragging at her skirts.

Pretty in an unconventional kind of way, she looked more like a farm girl than a Chassidic wife, and it took a few seconds to figure out why. The suntan, of course, and also the fact that there, on the other side of the world, the Chassidim let their women keep their own hair. Hers was crinkly, pulled back tight; her unlined skin suggested that the gray in it was premature.

"Good *shabes*," she said quietly. "I'm Rabbi Israel's wife." If you blinked, you could have missed her smile, but I felt immediately that this wasn't unfriendliness, but shyness. Clearly less suited for her job than Rabbi Schmuckler's German-Jewish baroness, the rebbitzin seemed like one of those women who can house an army all their lives and still feel nervous whenever a guest walks in. Her manner was patient, determinedly cheerful, and slightly exasperated, like that of a wife whose husband regularly invites crowds home without telling her. And later, seeing pictures of Eleanor Roosevelt and even Mamie Eisenhower, I would think with great sympathy of Rabbi Israel's wife, and of all the quiet women who think they are marrying one man and find themselves wed to a nation.

"Come in," said the rebbitzin, without offering us tea, or a chair, or any of the small niceties which come so naturally to some hostesses. We remained standing near the door, while the cooking went on undisturbed on the other side of the room. And when the rabbi's wife saw us staring at the copper on the walls, her eyes followed ours and she stared along with us, as if she too had never seen it before.

"That's some collection," said Clara.

"My husband's," said the rebbitzin.

Imagine our mortification when Zalmen said, "Your *husband* collects *frying pans?*" But for all the embarrassment, the Zalmens of the world have their uses. If the loudmouths don't often bear God's messages, they *do* get things moving sometimes by saying what no one else will. Zalmen's tone seemed to have called up the rebbitzin's loyalty; challenged, she told the story in more detail than she might otherwise have gone into.

"When Rabbi Israel was a boy, he and his brothers played and fought so roughly, they smashed everything in the house. Their mother's attitude was: The more they break now, the less they'll have to fight over when I'm dead. Which was exactly what happened—and why my husband left Budapest with no keepsakes from his childhood but his mother's indestructible copper skillet.

"Because it was the only memento, it assumed special importance. That frying pan was Rabbi Israel's friend from home in a foreign city, a friend he could cook his meals on. For weeks after he showed up at the *shul* to which my parents belonged, he was known as the Hungarian with the frying pan.

"In that congregation, my father was the one who invited every stray Jew home for supper. At our table, Elijah the Prophet had a place set not just on Passover, but every night.

Papa was so generous, he gave me in marriage to a Hungarian with a frying pan—simply because, I've always thought, he was the first to ask. And if my husband had brought one copper skillet from his family, Papa gave us, as a dowry, a dozen—and a house in which to hang them."

At this point, I pictured the Schvartze Rabbi as some kind of golem and waited for his wife to tell us how it felt to be married off, like Leah, to the troll from under the bridge. But she wasn't talking about arranged marriages; her subject was frying pans.

"On the morning after the wedding, my husband went off to *shul* and I started fixing up our new home. The first thing I did was to polish my mother-in-law's skillet and hang it in the kitchen with the dozen from Papa.

"But when Rabbi Israel returned to dinner and saw his mother's skillet up with the others, I was sure from the look on his face that the marriage was over. He drifted from one pan to the other, studying them as if they were masterpieces in a museum and not just something to fry blintzes in.

Finally he said, 'Which is mine?'

" 'That one,' I said.

" 'Are you sure?'

" 'Yes,' I said, and I was. I'd just spent a half hour shining it.

" 'Two days ago,' he said, 'I would have bet that I could pick Mama's frying pan out in a copper market. But there's my best friend, polished and hung with a dozen like it, and I couldn't tell. Don't you see what that means?'

" 'No.' This was before I'd learned that my husband's meanings sometimes take days to come clear. 'I don't.'

" 'It means I could have stayed in Budapest. Because the Chazzer Rabbi's disciples were nothing but frying pans—nearly identical, a little too highly polished. And after the master died, what difference did it make which one was chosen to cook dinner?'

"For the rest of the evening, my husband seemed humble. But the next night, when several hundred of the Chazzer Rabbi's former followers knocked on our door, he wasn't so modest. He received them with open arms and 'I told you so'—like every Jewish father greets his prodigal sons.

"Except that these Chassidim weren't asking his pardon. On the contrary, they were accusing, demanding: 'Where's El Dorado?'

" 'Such marvelous people, the Jews,' said my husband. 'So adaptable. Ten minutes in South America, and already they know about El Dorado. If I knew where El Dorado was, children, what would I be doing in Montevideo?'

" 'But the letter!' They were all yelling at once. 'You said you'd been there.'

" 'What letter?' asked my husband.

"Since then I've often wondered what he would have done if they'd produced it. But I think he was counting on the fact that his letter was one of those treasures that get left behind precisely because they're so valuable; everyone assumes that someone else must be bringing them.

"The whole crowd looked toward one old lady. And when she turned her palms up and shrugged, someone cried, 'The letter you sent Yentie Raisl.'

"My husband approached the old woman and lifted her wrist as if taking her pulse. And from that one gesture, I understood that in marrying Rabbi Israel, I had wed the whole block—and the biggest gossip in Budapest.

" 'Yentie Raisl,' said my husband. 'You must have dreamed it.'

" 'How about us?' asked the others. 'We all dreamed this letter?'

" 'You all dreamed it,' said the rabbi. 'Therefore it is an especially significant dream. And its meaning is, Here in Montevideo, your souls will be clothed in gold.'

"It's not so stupid," said the rebbitzin, "leaving Budapest for El Dorado—except that there *is* no El Dorado. And these Hungarians were certainly smart enough to know a dream from a letter. But here they were, on one-way tickets, thousands of miles from home. A golden soul sounded better than no gold at all.

"As they tried to remember themselves somewhere in Budapest, reading Rabbi Israel's letter, they found that the old country already seemed like a dream. And so my husband got his congregation at the same time as a reputation for interpreting dreams.

"After less than a hour in Uruguay, these Chassidim had not only a rabbi, but also a place to park their things while they went out to look for lodgings. That night, most of them stayed in hotels, and so left their heavy luggage with us.

"In the morning, my husband said to me, 'Wake up. The angels have decorated our home.'

"In the middle of the night, apparently, the angels had gone through two hundred sets of baggage, sorted out all the copper pots and pans, polished them, and hung them on our wall. I was amazed, but not half so shocked as the people who came back to claim their possessions and discovered that their hampers no longer clanged like brass bands.

"'Take them!' Pointing to the wall, Rabbi Israel dared them. 'If you can pick out your own! But I find it hard to believe that you would trust me with your souls and not your frying pans.'

"The crowd became speechless. For this, they reasoned, was another example of the divine *chutzpah* for which so many great holy men were known. And surely, a rabbi who stole the frying pans out from under his disciples' noses must be even holier than one whose nerviest act was to envy pigs.

"Well, when people hear you're collecting something, it comes to you. Late arrivals from Budapest immigrated with nothing but skillets for the rabbi. Travelers and businessmen brought back copper from Brussels and Tangiers. And when anyone in the congregation died, what did they leave the master?

"All through this early collecting of frying pans and followers, I walked around with a lump in my throat. One thought choked me, but I couldn't put it in words until one night I took a deep breath and said, 'I can't do all that polishing.'

"My husband nearly fell out of bed laughing. Not to worry, he said. Grown men and women would vie for the honor of doing it. And this, like so much my husband promised, has come true."

The rebbitzin stared at us, as if to make sure we believed her. But why would we doubt? As evidence, the shine on those pans would have held up in court.

She was still watching us when we heard a commotion and Chassidim began rushing into the room, pushing four at a time through the narrow doorway like circus clowns squeezing out of those tiny cars.

Without any introduction, we recognized Rabbi Israel. Like the others, he wore a long coat, black knickers, and high socks. But whereas the others' socks were black, Rabbi Israel's were striped every shade of the rainbow.

The colors, I thought. The colors.

"Who's the guy's haberdasher?" whispered Zalmen. "The man should be shot." And yet Rabbi Israel didn't look like a man wearing criminally loud socks—just the opposite. Like a bluebird, or a field of purple weeds, like any spot of bright color in nature—those socks made me silently thank God.

Even dedicated ensemblists like us saw immediately that Rabbi Israel was a star. Something about him commanded our attention, and we paid it in full. Like the other Chassidim, Rabbi Israel was walnut brown. But his hair was shinier, his eyes blacker and brighter; he was lighter, somehow, on his feet. He wasn't so dirty as Rabbi Schmuckler and Dr. Zweivel had led us to believe, but neither was he clean. All in all, he looked like a cross between the Baal Shem and Emiliano Zapata, and suddenly I had the most unsettling thought: If this is a golem, no wonder maidens sacrificed themselves to be married off to the troll under the bridge. And I cried to think that Benno wasn't enough for me, that also I could have such thoughts about this Chassidic bandit.

By now, the house was so full of men that the walls seemed to bulge—which was lucky, because we were pressed up against them. Squashed belly to back with that rude, suntanned horde, we were ignored but not unwelcome. Standing on tiptoe and craning my neck, I braced the back of my head against a copper pan to keep from being lifted off my feet.

The sight lines alone were a miracle. From the last row, I could see Rabbi Israel standing at the head of the table, raising a soup ladle like a baton.

Only when he struck the skillet nearest him did I realize the drawbacks of standing room. When the clanging went off in my head, I jumped away from the wall so fast that I scratched my forehead on the rough material of a Chassid's jacket.

My God, the reverberations! Our bones rang and the fillings chimed like church bells in our teeth. In one second, that bong stopped all motion, all conversation; the echo went on for a few minutes more. Clara and Zalmen had their hands over their ears, but Benno's eyes were wide open with pleasure. And Dalashinsky stood there with one finger in the air, like an idiot who imagines that noise can be gauged and charted like the wind.

It was hard to tell precisely when the noise stopped and the ringing in our ears took over. By the time we could hear again, we'd missed a few blessings and the rebbitzin was about to light the candles.

As the lamps dimmed, my heart sank. This was the moment I'd been dreading, when everyone, Dalashinksy in particular, would blame me for the loss of his family heirloom. But soon I forgot Dalashinsky and gasped along with the rest, who were oohing and aahing like spectators at a fireworks display. For as Popolescu said, you must take my word: The effect of those candles reflected in hundreds of reddish pans was twice as spectacular as the noise.

It took six women to carry in the enormous braided *challah* and heft it onto the table. After the blessing, Rabbi Israel broke off a hunk and tasted it with an expression which made me think of Benno at our most private moments of passion. With every nibble, the rabbi's disciples swayed toward him like willows over a pond.

Meanwhile, we were collecting our own little circle of guides and interpreters who were only too happy to discuss Rabbi Israel's slightest move; they reminded me of myself at *The Jewish Seagull*, reading Benno-Trigorinstein's every gesture for secret codes.

In a tone of sheer wonder, an old Chassid whispered, "The rabbi eats."

In the other ear, a younger disciple, a real sociologist, was expounding on the differences between his master and the others.

"Go to the Bratslavers, the Satmars, the Vilners. Go on Friday night and you'll see. First the rabbi eats, soup to nuts, then the rest of the community fights over his crumbs like pigeons in the park. In all the world, in all history, our rabbi is the only *tzaddik* who cooks omelets for his disciples."

Omelets?

Sure enough, the women were setting two large glass bowls on the table in front of him. And the rebbitzin, with children still hanging from her and the baby in one arm, brought in a large wire basket full of eggs.

Rabbi Israel cracked the first egg against the side of the bowl and, with dramatic movements more suitable to juggling than separating eggs, divided the yolk from the white and deposited them in separate bowls. The whole room was silent as he did it again and again, until it *was* like watching a juggler, or an acrobat doing triple flips. For by the ninth or tenth egg, the rabbi was holding the two halves of the shell, one above the other, a foot apart, and slipping the yolk back and forth directly over the bowl of whites.

I noticed that the Chassidim were counting to themselves. I too began to count and it's remarkable how counting, like hard work and kisses, will occupy your mind, leaving no room for anything but the number of yolks and whites in those bowls.

I should have kept an eye on Rabbi Israel's hands. Watching his face, the only way I knew he missed was the Chassidim's groan, and the solitary yolk floating in the bowl of whites. Even so, it was just as well. I'd been paying attention to how it is possible to separate thirteen eggs and mess up the fourteenth without a frown, a wince, or even an extra blink. Shrugging, the rabbi picked up one bowl and dumped the contents into the other, into which he proceeded to break the rest of the eggs. Then he took an egg beater and began whipping them till his arm was a blur.

"Every Friday night he sets out to do it right," explained the "sociologist." "But he never manages to separate more than fifteen without breaking a yolk and giving up."

"And why not?" asked the old Chassid who'd said, "The rabbi eats." "Aren't yolks and whites the same in the eyes of God?"

"They don't whip up the same," said Clara.

"That depends who's whipping them," said a young disciple in the unmistakable tone of people who know—or claim to know—about cooking.

Rabbi Israel carried the bowl over to the stove and slowly poured the eggs into several large copper skillets. With his bare hands, he tilted the pans while poking at the eggs with a fork.

"The rabbi's hands are like potholders," said the pious old Chassid.

"No seasonings?" asked Natty. "Salt and pepper?"

"Just wait," said the "cooking expert." "Wait."

At last Rabbi Israel cried, "done!" Then he motioned to two disciples, who *did* use potholders as they helped him carry one of the skillets across the room.

Nearly swooning now, our "sociologist" said, "Have you ever in your life seen a rabbi feed his court like a mother bird feeds her chicks?"

I resisted saying I'd never seen any mother feed her babies on the point of a knife. But that was what Rabbi Israel was doing, cutting pie-shaped wedges of omelet, spearing them, placing them directly into his followers' mouths. And yet he was handling that butcher knife so tenderly, it could have been a baby spoon.

He'd finished two pans and started a third before he got anywhere near us. As he did, I could feel the cast's uneasiness, and my own—a discomfort reminiscent of those moments at Gentile weddings when everyone kneels or steps forward to kiss the cross. This was silly; we were all Jewish. Surely that omelet was kosher as could be—but I was terrified to eat it. All Papa's warnings came back to me, and I thought: If a person can get in trouble just by breathing South American air, imagine what can happen from eating from a communal knife with a bunch of dirty Hungarian-Uruguayan Chassidim!

But all my worries disappeared when Rabbi Israel got close enough for us to see what was in that pan.

What we had taken for an unseasoned omelet was, in reality, a work of art. A miracle of a one-dish meal!

Only looking straight down into the skillet could you see the pattern, the perfect triangles of green peppers, red pimientos, purple onions, celery fried a translucent jade, a brilliant cornucopia of an omelet bound together with the yellowest eggs. So that was what the women had been doing—slicing, sautéing, arranging vegetables in the pan so that the rabbi could slip the eggs in without disturbing the grand design.

"It's Rabbi Israel's own recipe," explained the cooking expert, as if we might have identified this bizarre cuisine as Hungarian or Uruguayan. "He came up with it so that he could give to each of us according to our needs."

First, this sounded suspiciously like something Jesus Christ might say. And I wondered what guidelines the Rabbi used to decide who needed green pepper and who needed potato. I was wary, as always when I heard about teachers, directors, gurus, holy men of every stripe who controlled their disciples by "having their number." My instinct was, Not *my* number, you don't. In this spirit, I was fully prepared to give Rabbi Israel a firm no thank you; lying if necessary, I'd pretend an allergy to eggs. . . .

Nearby, I heard Rabbi Israel, his voice surprisingly husky for such a slight man, saying, "Mr. Frumkin. Good evening."

Well, it's the oldest trick in the book. You go to a holy man, out of the blue—and somehow he knows your name. And like so many old tricks, it still worked; I watched it cast its spell on Feivel. Like a good little birdy, Feivel opened his mouth. He chewed, he tasted, he swallowed.

"The flavor . . ." he said. "It's . . ."

"Herbs," said Rabbi Israel.

Herbs! What could have pleased Feivel more, except perhaps to hear that the chickens who'd laid the eggs lived out in the sunshine on a diet of wild nuts and berries?

"Miss Appleman," said Rabbi Israel, and Ida the cynic took less than a second to open up. She chewed, swallowed, then raised one eyebrow at the rabbi and said, "Caviar?"

Caviar? In Montevideo? And suddenly I realized that for all Ida's sarcasm, what she wanted most in the world was a man to get her caviar in Montevideo. It hurt me for Ida, that her number should be so easily gotten. My teeth clenched, and I tilted my chin up, just as my Hannele would, years later, as I filled the spoon so hopefully with strained peas. For by now, Rabbi Israel was standing in front of me with a piece of egg on the point of his knife.

"Miss Rappoport," he said.

Shivers ran down my spine, and I thought again of how cagey Chonon's dybbuk had been to conceal his name from Rabbi Azrielke. Names are powerful—and it's different, just different, when the holy man you've never met before says yours.

My mouth dropped open and why not? Eating a little kosher omelet wasn't exactly kissing the cross. I tasted eggs, milk, butter, cabbage—sweet and slightly crisp—lots of salt and black pepper. And I knew then that Rabbi Israel had my number.

It was Mama's special dairy-holiday cabbage *kuchen*! I made it myself for Benno on Sunday nights. And all at once, I thought: So what if I'm selfish, rotten to the core? I could still cook cabbage *kuchen* on Sunday nights! And who knew? Maybe Benno and I would have a child someday, a daughter who would recreate Mama's specialty for her husband and children. (Later, I would visit Hannele—now Harriet—in Seattle, where at a ladies' lunch, she served this very cabbage *kuchen*, so tasty that the ladies all asked where she'd gotten the recipe; and it hardly bothered me at all when Hannele answered, "Julia Child.")

So in one mouthful, Rabbi Israel's omelet transported me from Novyzmir to Attorney Street to Fourteenth Street and into the future to Seattle, a journey which filled me with such nostalgia, hope, and just plain relief that I started crying too hard to swallow.

Rabbi Israel watched patiently; no one since Mama had shown such interest in whether I ate the cabbage *kuchen*. When at last Rabbi Israel reached out and gently brushed away my tears, his touch made me shiver harder than his saying my name; and only then did I understand how different it is when it's *your* number the holy man's got.

I looked at Rabbi Israel; I looked away. I wanted him to single me out; I was shy. I was used to those moments when strangers begin to seem "human," but not to those when humans suddenly seem like something more. And yet I remained objective enough to marvel that this wild-Indian golem of a Chassid should have the sex appeal of a Valentino. When Rabbi Israel moved on, I felt let down, just as I had after *The Dybbuk*'s first few rehearsals—before I found Benno waiting.

"Mr. Brownstein," said the Schvartze Rabbi, and I noticed that Benno too was having difficulty swallowing.

Later, Benno would ask me if I'd been thinking, as he had, of the dream he'd had back in New York, the dream in which the Prophet Elijah showed him how to cook a five-course meal in one pan.

I had to tell him: No. When you're tasting three generations in a piece of Mama's cabbage *kuchen* which a Uruguayan Chassid is feeding you on the point of a knife, you don't think about someone else's dream from six months ago. Though maybe I would have if my slice had tasted like Benno's.

By sight, he said, you couldn't identify the particles baked into the egg. But as Benno chewed, he tasted pot roast, then green beans, fried potatoes, honey cake, and coffee—in short, the five courses in Elijah the Prophet's meal. From that moment, said Benno, he was waiting for Rabbi Israel to ask us to do the tango. But I was waiting to see what he had in the skillet for Dalashinsky.

He didn't say, "Mr. Dalashinsky." Because I think he knew: Of us all, only Dalashinsky was used to strangers knowing his name; he expected it. Besides, Dalashinsky couldn't have been paying closer attention—though only later, in our last and most famous New York performance of *The Dybbuk*, would we understand how and why.

Dalashinsky ate his portion of egg very slowly, swallowed it all, then said, "Amazing. This tastes like a certain noodle *kugel* I used to get in a little waterfront dive on Fulton and Front. The owner's wife. . . ." Dalashinsky's voice trailed off as he went into a kind of trance, a reverie so deep that Feivel, recovered from his own transport over the herbs, had to do his job of keeping Dalashinsky moving.

Gesturing toward the pans on the walls, Feivel said, "That's some collection you've got, rabbi."

Rabbi Israel shrugged modestly. "It keeps out the heat in summer, the damp in winter. Copper's marvelous insulation."

Insulation! At this, the room buzzed like a courtroom in a "standback" melodrama when a witness has just dropped a bombshell.

"Now I'm hungry," said Rabbi Israel. Returning to the table, he helped himself to a piece of omelet. I thought it was a cheat that we couldn't see what his portion contained. But apparently, this wasn't the point.

"It's a miracle how he lives," said the old Chassid. "He never eats more than one bite."

"What's *his* secret ingredient?" It was Ida who'd asked, from which I gathered that the effects of the caviar must have worn off.

"Whatever's left over," said the Chassid.

After one bite, the rabbi put down his knife and picked up a cup. He gulped five cups of wine in quick succession, then shook his head like a swimmer with water in his ears. I looked for

Dalashinsky, who—just as I'd anticipated—seemed dismayed to see Rabbi Israel indulging in the sort of cliché you'd expect from the melodrama drunkard who's just had a stiff one.

Rabbi Israel filled his lungs and began the final blessings, a boozy and heartfelt welcome to the Sabbath Queen. He dabbed at his eyes, then said, "Enough eating. Let's have some entertainment."

Always the perfect audience, we waited for the singing and dancing and jumping around, whatever these crazy Chassidim did Friday nights. We were paying the kind of attention we wished for from our own audiences, waiting so attentively that it took us a long time to realize that Rabbi Israel meant us.

"Come on," said the rabbi. "A little *shabes* theater."

Shabes theater? This was like asking for a little kosher pork. In New York there were rabbis who'd devoted their whole careers to trying to stop Yiddish theater from desecrating the Sabbath, rabbis who couldn't mention Babylon or Sodom and Gomorrah without dragging in Second Avenue. But was *shabes* theater any more peculiar than suntanned Chassidim or, for that matter, a rabbi who cooked?

"I too have read Anski," said Rabbi Israel, thus winning what was left to win of Dalashinsky's heart. "And how we would have loved to see the Yiddish Art Theater do him! But I could have predicted that when I went to buy tickets for our community, Rabbi Schmuckler would be all sold out. It would have been different if the theater were still standing, but as you know, it burned. . . . Who can understand God's will? So if you wouldn't mind . . . since you're here, maybe you could do something, an act, a scene, two lines, anything. . . ."

What actors can resist such an invitation?

"Let me think," said Dalashinsky.

Ordinarily, he would have picked some dazzling one-actor, some acting class showpiece starring himself. But we didn't ordinarily play for the Schvartze Rabbi and his disciples in copper-lined houses in Montevideo. The circumstances were extraordinary enough to shake us all out of character, and so, like a hired band at a wedding, we found ourselves taking requests.

"Please," said Rabbi Israel. "Anski's *Dybbuk*."

So. The magic word had been spoken. The moment had come to talk of dybbuks and Feivel, God bless him, seized it:

"Frankly, that's our problem." Feivel hesitated, and I realized with panic that the dog could have lifted its leg and Feivel wouldn't have budged. Finally, though, he gestured in my direction and said, "She's been crying like that since the night before last."

Climbing onto a stool to see above the crowd, Rabbi Israel pointed at me and then—as if he were a teacher and I an unruly kid in the back—said, "Stop crying."

For two days and nights, people had been asking me what the trouble was, assuring me that my troubles weren't so bad. Once, when we were alone, Ida had tried slapping me, but all she could muster was a tentative pat. Yet no one in all that time had thought of just telling me to quit. And miracle of miracles, it worked. Though I was no less unhappy, I stopped crying.

"All right," said the rabbi. "On with the show. Lights!"

Turning down one of the lamps, Rabbi Israel motioned for his disciples to dim the others. Who would have thought that the Schvartze Rabbi would be one of those amateur lighting geniuses, like those teenagers who practice with flashlights and scrims on their bedroom walls? Somehow he had positioned the lamps so that at a certain magnitude, the beams would hit the copper pans and bounce back in a solid circle on the center of the floor.

Showing an actor a spotlight is like showing a flame to a moth—and we flew toward that one. "Why has the soul fallen from the heights to the depths?" we sang. But before we could get to the part about the ascension being in the descent, Rabbi Israel began fiddling with the lights.

Years later, Benno and I were doing a benefit in an old-age home when, right in the middle of *"Rozhinkes und Mandlen,"* I saw some old ladies up front switch off their hearing aids. Discouraging, to say the least. But when it came to difficult audiences, those Schvartze Chassidim took the cake. They were relatively attentive when the men were onstage, but whenever a woman entered, they kept checking with their rabbi. Was it all right to pay attention?

If this wasn't distracting enough, we were physically disoriented by the darkness, the flashes of light which wandered according to Rabbi Israel's whim, and by the absolute lack of props and sets, which made Rabbi Schmuckler's parlor look, by comparison, overdecorated. When Clara, Ida, and I were supposed to approach the ark, we walked off in three different directions. No matter how I tried to look and not look at Benno, I kept looking at Rabbi Israel, who was pacing the perimeter of the spotlight, less like a theatergoer than a referee.

As I bent toward my "grandmother's grave" to invite her to my wedding, I noticed that the floor was carpeted with bits of egg and vegetable, as if a whole nursery school had just eaten lunch; the peas on my *bubbe*'s tombstone did nothing for my sense of illusion. Despite all Dalashinsky's breathing lessons, we were afraid that if we stopped to breathe, we'd never get going again. And also we were holding our breaths in anticipation of my dybbuk's grand appearance.

Yet maybe my dybbuk was intimidated by the Schvartze Rabbi, or still smarting from the indignity of being ordered to quit crying. When Menasha-Zalmen advanced on me with that obviously snotty handkerchief, I proclaimed my refusal to leave my predestined bride in Benno-Chonon's otherworldly growl. For once, I was possessed by the right dybbuk, and at that tragic juncture, the whole cast looked half silly with relief.

We kept going without intermission or even the two-minute break we usually took to set Rabbi Azrielke's study. Why bother? We had no props. Even the *challah* had been eaten. And the one illusion we didn't need to create was that of a holy man's home.

We looked for Dalashinsky, who normally would have been praying in some corner, preparing his Rabbi Azrielke. And we found him standing at the edge of the spotlight, shifting his weight from one foot to the other and scratching his head.

How often had Dalashinsky told us that all the best actors had their "off" nights, always in a tone meant to imply all but him. Yet "off" is a compliment for what Dalashinsky was in the Schvartze Rabbi's house. Since then, I have considered the obvious explanations. Just as amateurs grow constrained in the presence of professionals, so perhaps Dalashinaky felt self-conscious about playing a holy man in front of a real one. Or maybe he, like my dybbuk, was simply intimidated. But I have never come close to explaining his awfulness that night, his stalling and stumbling through Azrielke like a novice sweating out his first walk-on.

As I watched him flub whole lines and emote like a madman, I felt that faint disgust which is the other side of hero worship. Beneath that wonder worker, I saw Dalashinsky, but not the inspired storyteller who'd moved me almost to tears with his tales of the constellations. The Dalashinsky I saw was an affected old man, all vanity and false puffing, an old has-been who couldn't even fake sanctity in the presence of a saint. And though this was the ensemblist's nightmare, that I would face Rabbi Azrielke and see only Dalashinsky, I wasn't as upset as I might have been; oddly enough, I felt better than I had in weeks.

That night, Dalashinsky didn't bother miming the story about the Baal Shem and the tightrope walker; he was just getting through. And by the time he reached the last line, "If only that tightrope walker had developed his soul as fully as his body! What deep abysses he could cross on the thin rope of life!"—our unbroken line was stretched thinner than twine.

Maybe that was why Rabbi Israel didn't hesitate to carry a chair "onstage" and sit down at Rabbi Azrielke's table. He propped his chin on one hand and, like a Talmudist initiating a debate, smiled and said, "Here I must take exception."

At this, the Yiddish Art Theater nearly jumped out of its collective skin. On Stuyvesant Place, coughing was a cardinal sin; once Dalashinsky stopped a show and gave refunds because some poor guy in the last row was snoring. On this tour, he'd learned to put up with haggling pimps, squealing babies, and their sandwich-eating mamas. Still, no one had ever dared stroll onstage in the middle of Dalashinsky's big scene and take exception!

Again we awaited an explosion; again we saw how different Dalashinsky was on the other side of the world. In New York, he would have kicked the table over. But here he was leaning on it and asking, "Rabbi, on what grounds?"

"On the grounds that it couldn't be true."

"True? Rabbi, truth—"

"Anski must have made that story up. And if you don't mind my saying so, it's not such a hot one."

Don't mind this insult to the sacred text? At home Dalashinsky would have challenged him to a duel, raised voices at thirty paces. But now all he raised were his eyebrows and his inflection as he asked, "How do you know?"

"Because I can't believe that the Baal Shem would have nothing better to do than to stand on the sidelines and heckle the acrobats. But wait a moment! Wait! Maybe Anski got it wrong. It's coming back to me now—a story about the Baal Shem and some acrobats. I remember hearing it from the Chazzer Rabbi. I remember the night he told it, and also what happened on the following day. But here (before this gets any more complicated) is the Chazzer Rabbi's story:

"One day, a circus came to Medziboh, and the whole town turned out to watch a young man walk a tightrope between the riverbanks. When the acrobat bounced up and down over the deepest part of the gorge, the Baal Shem, who was in the crowd, looked unimpressed, nor did he join in the cheers and applause. He did, however, drop a penny into the hat which the circus children passed around.

"The Baal Shem waited till the daredevil had taken his bows and the rope had been hauled in and coiled. Then he went to the edge of the precipice and stepped out over the chasm. Walking on air, one foot in front of the other in a perfect straight line, the Baal Shem stole the show. He got halfway out, then turned and walked back onto solid ground, where now the townspeople saw that he was weeping.

" 'You can dance on the earth, on a rope, in thin air,' he said. 'But there's no lasting pleasure in the horizontal. The only real joy is in walking the tightrope which leads straight to God.' "

Rabbi Israel paused, then winked at us and said, "Before you take this too seriously, let me go on.

"We ourselves had just one night to meditate on the Chazzer Rabbi's story. Because on the morning after he told it, a traveling circus showed up in our own city, Budapest.

"For us, such coincidences were an everyday affair. The joke was, with the Chazzer for a rabbi, you didn't need a doorbell to know when company was coming. For a rabbi who could hear a cat cross the road in the next town over, the footfalls of an approaching circus were hard to miss. Often the rabbi said, 'Tell a story, any story. Then sit back and wait for it to come true.'"

Hearing this, I began nodding frantically, but Rabbi Israel did me the courtesy of ignoring my foolishness and went on.

"Here in Montevideo, the nip of that Budapest wind seems like something in a winter night's dream. And it's a mystery why anyone should want to remember those dismal early springs, when the cold had gone on so long that April stung worse than February. But to do so, I have only to recall that blustery afternoon when we went to watch the acrobats, and once more that river wind boxes my ears like a schoolyard bully.

"Only the young acrobat walking the rope in his skimpy tights looked warm; we did the shivering for him. Like the Baal Shem, our Chazzer Rabbi kept quiet till the boy was safely back on terra firma. Then he went over to the performers and asked if he might try out the rope.

" 'Be my guest, Pop,' said the circus master.

"We disciples had to pinch each other to keep from crying out, 'Don't do it!' But who were we to give the master advice? And the fact was, he did seem to know what he was doing.

"Where could he have practiced, that frail old man, to manage so nimbly in those heavy boots, that fur *streiml*, that loose coat flapping around his shins? Like a true professional, he tested the rope with one foot, then bent his knees, flexed his toes, and skipped out to the center. Thirty feet over the snow-swollen river, he hopped first on one foot, then the other, then skittered back, spry as a rooster.

" 'Thank you,' he told the leader of the troupe.

" 'Thank *you*,' said the circus master.

" 'One thing,' said the Chazzer Rabbi. 'There's a frayed section in the middle of the rope. You should fix it.'

"The manager looked doubtful. But sure enough, when the rope was pulled in, we all saw the spot where the strands frizzed and the twine was almost worn through.

" 'A million thanks.' The manager put his hand over his heart. 'We didn't know. . . . I hate to think. . . .' But the Chazzer Rabbi had already turned to the young tightrope walker.

" 'How old are you?' he asked.

" 'Fifteen,' boasted the boy.

"The Chazzer took this in, then turned back to the troupe leader and said, 'When you're working with children, you should use a net.' "

Rabbi Israel delivered this line so pointedly, there was no mistaking the fact that he meant it for Dalashinsky.

That's right! I wanted to shout. Dalashinsky, are you listening? Don't encourage us to let dybbuks in unless you also know how to let them out. Don't allow your children to walk tightropes unless you're underneath with your arms out!

"All right," Rabbi Israel was saying. "Pardon the interruption. And now, if you don't mind, we can get on with the play."

We? Get on with the play? So now Rabbi Israel was directing —and Dalashinsky was taking directions like a chorus boy. Swallowing half his lines, Dalashinsky finished the scene, and the cue came for me and my dybbuk to enter that circle of light.

"Who are you?" said Rabbi Azrielke.

"Rabbi of Miropol," said my dybbuk voice. "You know who I am."

"Who are you?" he repeated.

I had hardly opened my mouth when Rabbi Israel leaped into the spotlight. Part badgering, part seductive, he zeroed in on me like a "standback" detective confronting his prime suspect in the final act.

"Paco," he said. "Why not tell us your name?"

"Paco Engelhart," I said—and my dybbuk took over.

Suddenly I was babbling in Spanish without comprehending one word. All I knew was that Mamie's name kept coming up, and that while *I* may not have been understanding, Rabbi Israel obviously was. He was nodding in such a way that I thought, How pleased Dr. Zweivel would have been if I'd spilled the beans to *him* like this. But of course my dyybuk was the type who'd be closed-mouthed with the psychiatrist—and jabber away at the Schvartze Chassid as if there were no tomorrow.

Meanwhile I kept talking until I began to feel faint. I had to blink to focus, and when Rabbi Israel's image came clear again, I said, "Rabbi, what did I say?"

"You mean, 'What did my dybbuk say?'" he said, and I felt that he wasn't so much correcting me as stalling for time.

He hemmed and hawed a bit more, then began, "In a nutshell, your dybbuk said that he'd stopped loving Mamie. It wasn't that he was jealous of the diamonds or of the man who gave them to her; but the diamonds *were* what killed it. For when he watched her fall in love with those glassy chips of stone, he realized that she wasn't the girl he'd thought she was. His predestined mate from forty days before birth wouldn't have carried on so over those shiny playthings meant for babies and dimwits. And from then on, he couldn't look at Mamie's hands without imagining them fat, old, and slack, with loose skin ballooning out around tight diamond rings.

"That night he'd tried to manufacture diamonds was his last attempt to salvage things. Perhaps, he hoped, the process of creating diamonds with Kabbalistic spells might help him glimpse the magic Mamie saw in them. But in the morning, all he saw was Mamie wailing over some grimy rocks; all he wanted was to leave.

"Not that it was painless for him. This was the first time he'd been in love, and the fact that a predestined passion could cool because of some diamonds wounded him so that he crawled home to Mama's nest. There he reached the conclusion that love, like diamonds, was for babies—except that diamonds lasted. The enduring concerns were the mystical ones; it was no accident that the Kabbala was more venerable and widely read than *Romeo and Juliet*. Freed from the physical, he devoted himself to his studies. One day, out walking, he saw a plane fly overhead and thought, If it's all a matter of rising up toward God, why not give yourself a two-thousand-foot head start? That plane, to him, was not just an emanation, but an invitation from the Highest: Come closer.

"People talk about the rapture of the deep, he said, but the first time he went up alone he experienced the ecstasy of the heights. He sang to himself, and though his normal singing voice was a croak, airborne it chimed like an angel's. The more he flew, the more he began to view himself as some sort of messiah. He dreamed of doing something for history and for the people of Buenos Aires, of putting on a performance so magnificent that its memory would change their lives.

"Which is, I suppose, what he did. Seeing a plane crash into the sea has to change a person, but not by very much, or for very long."

I believe that my dybbuk had said all this. But whereas I'd heard him speak with deep emotion, the sentiments, in Rabbi Israel's translation, sounded simply naïve. It saddened me that this aviator had died as such an adolescent, but what depressed me more was the suggestion that Paco and Mamie had stopped loving each other.

For this, as you can imagine, was the last thing I wanted to hear. It mustn't end this way, I thought. Because like all sad endings, it reflected back and cast the entire story in a lousy light. To me, it confirmed what my dybbuk's mother had said about her son and by extension about me: We had ice cubes for hearts. Leaving someone because they liked diamonds was not so very different from nearly sacrificing them because God asked. How could he have loved her if the greatest joy he remembered from this life was the ecstasy of the heights? And if you don't really love, it's easy to give up your beloved. So what if the sacrifice is for nothing, if you're no more a great actress than Paco Engelhart was the messiah of the Buenos Aires airways?

Now when I cried, even Rabbi Israel looked slightly irritated.

"See what we're up against?" said Feivel. "Rabbi, she doesn't speak Spanish. Hard as it is to believe, could it be that a dybbuk . . . ?"

Tempted to poke Feivel for implying that the wonder worker of Montevideo might find dybbuks hard to believe in, I was taken aback when Rabbi Israel said, "Yes, it *is* hard to believe. Even after witnessing so many of the Chazzer Rabbi's miracles, I had trouble accepting the idea of dybbuks. With my own eyes, I'd seen the Chazzer walk on air. But where were those restless spirits, those bodiless souls which I pictured like grapes without skins? And the truth is that I might never have believed in vagabond spirits if not for modern technology."

I saw Benno and Zalmen exchange looks. This Chassid straight out of medieval Hungary was talking about modern technology?

"The Chazzer Rabbi," Rabbi Israel continued, "had one of the very first radios in Budapest. This was no elegant piece of furniture, but a simple box with earphones, antennae like a cockroach's, and knobs you had to tune constantly. The Chazzer passed the earphones from disciple to disciple, and when I put them on, I heard someone playing the violin.

" 'Playing the violin in *Vienna!*' said the Chazzer, and we believed him. Because if a plain pine box could fiddle better then Beryl the one-man band, anything might be true.

"What this changed, among other things, was my attitude toward dybbuks. I thought, What receiver could be as marvelous as the human brain? If this contraption can pick up music from Vienna, who's to say that the mind can't receive information about a departed person, memories stored in the thoughts of the living . . . ?

"And as for human radios"—Rabbi Israel was playing to us now—"artists must be among the most finely tuned of all. So what's so incredible about this young lady picking up a little static?"

"My theory of dybbuks exactly," said Dalashinsky. "I'm always telling these children of mine that we're like rain barrels, open to the sky. Anything can fall in, even frogs."

"Rain barrels are too simple," said Rabbi Israel. "The fact is, frogs rarely drop in. Mostly, it's water and leaves. But it's not uncommon to tune Vienna in on the radio and get Timbuctoo. Sometimes it's just as interesting, if not more so. And certainly, none of it hurts."

This was *my* theory of dybbuks! As of right now! It was so logical, so reassuring. I'd picked up some static; none of it hurts. I was crying with relief, but who cared anymore for the reasons behind my tears?

Only one question still disturbed me—and Benno asked it.

"Rabbi," he said. "What can we do about it?"

"Turn off the radio," said Rabbi Israel.

Later, when I would read about gurus who said things like "Turn off the radio," I'd feel great sympathy for the kids who gave up everything to follow them. It's so simple, your heart responds, of course! Turn off the radio! Only later do the complications set in, and so it took us a while to wonder if, in our case, turning off the radio might be a gentle euphemism for an exorcism.

"Can you do it?" asked Feivel.

"I won't promise. I can try. Also, I'm not saying for sure it *is* a dybbuk. We'll see. Come back tomorrow night."

Tomorrow night? No one relished the prospect of spending twenty-four more hours with my crying. Besides, tomorrow was Saturday. The boat was leaving Sunday, and (for all that comforting talk about radios) it still scared us to think about sailing with me in hysterics.

"Rabbi," said Benno. "Couldn't you . . . ?"

"It's *shabes*," said Rabbi Israel. "I don't touch the radio on *shabes*."

"But you cook!" said Clara.

"Smart girl," said the rabbi. "She's got me."

"All right, tomorrow night," said Feivel, before his wife could get any smarter. "Here?"

"Are you crazy?" said Rabbi Israel. "Do you think I'd knowingly invite a dybbuk home to my wife and children?"

"A possible dybbuk," I said.

"A possible dybbuk," said the Rabbi.

"Where then?" asked Feivel.

"The kosher *frigorífico*. At ten."

Frigorífico? Even after our interpreters translated the word for us, we couldn't believe it. And yet we did believe that we needed Rabbi Israel's help. So we nodded so graciously, you'd have thought that we were planning a rendezvous under the clock at the Biltmore. Unless you knew Spanish, or the Schvartze Rabbi's mind, you would never have dreamed that we were arranging to meet at a kosher meat-packing plant in the slums of Montevideo.

10

WHAT COULD BE SWEETER than lingering on the edge of sleep,
knowing that something good is in store for the day but not
letting yourself wake up enough to remember just what. Brides,
so I'm told, sleep like that on their wedding day, though this was
never my experience. Only I, crazy Dinah, possessed by a
dybbuk in a hotel bed halfway around the world, could have
slept on that edge between peace and excitement, all morning
and partway into the afternoon of our second and final visit to
Rabbi Israel.

For though the Schvartze Rabbi had scrupulously promised
nothing, what I'd taken away from his home was an armload of
promises to snuggle up against in my sleep. My so-called
dybbuk would turn out to be nothing more than a little inter-
ference, wacky reception, an electrical squall in the brain; none
of it hurts. Did a radio feel pain when somebody turned it off?
And maybe it wasn't a dybbuk at all, but something else, some
tourist complaint which would disappear on its own. . . . I
drifted under the blanket.

Then from the depths I heard Ida. "Dinah, wake up. In the
grave, you'll get plenty of sleep."

My first thought was, Who wakes a bride like this on her
wedding day? And my second was that it wasn't a wedding in
store for me, but an exorcism.

And what had Ida woken me for? To sit in my room while
the others checked in on me? Years later, when Benno was

having his operations, the morning-after nurses reminded me of the Yiddish Art Theater that afternoon. The hollow cheer, the breezy assurances that I would soon be well made me feel, as poor Benno must have, that I was as good as dead.

The night before, Rabbi Israel had sent one of his disciples to help us find our way back to the hotel. Our guide, the young man I'd come to think of as "the cooking expert," spent the whole distance talking food. His idea of conversation was to grill us, so to speak, on the subject of our favorite dishes. I listened till Zalmen said, "No contest! My dear mama's *tzimmes* with carrots and prunes." Then I put my hands over my ears. For how could I keep rehashing Rabbi Israel's every word when Zalmen was going on about *tzimmes*?

Tonight, though, we were on our own, guideless, and so Feivel made us leave hours early, while we still had light. We took the same bleak walk as the evening before, only now, following the directions which the disciples had repeated fifty times, we didn't turn at the Calle Judea, but kept on another few blocks.

Even if it hadn't said in big letters, KOSHER FRIGORIFICO (*frigorífico* transliterated into Yiddish), it would have been hard to miss. And I thought, If this is my downfall, Rabbi Israel couldn't have picked a better setting. White stucco with pale blue trim, the meat-packing plant was a Jewish fortress to make Masada look like a sand castle. And yet this bastion was unguarded except for a small mezzuzah beside the half-opened door.

Entering through a dark hallway, we were hit head-on by the smell of blood and raw meat. Aha! I thought. (Again I was second-guessing the rabbi.) He thinks the stench of death will draw my dybbuk out like a child lured home by the smells from Mama's kitchen. In this freezing cold, cooler even than the chill of the grave, even a restless spirit won't play around!

But it wasn't till we passed through a second doorway that I understood. Rabbi Israel was staging our rendezvous in that warehouse to teach us a thing or two about theater.

The dimensions alone made Stuyvesant Place look like a

closet. And as a setting for a drama of life and death, what could beat those rows of beef carcasses dangling from hooks? I thought of *The Dybbuk*'s little "cemetery" and was glad we'd left the flats and cardboard tombstones in Buenos Aires. For sheer eeriness, this *frigorífico* made the Expressionists' best work seem like a joke.

The white tile walls ricocheted every footstep, acoustics so perfect we could practically hear ourselves breathe. The lighting was bizarre and terrific, a few bright lamps reflected like a rainy night on Broadway in the wet (I didn't want to know what with) floors. You'll think I'm exaggerating when I say that the whole scene had a gray-green tinge; but gray-green is what I remember. And the sight lines? From five hundred feet, you could count the stripes on Rabbi Israel's socks.

Skirting the puddles, we flew toward him down the center aisle. At the edges of my vision, giant sides of beef zipped past, but I was so thrilled, so optimistic—those curved ribs grinned at me like smiles.

A *minyan*, nine Chassidim plus Rabbi Israel, sat on chairs in a semicircle near the far wall. I counted those ten little men with their black coats and suntans, remembered the huge crowd in the rabbi's house last night and thought, Heaven help me. This is really going to be something if he's keeping it down to a *minyan*.

Suddenly I got as frightened as I should have been for the last two weeks, as any normal woman would have been to find herself speaking in an unknown language and someone else's voice. Just as when I was pregnant with Hannele and didn't get nervous till the night before she was born, so with my dybbuk, I saved it till my delivery was near.

Halfway to Rabbi Israel, my knees went. I sagged, then felt hands at my back and elbows. I turned, and there on both sides of me were Clara and Ida.

I was trembling in expectation of God knows what. Embarrassment at the very least, worse than crawling into that mock-up coffin with the whole cast watching. And possibly, physical pain. I took it for granted that Rabbi Israel would stare into my eyes, ranting and raving like Dalashinsky playing the wonder worker of Miropol. And though I noticed that this Chassidic *minyan* didn't seem to have candles, shofars, or shrouds on hand, I still anticipated all the trappings of mumbo jumbo. It wouldn't have surprised me had lightning crackled out from Rabbi Israel's fingertips.

But what I didn't expect was for Rabbi Israel to stand to greet us, then say, "If there's one thing which attracts evil spirits like flies to honey, it's a secret marriage."

It's impressive enough when a stranger knows your name; still, powerful as names are, they're easily discovered. But when a holy man has magical access to your most intimate secrets, you're *his*. If at that moment Rabbi Israel had suggested that I leap off the *frigorífico* roof and fly up toward heaven, I might have at least gone up there and flapped my arms.

I was speechless, as were Benno and Dalashinsky. We left the hubbub to the others, who could only assume that Rabbi Israel meant Paco and Mamie.

The rabbi focused on me and said, "Miss Rappoport, do you feel well enough for a party?"

"What kind of party?"

"A wedding."

"Whose?" I asked, though somehow I already knew.

"Yours," said Rabbi Israel.

I have always thought that there are two kinds of déjà vu. The first comes from nowhere and means nothing more significant than some static on a nerve. Walking down the street, you see an empty orange soda can in the trash and you feel you've been there before. The other comes at the truly important times, the ones you've imagined so often (though maybe inaccurately) that when they finally happen, it's only half a surprise.

And so when I heard Benno cry out, "Rabbi, she's already married! To me!" I didn't turn around. Happy as it made me, I'd heard it before.

"I know that." Rabbi Israel was smiling. "The important thing was that you should shout it from the house tops."

Meanwhile it was like the climax of a "standback" drama: Stand back! Miss Rappoport the basically sensible girl is actually your long-lost wife! Benno and I ran to each other's arms, while all around us the others were saying, "*Mazel tov!* Why didn't you tell us?"

As Benno and I hung on for dear life, I squeezed him till my arms hurt, then reluctantly let go, walked a few steps away— and fainted.

My last conscious thought was, I must be an actress! I'm taking notes on my own faint! Everything glittered, then grew dim. I was exhausted. But instead of sinking like an elephant—a Dalashinsky faint—I had one arm out, groping for a dry place on which to land. Someone caught me and lowered me, and I filed it away for the future that I didn't care who it was.

Later, Benno would say that he'd felt responsible for having hugged me too hard and cut off my oxygen. But even out cold, I knew that Benno's embrace wasn't why I'd fainted.

When I opened my eyes, I was stretched out on the tiles with Benno cradling my head. And Rabbi Israel was dusting his palms together.

"So much for this dybbuk," he was saying. "Now someone, please, help her up."

Was this all there was to it? Could I have heard him right? No shofars, so shrouds, no lightning, no physical pain? A fainting spell—was my dybbuk really gone? Except for a cottony head and jelly legs, I got up feeling wonderful. And yet, like a hypochondriac after a checkup who insists that the doctor tell him he's healthy a dozen times, I needed to hear Rabbi Israel say it.

"She'll be fine," he said. "No more dybbuks." Then his gaze narrowed to Benno and me and he said, "As we know, you're married before the state of New York. But don't you think it's high time you got married before God?"

"Yes!" He didn't have to ask *me* twice.

"Mr. Brownstein?"

After a minute, Benno said, "All right."

Later, Benno would tell me that, in that brief hesitation, he was imagining the delights of someday telling our children that their mama and papa were married by the wonder worker of Montevideo in a kosher *frigorífico*. And I knew that things must have been all right if Benno was imagining children.

"Come with me." Rabbi Israel beckoned us through a door which led into an open courtyard. And there under that moon and starlit sky were more Chassidic men, women, and children than could possibly have fit in Rabbi Israel's house. And I understood the real reason he'd staged this in the *frigorífico*. Not for the theatrics—for the space!

And the colors! The colors! The first thing I noticed was the bridal canopy woven entirely of ribbons—the best French velvets, Florentine silks, embroideries which must have traveled all the way from Budapest. The rebbitzin and three other women held it up until Rabbi Israel poked Ida and Clara and said, "Go. Take it."

As soon as my friends had the *chupah* steady, Rabbi Israel took Benno's elbow and ushered him underneath it. And just as I was wondering, What about me?, the women came over and got me and began to lead me in circles around Benno.

If I'd wanted mumbo jumbo, I got it now. To this ceremony, Rabbi Israel invited not only God, but a guest list of ninety-nine angels. At one point in the service, he paused and pointed at some women who began to shriek and moan like the chorus in a Greek tragedy.

"For the demons' benefit," he whispered. "We don't want them to think we're having too good a time."

When the moment came to break the glass, Rabbi Israel handed it to Benno and whispered in his ear. Normally this custom involves a glass neatly wrapped in a napkin for easy disposal, a civilized little crunch of the heel. But at our wedding, Benno pitched the glass against the wall—and I felt proud that Benno could hit the bull's-eye from a hundred feet with a real pop and crack. I also remember being relieved that this was the opposite wall from the long table on which they were keeping the food; and more than anything else, this sensible housewifely thought reminded me that I was already married.

Still, it did feel as if Benno and I were getting married for the first time. Mumbo jumbo or not, this service was more elaborate and certainly more heartfelt than anything we'd gotten from that red-nosed pol at City Hall. And this time, we got rings.

"Plain gold bands," said Rabbi Israel. "No breaks in the metal and please, no diamonds." Then he said, "Kiss the bride."

For that public kiss, we used all our practice in alleyways to create for ourselves the illusion that now too, no one saw—that only God and the two of us witnessed that kiss, which would have gotten us thrown off the stage at Stuyvesant Place.

The next thing I knew, I was shoved down into a chair, which was then lifted up by four Chassidim. The reason it took four was that each had only one free hand, the other being occupied with a bottle of brandy. Both *my* hands were gripping the seat beneath me, except when I waved at Benno, who was bobbing over the crowd on a chair of his own.

"Let's eat," said Rabbi Israel, and I landed. Thump.

Benno and I were steered toward the head of the line. There were thirty or so different dishes, but we put a spoonful of everything on our plates, delicious morsels of this and that which made Rabbi Israel's omelet look like cooking class.

Only the women and children ate; the men were too busy drinking. And when Benno and I finished, we joined them. I realized how unheard-of it was for Chassidic men and women to be celebrating together, but no more so, I decided, than for suntanned Chassidim to hold weddings in the courtyards of *frigoríficos*.

After a while, Zalmen held up his glass and said, "A toast! To love!"

The men with their brandy, the women with their wine, even the children with their cups of creamy milk—the whole place toasted love.

Then Leon Dalashinsky raised his glass, closed his eyes, sighed and said, "To youth, love, and beauty!"

The sob in his voice reminded me of the day he'd shown me those silvery dolphins off the *Veracruz*. In light of everything which had—and hadn't—happened, I couldn't help being moved. And yet some part of me thought, Hypocrite! How easy it was for Dalashinsky to toast youth, love, and beauty here in Montevideo, while his poor Hinda was freezing home in New York with the three screaming kids. This new sympathy for Hinda made me realize how much I'd changed toward Dalashinsky. The lost youth, love, and beauty I pitied was not his, but hers.

This fine point escaped the Chassidim. Youth, love, and beauty? They toasted.

Benno and I brought our glasses together and made a silent toast to souls betrothed forty days before birth, to the two halves of an orange. And the tone of the cheering suggested that the crowd was interpreting our look as something earthier than it was.

Finally it was Rabbi Israel's turn. He raised his glass and with the other hand, struck a match, then held it up so we could watch it burn. Astonishingly, the plain wooden match burned so slowly and for so long—Rabbi Israel put down his glass, lit a cigar, took three puffs, put down the cigar, picked up the glass, drank—then blew out the match.

"To light," he said.

To light? Why not? The Schvartze Chassidim and the Yiddish Art Theater toasted Rabbi Israel's match trick.

Did I mention that our glasses were refilled between each toast? And that wasn't the end of the drinking. No wonder I can remember lots of hugging and kissing, talking to Benno, to Ida, to Feivel—but not one word that was said. Also I was distracted, I kept looking for Rabbi Israel. But whenever I located him, he was off in some corner, talking nonstop to Dalashinsky. And the greatest miracle so far was that Dalashinsky was listening.

Together, they were unapproachable, and frankly, I was just as glad. I was bashful of Rabbi Israel. At the same time, though, I was slightly envious that Dalashinsky was being singled out of our so-called ensemble for such an intense and private conversation. I consoled myself with the thought that whatever went into Dalashinsky's ears would filter eventually down to us all.

I waited; I didn't mind. And finally Rabbi Israel came over to me.

"*Mazel tov,*" he said.

"Thank you," I answered, then realized that if I didn't ask now, I might never get another chance. And though it wasn't the most important question on my mind, I said, "Rabbi, one thing. How did you know my dybbuk's name?"

"Through the grapevine." Rabbi Israel laughed. "And what's so miraculous about a grapevine? It's no more incredible than that I should send one of my disciples along to find out the Yiddish Art Theater's favorite foods so that we might serve them tonight."

At this, I put two and two together, and remembered eating a helping of *tzimmes* just like Zalmen described.

"Now *I* have one thing." Rabbi Israel was staring at me, and if lightning wasn't crackling from his fingertips, the glow in his eyes made up for it.

"Next to secret marriages," he began, "there's no time which attracts evil spirits more than the moment when someone discovers that love—first love, especially—doesn't stay the same forever, that passion can cool because someone snores, or scratches his head, or goes crazy for diamonds. But the tragedy is that this dybbuk of yours died young, before he'd lived long enough to realize that love has more lives than a cat; it's like parents who die before their children have grown out of thinking that Mama and Papa are the villains.

"Yet I promise you, love doesn't just vanish. The proof of it is that this dybbuk bothered coming back to tell this girl in Buenos Aires that he'd found more diamonds in the clouds than she'd ever received from her rich old man. And that Chonon kept returning to claim Leah."

Rabbi Israel pointed up at the moon, as thin and grainy as a curve of white chalk on that blackboard of a sky. "To think that love doesn't return is like a child seeing the new moon and thinking that the old one is gone forever."

So. Another déjà vu. For this too had happened before. Benno and I had already fallen out—and back in. And judging from that kiss under the canopy, the encores weren't so bad. I wanted to hug Rabbi Israel, but needless to say, I didn't. For once, I was too nervous even for jokes.

"Wait," I said. "Something else." Then, without being able to frame one coherent sentence, I managed to tell Rabbi Israel about my real worries—about Mama and Papa, about Benno, my cold-heartedness, my dybbuk's mother's harsh warnings, about abandoning your loved ones and climbing that mountain for nothing. . . .

When at last I'd finished, Rabbi Israel was smiling.

"It's true that art won't put its arms around you in the middle of the night," he said. "But really, who's making you choose?

"And now, please." Rabbi Israel had already turned away from me and was clapping his hands like a watchful host who's just noticed that the party has begun to lag. "Gentlemen!" he called out. "Some music!"

A band was brought in. And though the Chassidim were all pretty unkempt, these men were so especially overgrown, there was no mistaking that this was a real Jewish wedding band. They arrived with the usual equipment, two fiddles and a mandolin, but when they began playing, it wasn't your typical folk song, your Yiddish good luck to the bride tra-la-la.

They were playing—what else?—a tango.

Suddenly everyone was prodding Benno and me. "Let the bride and groom have the first dance!"

Benno and I shook our heads. What did we know from the tango? But when Rabbi Israel said, "I insist," we traipsed obediently into the space they cleared for us in the center of the courtyard.

From the minute I slung one arm around Benno's neck and extended my hand to meet his, it was a perfect tango. It *was* the dance of love and death and, halfway through, I fell madly in love with Benno all over again. What was happening between us was private, yet the music seemed to cover us like a blanket. I didn't want it to end, partly because of the pleasure and partly because I was afraid of what would occur when the blanket was pulled off.

But when the music stopped, all that happened was that Benno and I looked at each other and thought the same thing.

"Let's get out of here," he said.

I have always regretted that we didn't stay to thank Rabbi Israel once more. Yet somehow I feel certain that the way we rushed out of that *frigorífico* and back to the hotel was thanks enough.

"Your place or mine?" asked Benno.

"Mine. Ida will have the sense to get another room, but I'm not so sure about Zalmen."

Nowadays, I know, it's customary to tell everything. But I've always been too modest for such confessions. And besides, even if I wanted to, these things are impossible to explain. No words in any language fit the act, and though everyone knows what you're talking about, no one does. For how can you describe a night when something which has happened to nearly everyone seems as if it has never happened before?

Without going into detail, let me say: That night, we didn't joke about heaven. We were there. In that dark room, we shone, bright and round and perfect as an orange.

And yet we weren't so dazzled that we missed the dawn. When light began sifting in through the curtains, we jumped out of bed.

"It's Sunday," said Benno. "Let's go home."

What is it about church bells which lifts the heart and makes even Jewish feet step livelier? On that brilliant Sunday morning, the carillons of Montevideo rang us down to the harbor.

Benno and I led the parade, for though we hadn't slept, love seemed to be exempting us from the physical price of drinking and dancing and staying up all night. Stumbling behind us, the rest of the cast appeared to be paying in full.

Maybe that was why, after all the hugging and kissing of the night before, they were keeping their distance now; perhaps it was the sense of betrayal which comes when, in the clear light of day, you see that your near and dear have been holding out on you. Of them all, Zalmen seemed most outraged by this poke in

his sharp eye for hanky-panky. When we'd come down to break-
fast, he'd led the others in a halfhearted, almost mocking cheer.
"Since when have you lovebirds been married?" he grumbled.
"Since fall," I said. "The third week of rehearsal."

"Jesus," said Zalmen. "If *I* didn't pick up on it, maybe you
two *can* act."

Ida wouldn't acknowledge my presence at all, but Clara said,
"Dinah, Benno, why did you keep it from us?"

Benno and I just shrugged, for such was Dalashinsky's power
that nothing could have induced us to point and say, "He forced
us." And such was Dalashinsky's confidence that he had no
hesitation in answering for us:

"For artistic reasons," he said.

This the Yiddish Art Theater could understand. For artistic
reasons, they would have kept their own grandmothers under
wraps. Then the full import hit them: Dalashinsky had known.
Which only made them resent me and Benno more, for the extra
bond which, they imagined, tied us to Dalashinsky as a conse-
quence of sharing this great secret.

But fortunately, as we neared the waterside, each lungful of
fresh sea air affected us like two weeks at a sanatorium. Sunlight
bounced off the water and onto that proud, clean white Viking
of a ship, the *S.S. Copenhagen*. Heading towards it, we breezed
through customs with a quick stamp-stamp, click-click, and all
was forgiven.

One look at that boat and the whole cast embarked on a
honeymoon. With one foot still on the gangplank, Clara was
blabbing our whole story. Captain and deckhand alike heard
how Benno and Dinah had been secretly married, then really
married, just last night. . . . Already, I noticed, my dybbuk had
been edited out of Clara's version. And though the cast made
fun of her big mouth, they liked it that everyone knew. It set the
tone of things—raised it, if the truth be told. After hearing our
adventures, those melancholy Danes couldn't have been jollier,
and from the first night out, the crew couldn't do enough for us.

Eighteen days on the *S.S. Copenhagen*—and not one word of
complaint. The most nervous immigrant, the most chronic

bellyacher couldn't deny the temptations of those breakfasts, fresh rolls and fifteen kinds of smoked and pickled fish, those dinners of tournedos which needed no chewing, topped with a choice of five different French sauces. Every night, the wedding party started up anew, and though it would have gone on without us, Benno and I presided. Every night, the captain got drunk, and it was all we could do to dissuade him from marrying us all over again.

Like the *Veracruz*, the *Copenhagen* carried a cargo of beef, but this time no one complained of the smell. Perhaps it was the consolation of those marvelous tournedos which resigned them to the proximity of all that meat, or the aromatic reminder of Rabbi Israel's *frigorífico*.

And if the boat pitched now and then? Benno and I rolled harder, creating such light—if there had been moths on the open sea, they surely would have flown in. And this despite the fact that we had no porthole; we were literally underwater. To us, though, this wasn't a problem, but only a reason to surface occasionally for air.

With no window, we couldn't tell what time it was. And yet I had no doubt that it was the very middle of the night when Benno and I were awoken by the ship's whistle blaring a series of blasts so frantic, I sat straight up.

"Fire!" I said, though I didn't smell smoke. "Collision!" Why hadn't I felt the crash?

"Hush." Benno reached for me and drew me close. "We're crossing the equator."

Maybe everything is easier the second time. This crossing, I felt no desire to run up on deck for the akvavit and party hats, the King Neptunes and dancing bears. And how could I worry about falling off the edge of the planet when, just a few hours before, I'd imagined that Benno and I had transcended gravity, or at least discovered a gravity of our own?

On the night before we reached New York, the captain asked if we would mind doing a little play for him and the crew. He'd hesitated, knowing that this was some sort of honeymoon, but wasn't there something . . . ?

"Like what?" asked Dalashinsky.

I was, if possible, more surprised than I'd been to hear him ask Rabbi Israel a similar question. Did this mean that the Yiddish Art Theater was going into the business of taking requests?

On that voyage home, you must understand, everything Dalashinsky did—from his gorging at breakfast to his picking at supper—irritated me physically, and struck me as evidence of inferior character. Fresh from those long afternoons in Benno's smooth arms, I'd look at Dalashinsky and see nothing beyond his old man's crepey skin. One night, I showed Benno the Warrior of Masada, and when he said, "Dinele, sweetheart, that's Orion," I blushed in the darkness for every word I'd ever exchanged with Dalashinsky. I could feel my respect for him dwindling, but I felt more relieved than diminished.

And so when the Danish captain put his head down in his arms to mull over his request, I almost knew what it would be and waited with something like glee till he roused himself enough to mumble, "Hamlet."

We gulped. Even I, who'd expected to see Dalashinsky demeaned, hadn't anticipated this.

"Hamlet?" said Feivel. "Leon, we don't know Hamlet from a hole in the ground."

"No one's got the script," said Ida. And then, to show us that she hadn't forgotten the inhumanity of our luggage limits, she added, "I left my boyfriend at home. I should bring along Shakespeare?"

"You know the story, children," said Dalashinsky. "One or two of you must have seen it, or—though I know it's too much to hope—read it. At any rate, you've read reviews. If you're actors, you can improvise."

Improvise Hamlet? The sin of the Thomashefskys committed against the most sacred of sacred texts?

"To be or not to be, that is the question," said Dalashinsky. And bang! We were off like racehorses!

That night, we played Hamlet like Goldfaden—with a lamp, a sheet, and two swords. As the ghost of Hamlet's father, Feivel knotted a tablecloth around his shoulders, powdered his face with some flour from the kitchen, picked up the nearest candle-stick, and walked the "ramparts" of stacked chairs. A curtain was borrowed from the window for Zalmen's Polonius to hide behind, and midway through the scene, Dalashinsky slid the curtain rod out to use as a rapier.

Primitive, true, but we'd grown used to primitive conditions. Without the sacred text to impede us, we zipped through *Hamlet* in twenty minutes. If it wasn't Shakespeare, well, we got the story across, and to paraphrase Popolescu, Shakespeare should only have written so well. The Danes went wild for it, the sword fights in particular.

I played Ophelia, hamming it up like the Saraleh Bernhardt I was, sniveling, singing little ditties, shredding the floral center-pieces and strewing the petals about. The sailors didn't know the difference, and in a way, I think, it reassured the cast that I was so awful. Clearly, I couldn't have been basing my big mad scene on my own emotional memories of being possessed by a dyb-buk; my dithery Ophelia couldn't have been less like Dinah Rappoport transmitting urgent communiqués from beyond the grave.

Since then, I've often wondered if that was why Dalashinsky agreed to do *Hamlet* and cast me as Ophelia. Did he mean to test my sanity against that poor cracked Danish princess? Was he banking on the chance that I'd come out of it with nothing worse than a bad acting job? Did he intend to convince us, with all this, that as Rabbi Israel had promised, I'd be fine?

I might have thought so then, except that I was in such a frame of mind about Dalashinsky, I couldn't believe that he would do anything for anyone else. And what I decided was later confirmed by the evidence of his next performance.

He staged that *Hamlet*, as he did everything, as preparation, as further preparation for the part he would play over the fol-lowing weeks: that most peculiar role of being "out of charac-ter," that confounding of all our ideas of him, which would culminate in the meeting he called, not long after our return to New York.

11

THE TROUBLE WITH MY MEMORIES of my family's first arrival in America is that I was a grumpy ten-year-old with a limited perspective. I would have seen anywhere they took me as a geographical manifestation of Mama's and Papa's shortcomings. Ellis Island, for example, was the kind of place where they worried too much. And the first time we sailed past the Statue of Liberty, I thought, How typical of them to set their sights on this big green cow with her dumb spiky hat!

In this too I was grateful for a second chance. For as the S.S. *Copenhagen* passed the Statue of Liberty—at sunrise, with mist on the water and a pink-blue sky—she not only lifted her lamp, but appeared to turn in a graceful arc, holding it steadily toward us. And I thought, just as my parents must have, Thank God.

On that unseasonably warm March morning, New York was as interesting as a foreign country, only better: We knew the language and our way around, we even had a place to stay. Benno and I took our luggage to our apartment—a little dusty but shipshape—then rushed over to Attorney Street.

Mama and Papa couldn't believe that I hadn't been shanghaied; nor I, that they were alive and well. Because we couldn't trust our eyes, we had to hug each other—though we'd never been much of a family for hugging—fifty times. Mama was crying so, it took her a good five minutes to ask, "How was it?"

"Terrific," I said. Wild horses couldn't have dragged the word "dybbuk" out of me.

"What now?" Papa couldn't help asking Benno. "Any plans for the future?"

"Vacation," said Benno.

And so in that foreign country, New York, Benno and I took the best kind of vacation: We rarely thought about the past or future, and never about work. Mostly we stayed home, enjoying the privacy and freedom we hadn't tasted since the weekend after our first City Hall wedding. Occasionally we'd go out, arm in arm, tight against each other through the windy streets; we'd come home with bags of baked farmer cheese, pickles, knishes, all the foods we'd missed, without knowing how much, on our travels. Secretly it pleased me to recall how, the first time, we'd hardly dared breathe the word "honeymoon"; whereas now, easier with one another, we joked about our second one.

But for all our not thinking about the future, when Feivel sent a message saying that Dalashinsky was calling a meeting, we were so glad he still *wanted* us at a meeting, we didn't mind that the honeymoon was over.

The meeting began like so many others.

"Children," said Dalashinsky, "the time has come for us to consider our next production."

As usual, the actors had their suggestions all ready, and it was amazing how each of these ensemble players would propose dramas with ready-made starring roles for his or her types.

"What about *Mirele Efros*?" said Clara, as if she hadn't nominated this older-woman's vehicle a thousand times.

"Falstaff—I mean *Henry IV*," said Zalmen.

"Perhaps *King Lear*," mused Dalashinsky. "But certainly not till the end of the season. . . .

"My chickadees," he continued after the briefest pause, "what would you say if I proposed a one-night slam-bang triumphal return engagement of Anski's *The Dybbuk*?"

Feivel answered, "I'd say, 'Leon, there's a thousand bucks' worth of equipment in crates which Popolescu is holding for ransom in Buenos Aires.' "

"To hell with Buenos Aires," said Dalashinsky. "Down with the old, up with the new. What I'm suggesting is an entirely new production—new lighting, new scenery, new special effects. . . ."

"For one night?" Feivel was practically whining. "What you're suggesting is financial suicide."

"Trust me," said Dalashinsky.

It struck me how out of character it was for this genius who so hated clichés to say, "Trust me"; for a man who'd always assumed our worship to be asking now for our trust. Yet no amount of uncharacteristic behavior could have prepared me for what came next.

"What I would like," said Dalashinsky, "is for us to have a wedding after the final curtain, for Miss Dinah Rappoport and Mister Benno Brownstein to be married onstage."

"No!" I cried. "Never! I'd sooner have an onstage funeral."

"That too can be arranged," said Zalmen.

Zalmen may have been joking, but I wasn't. For though my "No!" had come straight from the heart, my "Never!" had reasons behind it.

Partly, these reasons were artistic. To me, such weddings represented the dregs at the bottom of the theatrical trash can. Thomashefsky couldn't get through a run without marrying off some extra, and which wife was it Adler wed onstage at the final performance of *The Yiddish Romeo and Juliet?* Onstage weddings were come-ons, like the free dishes movie theaters would later give away. And what did free dishes have to do with art? Despite my nostalgia for the "old" Yiddish theater, I drew the line at the prospect of such a display and was shocked that Dalashinsky would stoop low enough to suggest it.

"I used to feel the same way." Dalashinsky read the look on my face. "But the one thing we should all have learned from our little trip south is that a wedding can be the height of theater."

"Granted," I said. "But a *frigorífico* in Montevideo isn't Stuyvesant Place. Or should I say, Second Avenue?"

"You shouldn't," said Feivel. "No one's proposing that we do the wedding in the *middle* of the play, but afterward. *The Dybbuk* will still be *The Dybbuk.*"

"Better," said Dalashinsky.

Perhaps this (together with my inability to believe that the

whole cast, except me, would so readily desert art for trash)
might have set my artistic doubts to rest and convinced me. But I
had personal reservations too.

After all, they were talking about *my* wedding. And though I
may have joined up for the colors, I hadn't signed on to parade
my personal life for a houseful of strangers. My marriage wasn't
a shill; it was serious business, arranged forty days before birth
and sanctified by the wonder worker of Montevideo.

"I won't be part of this carnival," I said. "What is this, the
Yiddish Art Theater or Luna Park?"

Dalashinsky didn't so much ignore me as cut me out, the way
a child will scissor one figure out of a group in a magazine.

"Children," he said. "Isn't it a pity that Miss Rappoport has
been married twice—yet her mama and papa have never once
danced at her wedding?"

I got furious. Dalashinsky, I thought, how dare you? Steal
from everywhere, use everything—but not my mama and papa!

"Can't you see?" I appealed to the others. "There are choices
to be made here. . . ." And even as I said it, I knew how I would
choose. Rather than prostitute what was left of my private life,
I'd retire, go on semi-permanent vacation. Benno could work,
I'd stay home, raise a family. . . .

I suppose my life in art might have ended right there if Dalashinsky hadn't turned to me with a half smile and a blankness in
his eyes which made it impossible to read secret meanings behind them.

"Miss Rappoport." Was Dalashinsky actually winking at me?
"Who's making you choose?"

This echo of Rabbi Israel stumped me—and made me realize
that the wonder worker of Montevideo was still somehow involved in all this. Suddenly, I felt certain that this wedding was
part of some pact made between Dalashinsky and the Schvartze
Chassid. And while I had no idea what was in it for Dalashinsky (at the time, I suspected the worst—pure showman-
ship and selfish ambition), I had faith that Rabbi Israel
wouldn't steer us far wrong.

All at once, I asked myself, Really, why choose? As Feivel

said, *The Dybbuk* would still be *The Dybbuk*. A ceremony afterward wouldn't compromise our art. What would be harmed by our giving my parents a chance to waltz at my wedding? Where in all Stanislavsky was it written that an artist couldn't do something for her mama and papa? Whoever said art wasn't wide enough to accommodate the daily kindnesses, the favors of family life?

Sensing that I was wavering, Benno took my hand and said, "Dinele, why not?"

"Why not?" repeated Natty. "We had such a good time at your last wedding, why not have another?"

"It definitely won't hurt business," said Feivel. "For publicity, this wedding will take care of the season."

"And it's true that your mama and papa will love it," said Ida.

"All right," I said. I was looking at Benno.

"All right," said Dalashinsky.

"First rehearsal?" Feivel picked up his pen and notebook, then put them down again when Dalashinsky said, "No rehearsals."

No rehearsals? What new Dalashinsky trick did this signify? We groaned, but Dalashinsky's voice swelled to drown out our groans.

"Feivel, have the posters printed up like wedding invitations. Put them up all over the neighborhood, uptown and down. Send one to everyone we know. Mail one to Rabbi Israel, if they deliver in that district. One to that Rabbi Schmuckler, and that psychiatrist . . . and also to that Mamie Ramirez. . . . And, Feivel. Send the first invitation to Miss Rappoport's mama and papa."

How could I not have been charmed, and so seduced by all the preparations and excitement over the wedding that I never once thought to worry about doing *The Dybbuk*? Or to wonder: If Mama had wept over Anski's dybbuk, how would she react to mine?

* * *

The posters went up on Sunday night. By Monday morning, the box office had sold out, with hundreds more turned away. And by Wednesday, when Benno and I went to Mama and Papa's for dinner, the poster was already framed and hanging on the wall.

"Just today," said Papa, "a million people came into the shop to wish me *mazel tov*."

Oh, Papa. Was this all he'd been waiting for, a ribbon shop full of well-wishers? If so, I was glad he could have it. Not only had he changed his tune about my garbage-picking spinsterhood; he'd even come to see the advantages of a secret marriage.

"They're all coming to the wedding," Papa said. And then, conspiratorially, "Of course, I didn't tell them you were already married."

This alone would have reconciled me to the wedding, if I hadn't already been won over by the fact that Feivel—on Dalashinsky's orders!—had sent Mama and Papa complimentary front row center seats.

Still, it bothered me when Mama asked, "Who's doing the service?" And I had to answer, "I don't know."

Twice, Benno and I had been to Stuyvesant Place, where Dalashinsky had posted a Pinkerton guard to keep his own actors away! Though this goon refused to take messages, we insisted that he ask Dalashinsky how we were supposed to do this show with different sets, different props, and no rehearsals. And the goon quoted "the boss" as replying, the play was the same.

Only Feivel got in, but he wasn't talking, except to say that we were expected at the theater at six on the evening of the show, which was scheduled for eight. To be safe, we got there at five, and found that a thousand people had come with the same idea.

Clearly, these weren't typical Art Theater-goers, who would have died before they'd show up in public three hours early for anything. These were hungry hearts: old ladies whose girlhood dreams were to marry Kessler onstage, couples who'd gone courting to see Jacob Adler's wedding, people who remembered when Boris and Bessie Thomashefsky's rival theaters both staged marriages on the same night, and who believed that this was the last one they might ever get the chance to see. I did pick out a few familiar Art Theater faces, a little bewildered by this open invitation to the philistines; they'd come early to arrive before the philistines could spread picnic lunches over their season seats.

These regulars looked as if they expected to be disappointed, which intimidated me—as did the mob of reporters from the Yiddish dailies, blocking my way and scribbling to beat the band. What gave me courage was the sight of Mama's cousin Greta, plowing through that phalanx of journalists and planting a kiss on my cheek; the knowledge that Feivel had sent fifty free tickets to my relatives; and finally the memory of Mama's saying, "Aunt Becky's daughter was married in the Eldridge Street *shul* with two cantors, and they thought *that* was a big deal."

My dressing room was full of flowers, but no more so than during *The Dybbuk*'s first run. The costume hanging by the mirror was the same dark shawl and white *schmatte* which had stood me in good stead from New York to Argentina. And my dresser, little Kitty Buchsbaum, was chewing what might have been the same piece of gum she'd had in her mouth when we'd said good-bye.

We stayed in our dressing rooms till Feivel knocked, then took our places in the wings and began chanting, "Why has the soul fallen from the heights to the depths?" I thought: Just as Dalashinsky promised, it was the same play.

And it was, only darker in every way. Even with the candles Feivel gave Ida and Clara, we tripped all over each other walking into that *"shul,"* and I recognized this ark as my former coffin, upended. Still, the velvet Torah cover felt exactly like the old one, as plush against my lips.

"Good evening, Chonon," I said.

Dalashinsky, were you paying attention? It *helped* that the audience knew that Benno and I were "engaged" in real life. They followed our every move like a bunch of peeping Toms seeing something real and secret up there in the shadows. And it *was* real. The history I shared with Benno was so much longer and more complicated; the attraction had grown to match. We looked, we couldn't look. We looked away.

What I noticed was that Benno's Chonon no longer talked so feverishly about scaling the heights of Paradise; to my knowing ear, he sounded like a man who wouldn't unravel Heaven's curtain with gloves on. But somehow Benno used this so that what came through was his awe and respect for whatever powers were out there. His Chonon had a greater profundity; watching, I felt that I could watch Benno without getting bored, every night for the rest of my life.

With each set change, we awaited the completely new production Dalashinsky had promised, but Brinnnits and its environs were nothing more than slapped-together versions of the sets which Popolescu had probably already broken up and sold for scrap lumber. By the end of act one, I'd begun to suspect that an exhausted Dalashinsky hadn't been able to come up with anything more than a little extra darkness.

There were subtle differences, of course. In the interim, Leah's father had become an art lover; the walls of Sender's house were hung with landscapes, greenish brown studies in heavy frames lit from below. When I figured out what they reminded me of—the "art" in Rabbi Schmuckler's home—I felt a twinge of that sadness which had me weeping up and down Montevideo.

But now, instead of losing control, I used it for the melancholy which deepened in the next few scenes and struck bottom in the loss of my beloved from forty days before birth. And once again it worked in our favor that the audience knew the truth and could imagine that this lovely couple, about to be married in less than an hour, had been suddenly, cruelly divided by death; that my predestined mate had been taken from me, his place usurped by Menasha, whose shaky hands were even now transforming the innocent marriage veil into some intimate, lewd article.

A fog of gloom rolled over the house—over everyone but Mama. For Mama, in her front-row seat, was saving her tears.

This time, she knew that her daughter wasn't really being groped by lepers and possessed by evil spirits. When this dybbuk business was over, her Dinele was getting married. And *then* she would cry.

So without a care for anything but Anski's sacred text, I prepared for my dybbuk. I constricted my throat muscles and called on whatever I might have learned about restlessness beyond the grave. Then I opened my mouth, Anski's dybbuk flew right out—and I let it fly.

"I have come to my predestined bride and will not leave her!"

"The bride is possessed by a dybbuk," announced Natty.

Curtain. Applause.

The program called for a fifteen-minute intermission, and later, Mama would tell me that the lobby was a party in itself, lemonade sold by the half glass and doctored with bootleg schnapps. Benno and I and our unborn great-great-grandchildren had our healths drunk to so many times that even my unsuperstitious mother got nervous and said, "Enough!"

We saw none of this. On Dalashinsky's request, we were herded into an empty dressing room while the stagehands moved in the sets.

"Let *us* do it," Ida yelled at her muscle-bound ex-boyfriend, who in returning to his old job had quit Ida. "We've had loads of practice." The crew ignored her.

That room was a setup. We were sitting ducks for the pale, overweight kid who barged in with a large package wrapped in brown paper.

"Directions were, I should deliver this between the second and the third act," said the messenger. He held a paper up for Feivel's signature, but when he began asking everyone to sign, Zalmen said, "Autograph hound!" and shouldered him out.

How had he sneaked in past the guard? We never could. But maybe that was the reason for specifying this particular intermission. Everyone, including the guard, knew that this was the time when Dalashinsky was preparing his Rabbi Azrielke, *davening* his heart out; he wouldn't notice if a few pennies changed hands and a little something was delivered. And so the fat kid charged in like those glorious messengers in the melodramas: Stand back!

Feivel examined the stamps on the package. "Argentina," he said.

"A bomb!" cried Zalmen. "Don't anyone touch it!"

But Feivel had already detached an envelope from the outside and unfolded a note: " 'For the happy couple,' " he read. " 'From your friend, Popolescu.' "

I ripped open the paper. And there in all their glory were Dalashinsky's mother's candlesticks. We all thought it, but Natty said it first: "We should put them in the scene."

"But Dalashinsky. . . ." said Feivel.

"Dalashinsky can use them." For once, Ida wasn't being nasty. Ensemble, we'd realized: Dalashinsky *could* use those candlesticks. Feivel carried them onstage himself.

At last it was time for the light to come up on the wonder worker of Miropol's study. And did it! Gone were the angles, the slanted beams, the cobwebs, dingy windows and seasick pitch. In their place, on the ceiling and all three sides, was copper flashing faceted to catch and reflect the light.

The audience gasped—at the dazzle, I assumed; though later, I would learn yet another reason for their surprise. Our eyes needed time to adjust, so it took several seconds for us to locate Dalashinsky at the copper table center stage. As he sat there holding the candlesticks, staring into the flame, his eyes shone brighter than copper. And only then did I discover what the real difference was.

From Dalashinsky's first line, it was *his* show. And as he'd promised, it was better than *The Dybbuk*—or at least any version *we'd* seen.

That night, his Rabbi Azrielke was a true wonder worker, a *tzaddik* powerful enough to materialize his mother's long-lost candlesticks from the other side of the world. Every word dripped wisdom, the simplest sentences came out with triple paradoxes built in. Complicated, I know, but this Rabbi Azrielke was nothing if not complicated, a spiritual jigsaw puzzle which Dalashinsky assembled before our eyes to form the very picture of holiness. You felt that Chonon's dybbuk was something personal between the rabbi and God, and while compassion entered in, compassion was but another name for Azrielke's Creator. You felt that if you had problems with a dybbuk or anything else, you would travel halfway around the world to consult him.

Gradually I began to think I knew what sort of bargain Dalashinsky had struck with Rabbi Israel during those hours of intense conversation at my wedding. In return for some private instruction, some key to the nature of a holy man which would enable him to do this new and most brilliant Azrielke of his career, Dalashinsky had agreed to do one good deed, to arrange this wedding for the benefit of his "children's" parents.

A pact, pure and simple, like Doctor Faustus's—except that Rabbi Israel wasn't the devil, and none of it hurt. What was wrong with Dalashinsky being human for one night in return for the chance to bring off this superhuman performance? Neither Mama, Papa, nor art was any the worse for it—quite the opposite!

That night, Dalashinsky told the Baal Shem and the acrobat story so movingly that its resonance reverberated through the house and our ears rang with extra interpretations.

The Baal Shem (it occurred to me now) said his piece about loose souls because he was human, imperfect himself. If he'd only thought harder, maybe *he* could have come up with the Chazzer Rabbi's line about using nets when you worked with children. How much more sensitive and responsible that would have seemed than (as Rabbi Israel said) standing on the sidelines and heckling the acrobats! What this made me feel was sympathy for the Baal Shem's limitations, for the hint of pomposity in his "loose souls" lament, and finally, for the flaws in us all.

Including Dalashinsky. For to me, this genius wasn't the same man who'd invented silly stories about the Jewish constellations, the self-pitier who'd compared our art to crabgrass and gefilte fish. This was Dalashinsky the Master, the Teacher, the Artist. I could learn from him, I could stand in awe. He could have stolen, cheated, done far worse than he did; for that performance, I would have forgiven him.

Though I would never give up as much as Dalashinsky had, nor "use" my life as he did, that evening I valued his sacrifice. Though I'd decided not to choose between life and art, I no longer faulted his choice. And I asked myself: Was it so bad to forget your children's names when, in one night, you could feed a houseful of hungry hearts?

Inspired, our whole ensemble played like one person. Even through the clouds of gloom and demonic possession, my Leah shone. I fainted like someone who knew what it meant to faint —the best faint of my career.

But when the curtain came down, the audience wasn't applauding my one-armed swan dive. They were bravo-ing Dalashinsky.

The cheering made our opening-night reception seem lukewarm. Once again, they were up on their feet, but now they were stamping them. Even so, when Dalashinsky whispered, "Quiet, please," the house got quiet so fast, we had only to wait for the balconies to stop shaking.

I ran back to my dressing room, which was as crowded as on that first opening night, but now with women—Ida, Clara, Mama, all my aunts and cousins. How lovely they looked in their furs and fancy dresses! How delicious their perfume smelled! They were playing their part in this Cinderella story, displaying the wedding dress (where had it come from? my fairy godmother?) against their own handsome bosoms.

"Look, Yettele!" One of Mama's great-aunts was turning out the label. "Saks!"

At this, the ladies swooned, and I could have kissed every one of them. For it had dawned on me that this was what Mama wanted her daughter to be married in—not some beat-up shroud, left over, one of Desdemona's nightgowns. Small as I was, the dress was smaller, but when I squeezed in, the ladies hugged themselves and said, "Beautiful! Beautiful!"

We were married onstage in front of a pleated white satin backdrop, the kind of scrim I'd see later, transforming Hannele's Hebrew-school gym into a makeshift *shul* for the children's Yom Kippur. The first thing Benno whispered to me was that Feivel had arranged to have all the trappings lent, free of charge, by a synagogue supply house. Luckily, we'd fared better with the *chupah*. The ladies of the Dalashinsky Fan Club had worked overtime. And if the canopy wasn't quite as magnificent as the one we'd left behind in South America—well, this set the tone for the wedding.

The Forsythe Street rabbi was a celebrity, so enlightened and urbane, he made Rabbi Schmuckler look primitive. Fresh from the ecstasies in Rabbi Israel's *frigorífico*, I felt this rabbi's enthusiasm—as well as the set of his mouth—to be stingy and mean. But I knew that Mama and Papa would certainly have preferred this man and this setting to that madhouse in Montevideo. To look down on them for this would have been like blaming Dalashinsky for the decline of the "old" Yiddish theater, like Hannele blaming Benno and me for moving away from the Lower East Side. So I kept it in mind that if our first wedding was for the landlord and the second for God, this was for Mama and Papa. And when was the real one for Benno and me? Forty days before birth.

Benno crunched the glass, then picked it up between napkins without dropping one splinter onstage. As the rabbi disposed of it, I was astonished to see a small wastebasket under the *chupah*, expressly for this purpose. For rings, we reused the plain gold bands from Montevideo. And when Benno slipped mine on my finger, we looked into one another's eyes and thought, Our present from Rabbi Israel.

"You may now kiss the bride," said the Rabbi. Our embrace stayed well within the bounds of good taste, no steamier than what I got, within the next half hour, from everyone else.

Even Dalashinsky kissed me, a dry little buss which glanced off my cheek. And as he congratulated the air over my left shoulder, I understood that the show was over for him. He'd done his star turn, and though he claimed not to hear applause, he'd heard. He was present in body, but his spirit had taken a hop, skip, and jump to our next production—which, he'd already announced, would be *The Merchant of Venice*; for him, the food at my wedding had less reality than Shylock's pound of flesh. And maybe it was just as well, for the sad truth was, you couldn't have scraped a pound together from those liver canapés. Catered by Moscowitz and Lupowitz, the food was like the rabbi and my wedding dress—in other words, not enough.

Without getting any less noisy, the crowd was beginning to disperse when Dalashinsky raised his champagne glass and said, "Quiet!"

Go ahead, I thought. Toast youth, love, and beauty with Hinda right here. Instead, Dalashinsky turned to Feivel and said, "Can we show them the presents?"

"Definitely," said Feivel. "But first I would like to announce the Yiddish Art Theater's gift to the newlyweds." He cleared his throat. "Thanks to the unprecedented financial success of this evening's performance, we will all receive our share of back pay from our South American trip!"

It took a while for it to sink in that this was the present he meant, and when it did, I thought, When you're in an ensemble, you even get wedding gifts ensemble. And what kind of present was money we'd earned ourselves? But how could I harbor such ingratitude when Dalashinsky, impatient as a child on the first night of Chanukah, was pulling back the curtain which partitioned off part of the stage—revealing dishes, furniture, linens, and a preponderance of copper pots and pans!

I pushed my way through the crowd till I found Mama. Pointing at Feivel, she explained, "When he brought over the ticket, he told me to tell the relatives that you and Benno wanted copper. I took his word, I wouldn't know what to get you anymore. Besides, you can always use copper."

Feivel must have given the same advice to everyone, for now, recalling the audience's reaction to Rabbi Azrielke's copper-lined study, I recognized it as a gasp of delight at having brought the perfect gift, a present to match the production. All Mama's and Papa's families combined couldn't have afforded this; these were tributes from fans. And though I knew the senselessness of equating gifts with affection, I have never felt so loved. So what if half these people were the snobs, the Art Theater bluestockings who'd come tonight mainly to save their seats from the philistine picnickers? Their hearts were as hungry as anyone else's, they too could love and bring presents!

They kissed me *mazel tov* and good-bye as if they *did* love me, as if we were family and they'd see me tomorrow. It disturbed me to think that tomorrow I wouldn't recognize most of them on the street. But I wasn't sad long. Soon only the cast, the crew, and my parents were left, and Dalashinsky was saying, "And now. The party within the party. I would like to invite you all at my own expense to a little café at the corner of Fulton and Front where the owner's wife makes the most remarkable noodle *kugel*."

Aha! The famous café! Dalashinsky was taking me there, just as he'd promised—and my friends and family with me.

"That's the one I told you about," whispered Benno. "Where he talked me into the Yiddish Art Theater."

"Benno," I said, "I know." Then I asked, "Feivel, what about the presents?"

"Leave them here," he said. "There's a lock on the door. They'll be here tomorrow."

To this day, that copperware graces my kitchen and dining room. Despite the work involved, I polish them myself; I like the smell. After Benno's death, I gave some to Hannele. And when she served that cabbage *kuchen* at her ladies' lunch in Seattle, she might have claimed that the recipe came from Julia Child. But when they asked, "Harriet, where did you get that marvelous copper skillet?" she hugged me—a brisk, no-nonsense Rappoport hug—and said, "From Mama."

Still, there was one present Feivel wouldn't entrust to the

Stuyvesant Place security system. A few blocks from the theater, he caught up with Benno and me and handed us a small package, postmarked like the candlesticks: Argentina.

"I think I know what's in it," said Feivel, and I did too. But if I really had, would I have opened it right there on the street, unfolding layer after layer, looking in vain for a card until I found in the center of the wrapping a perfect diamond, cut round, perhaps an eighth of an inch in diameter?

Later, this diamond got lost in one of our moves, and though it must seem strange that someone could simply misplace a valuable gem and not care, it's true. Such were my feelings about my double's wedding gift.

Places built up in your mind never live up to expectations. So it's a blessing that I'd never heard this café praised for anything but its significance for Dalashinsky and its noodle *kugel*.

It was a luncheonette, a nice one with a brass-railed counter, high stools, wooden tables, and a glass case full of cakes, but nonetheless a luncheonette. I checked to see how Mama and Papa were taking it, that their daughter's fancy wedding party was winding up in a luncheonette. But after all that champagne onstage at Stuyvesant Place, a cup of luncheonette coffee seemed to be just what the doctor ordered.

The owner, a dark little man, good-looking in middle age, shook Dalashinsky's hand and faded into the background from which his wife promptly emerged. A stout pretty woman with high Slavic cheekbones and Kalmuk eyes, she hugged the first ten people within reach and said, "Mister Dalashinsky! What a surprise!"

But was it? Did she normally keep a hundred dishes of noodle pudding ready and waiting in the pie safe (the same room, I thought, where Dalashinsky had studied his *schvartze* Othello)? Like the golem of Prague's water buckets, the plates kept coming. The sailors and stevedores got *kugel* also, and I wondered if this was on the house, or on Dalashinsky, or because, as Mamie said, "There was something about us which made everyone want what we had."

The funny thing was, it was just what *I* was in the mood for, rich with butter, cream, and sugar, spiced with cinnamon, studded with fat raisins, every wedge with the crisp golden crust of a corner piece.

"Bravo!" Natty Kauffman kissed his fork. "It's better than wedding cake!"

"Wedding cake?" said the owner's wife.

"This happy couple hasn't been married two hours," said Zalmen. On the threshold of his subconscious, he must have known that this was nowhere near true, but if he'd thought it consciously, he could never have smirked quite the way he did.

"A wedding!" The owner's wife clapped her hands. She went to the door and peered out, a ritual check for prohibition officers like knocking on wood for the spirits in the trees. Reaching under the cash register, she took out three large whiskey bottles and a tray of shot glasses.

One bottle later, the sailors had organized themselves into a band and volunteered. In a way, it was like being back on the *Veracruz*, except that this international crew was better than those mariachis. Their instruments were just what you'd expect from old salts—concertinas, ocarinas, a dozen variations on the accordion, never my favorite. But, oh, how sweetly they played "Over the Waves."

Many years later, in a dramatization of *Anna Karenina*, Dalashinsky set Anna and Vronsky's first waltz to "Over the Waves." The critics roasted him for picking this organ-grinder's monkey when, in all likelihood, aristocrats like Anna and Vronsky would have waltzed to Strauss. Dalashinsky defended himself on the grounds that melody and rhythm were more central to his purpose than sociology, but I knew that he'd chosen "Over the Waves" in honor of the night we pushed back the chairs in that waterfront luncheonette.

By popular demand, Benno and I went first. After two steps he hugged me tight and said, "Sweetheart, you waltz even better than you tango." On the second verse, Mama and Papa stepped onto the floor and soon I'd learned something new about them: Mama had once been a good dancer, and from the way she nudged Papa, little shoves with forty years behind them, I understood that Papa had never been light on his feet, and that this disappointed her. Still, I decided, as Mama must have: If the worst thing about a person is that he can't dance, you can live with it.

Next Feivel led Clara out, and Natty joined in with a stevedore who didn't seem to mind. Zalmen ran into the kitchen, then reappeared beside a cook with breasts which intimidated even Zalmen into waltzing at proper arm's length. I noticed Ida's stagehand asking her to dance, and I thought, For her pride, at least, she'll have that. The only one who sat it out was Dalashinsky, who was too busy paying attention.

From "Over the Waves," the band swung into some sort of hornpipe, and we all sat down. Then Dalashinsky motioned to the musicians for silence.

"What few people know about this *tzatskele* here"—the plaything in question was the café owner's wife—"is that she reads palms. And I am wondering whether, in honor of the occasion, she would consent to read the bride and groom's."

Not mine! I'd always taken an instant dislike to the kind of women who read palms. And after my recent troubles with dybbuks and doubles and all that mysterious business, the last thing I needed was a fortune-teller.

I put my hand into Benno's pocket, where Benno's hand found mine. Down the table, I noticed, Mama had her hands clasped firmly together, as did most of the Yiddish Art Theater.

Only Ida had her hand out. Perhaps she was hoping to hear that she and her stagehand would waltz into the sunset to the tune of "Over the Waves." But that would have fallen short of what the owner's wife found in her palm:

"I see professional success, not great success, but respectable. Then a husband—"

"What does he look like?" asked Ida.

"Darling, it's only a palm. I see three children . . . six healthy grandchildren—"

"Only six?" Ida, our cynic, was laughing with tears in her eyes. And suddenly it struck me that, in her own soft-spoken way, this woman with her palm reading and noodle *kugel* reminded me somehow of Rabbi Israel. She took one last look at Ida's hand and said, "Four boys and two girls."

Four boys and two girls! I'd heard fortune-telling before, but never anything so specific. I liked how she'd ended the story, not with sickness and death, but with the blessings, the number and sex of the grandchildren. It encouraged us all, and slowly our fingers unclenched.

I never thought to wonder, What kind of fortune-teller is this who has nothing but good news? Not once, for example, did we hear about the arthritis which would twist poor Clara around her cane like a corkscrew. Nor how quickly Dalashinsky's new humanity would desert him, leaving him more oblivious than before, an old egomaniac blowing his life up to fit the windy phrases of his memoirs, *My Life in the Yiddish Art Theater.* But who wants to hear such things at a wedding? Instead, we heard about artistic triumphs for Dalashinsky which would dwarf everything so far, true love for Natty, pleasures of the flesh and imagination for Zalmen, good health for Feivel and as ripe an old age as even a naturopath could want.

When Benno held out his hand, I didn't stop him.

"I see yet another shining career on the stage," said the owner's wife. "Yet this line is doubled and twined; you will share it with your bride. I see one child, a daughter who will marry happily and have two daughters. The worst I see is that, in later years, you will trip on the pavement and knock out a front tooth. And even this will be converted to good fortune: As a result of this accident, you will finally be able to whistle."

"Mr. Brownstein, you can't whistle?" said Dalashinsky.

"Can this be true?" marveled Papa. "Is my Dinele really marrying a man who can't whistle?"

The way they were teasing him, like two affectionate fathers-in-law, made me so happy that I put out my palm.

For the first time all evening, the owner's wife looked distressed and hesitated before speaking.

"What is it?" My heart was slamming against my chest.

"Please excuse my asking . . . but is this your first wedding?"

"No." It never occurred to me not to tell the truth. "It's my third."

"Well, then." She let out a deep breath. "Because it says here that you will be married three times."

"Bravo!" cried Benno. "That's all we need to know."

But it wasn't.

"What else?" I asked.

"What else?" She studied my palm a while longer, then curled my hand into a ball and held it.

"For the bride," she said. "For the bride, always: blessings, blessings, and more blessings."

ABOUT THE AUTHOR

Born in Brooklyn, New York, in 1947, Francine Prose attended Radcliffe College and taught creative writing at Harvard. Her five previous novels, *Animal Magnetism, Marie Laveau, The Glorious Ones, Judah the Pious* (winner of the Jewish Book Council Award), and *Household Saints* have attracted widespread critical acclaim. She has also published fiction and articles in *Mademoiselle, The Atlantic Monthly,* and *The Village Voice.* Having lived in San Francisco, Bombay, and Cambridge, Massachusetts, she now lives in upstate New York with her family.